Introducing Don DeLillo

Introducing Don DeLillo

Edited by Frank Lentricchia

Duke University Press   Durham and London

© 1991 Duke University Press
All rights reserved.
Printed in the United States of America
on acid-free paper ∞
The text of this book was originally published without index as volume 89, number 2 of the *South Atlantic Quarterly*.

"Opposites," chapter 10 from *Ratner's Star* by Don DeLillo, is reprinted by permission of Alfred A. Knopf, Inc. Copyright © 1976 by Don DeLillo.

" 'An Outsider in This Society': An Interview with Don DeLillo" by Anthony DeCurtis is an expanded version of "Matters of Fact and Fiction" from *Rolling Stone Magazine*, November 17, 1988. By Straight Arrow Publishers, Inc. © 1988. All rights reserved. Reprinted by permission.

"*Libra* as Postmodern Critique" and part of "The American Writer as Bad Citizen," both by Frank Lentricchia, originally appeared in *Raritan*, Spring 1989.

Library of Congress Cataloging-in-Publication Data
Introducing Don DeLillo / edited by Frank Lentricchia.
p. cm.
Includes index.
ISBN 0-8223-1135-6. — ISBN 0-8223-1144-5 (pbk.)
1. DeLillo, Don—Criticism and interpretation.
I. Lentricchia, Frank.
PS3554.E4425Z72 1991
813'.54.—dc20 90-15567

For Melissa Lentricchia and Emily White,
guardian angels of SAQ

Contents

Introducing Don DeLillo

Frank Lentricchia

The American Writer as Bad Citizen

For obvious reasons Don DeLillo's publishers are pleased to advertise their man as a "highly acclaimed" novelist, but until the publication of *White Noise* in 1985 DeLillo was a pretty obscure object of acclaim, both in and out of the academy. His readings are rare. He attends no conferences, teaches no summer workshops in fiction writing, never shows up on late-night television—or in the *New York Times Sunday Magazine*—and doesn't cultivate second-person narrative in the present tense. So he has done virtually nothing to promote himself in the approved ways. And the books are hard: all of them expressions of someone who has ideas (I don't mean opinions), who reads things other than novels and newspapers (though he clearly reads those too, and to advantage), and who experiments with literary convention.

What is characteristic about DeLillo's books, aside from their contemporary subjects, is their irredeemably heterogeneous texture; they are montages of tones, styles, and voices that have the effect of yoking together terror and wild humor as the essential tone of contemporary America. Terrific comedy is DeLillo's mode: even, at the most unexpected moments, in *Libra*, his imagination of the life of Lee Harvey Oswald. It is the sort of mode that marks writers who conceive their vocation as an act of cultural criticism; who invent in order to intervene; whose work is a kind of anatomy, an effort to represent their culture in its totality; and who desire to move readers to the view that the shape and fate of their culture dictates the shape and fate of the self.

In other words, writers like DeLillo are not the sort who are impressed by the representative directive of the literary vocation of our time, the counsel to "write what you know," taken to heart by producers of the new regionalism who in the South, for example, claim parentage in Faulkner and Flannery O'Connor, two writers who would have been floored to hear that "what you know" means the chastely bound snapshot of your neighborhood and your biography. (An embarrassing sign of the aesthetic times: one critic, writing for the *Partisan Review*, reported his happy astonishment that DeLillo could invent such believable kids in *White Noise*, because, after all, DeLillo has no kids.) Writers in DeLillo's tradition have too much ambition to stay home. To leave home (I don't mean "transcend" it), to leave your region, your ethnicity, the idiom you grew up with, is made to seem pretentious in the setting of the new regionalism, and the South is not unique: it makes no difference if the province is generic North Carolina or generic New York City, or if the provincialist is Reynolds Price or Jay McInerney. In the cultural setting in which Bobbie Ann Mason incarnates the idea of the writer and Frederick Barthelme succeeds his brother in the pages of the *New Yorker*, to write novels that might be titled *An American Tragedy* or *USA*—DeLillo's first book was called *Americana* (1971)—no doubt is pretentious. In this kind of setting, a writer who tries what DeLillo tries is simply immodest, shamelessly so. Apparently only the Latin Americans have earned the right to their immodesty. So American novelists and critics first look sentimentally to the other Americas, where (so it goes) the good luck of fearsome situations of social crisis encourages a major literature; then look ruefully to home, where (so it goes) the comforts of our stability require a minor, apolitical, domestic fiction of the triumphs and agonies of autonomous private individuals operating in "the private sector" of Raymond Carver and Anne Tyler, the modesty of small, good things: fiction all but labeled "No expense of intellect required. To be applied in eternal crises of the heart only." Unlike these new regionalists of and for the Reagan eighties, DeLillo (or Joan Didion, or Toni Morrison, or Cynthia Ozick, or Norman Mailer) offers us no myth of political virginity preserved, no "individuals" who are not expressions of—and responses to—specific historical processes.

But things are changing now for DeLillo: in 1984 he was given an award by the American Academy and Institute of Arts and Letters that honored his work to date; then *White Noise* won the American Book Award for 1985; then *Libra* was made a main selection of the Book-of-the-Month Club in the spring of 1988, hit the best-seller list for several weeks in the summer of that year, and got its author invited to do interviews on National Public Radio and NBC's *Today Show*. Uncharacteristically, *Libra*'s author assented. And best sign of all of cultural relevance in our day: the media political right has begun to take an active interest in DeLillo. The "highly acclaimed" author is now, in his newfound visibility, drawing his harshest notices.

In the midst of a presidential campaign in which he usually devoted his nationally syndicated column to the vagaries of Bush and Dukakis, George Will took time out to write an article on *Libra* in which he called DeLillo a literary vandal for writing about real people, a bad citizen for suggesting that John F. Kennedy's murder was not the act of a "lone gunman" but the production of a conspiracy, and a bad influence because a lot of people were now apparently reading DeLillo. Will's charge of literary vandalism and bad citizenship (What is this, anyway, China?) is the latest frightened judgment—with a long American history—delivered upon writers critically engaged with particular American cultural and political matters, writers with terminal bad manners who refuse to limit themselves to celebratory platitudes about the truths of the heart, and who

don't respect the definitive shibboleth of literary culture since the eighteenth century—the sharp and deadly distinction between fiction and nonfiction: as if everyone didn't know who Dreiser was writing about when *An American Tragedy* came out; as if Dos Passos hadn't named and butchered some famous names in *USA*; as if Doctorow's *Ragtime*, Coover's *The Public Burning*, and Mailer's *The Executioner's Song* hadn't worked that same territory.

Will is no lone gunman either: a few weeks before, a Pulitzer prize-winning columnist for the *Washington Post*, who writes under the name of Jonathan Yardley, had similarly described DeLillo's efforts to imagine the lives of real people as "beneath contempt." Yardley is angry because he thinks DeLillo has somehow cheated, that thanks to a conspiracy of literary radicals he has "quite inexplicably acquired a substantial literary reputation"; Yardley is convinced that *Libra* "will be lavishly praised in those quarters where DeLillo's ostentatiously gloomy view of American life and culture is embraced"; and he is worried because Oswald, like James Dean and Marilyn Monroe, continues to fascinate us, Yardley included. Brandishing the literary theory of Eudora Welty, Cumaean sibyl of the new regionalism, who declares that fiction must have a "private address," Yardley accuses DeLillo of committing an "ideological fiction." By ideology he means (on this he is as "liberal" as he is "conservative") any point of view which traces any problematic action to an institutional, structural, or collective cause, rather than a personal one: any theory of society which refuses the lone gunman explanation of anything, but particularly of social crisis. Or, as Will puts it: DeLillo's is "yet another exercise in blaming America for Oswald's act of derangement." But political fiction is not fiction that forsakes the personal in order to blame the public sector, which it surely does critically assess; it is fiction that refuses the opposition of the personal and public altogether. Since DeLillo does not produce happy evaluations of the effects of large public pressures upon individuals—has any interesting writer in America ever done so?—it follows for the media political right which believes that America is good and that only individuals go astray (the homeless bring it on themselves, as Reagan used to say), that DeLillo is something of a traitor to his country.

In the words of a *New Criterion* soldier who preceded both Will and Yardley in this vein, DeLillo thinks "contemporary American society is the worst enemy that the cause of human individuality and self-realization has ever had." The reality is otherwise, at least as it is seen in the *New Criterion*. Here in America we lead "richly varied" lives: if we do not, if there is any fault to be found, if anyone "is guilty of turning modern Americans into xerox copies, it is Don DeLillo." Two cheers for the media right: their censorious reflections on DeLillo's work—what consequences, anyway, ought to be visited upon the writer whose acts of invention are termed bad citizenship and bad influence?—are the best backhanded testimony I've seen in a long time on behalf of the social power of literature, for good or for ill, and an unintended but superb compliment to DeLillo's success in making his writing count beyond the elite circle of connoisseurs of postmodernist criticism and fiction. Not wanting to say so, the media right has nevertheless said in so many words, against its Will, that fiction does not have a private address and that DeLillo does to Oswald what we, for good or for ill, do every day to our friends, lovers, and enemies: he interprets him, he creates a character.

The telling assumption of DeLillo's media right reviewers is that he is coming from the left—as if the criticism of American culture is necessarily a Marxist plot and we've never heard of the activists on the political right and their agendas for social change; as if some of our most honored writers—I mean precisely those whom conservative intellectuals charge universities with forsaking, as we go whoring after the strange gods of minority cultures—as if Emerson, Thoreau, and Twain had not written savage critiques of America, not peripherally but centrally, as their life's work. It is true that DeLillo's heroes are usually in repulsed flight from American life. But what did Emerson say? He said: "Society"—he meant ours—"is a joint stock company in conspiracy against the manhood of every one of its members."

Should conservative intellectuals refresh their memories of American literature, they'd find that the canonical American writers—those who conservatives say best embody American values—are adversarial critics of our culture. The American literary way has from the start been fiercely antinomian, suspicious, even "paranoid," and how interesting that key word of contemporary jargon becomes when it characterizes the main take on our culture from Anne Hutchinson and Emerson to Pynchon and DeLillo. The main literary line is political, but not in the trivial didactic sense of offering programs of renovation, or of encouraging us to go out and "do something." Writing in the main line in effect stands in harsh judgment against American fiction of the last couple of decades, that soft humanist underbelly of American literature: a realism of domestic setting whose characters play out their little dramas of ordinary event and feeling in an America miraculously free from the environment and disasters of contemporary technology, untouched by racial and gender tensions, and blissfully unaware of political power; a fiction, to be sure, cleverly veneered with place (Tyler's Baltimore), brand names, and other signs of advanced consumer culture (Carver's cube steak, his Jim Beam). In the fashioning of such surfaces lies the entire claim of these writers to realism. But the deep action of this kind of fiction is culturally and historically rootless, an expression of the possibilities of "human nature," here, now, forever, as ever. This is realism maybe in the old philosophical sense of the word, when they affirmed that only the universals are real. The Jim Beam, the dope, the TV set, the cube steak, which all make apparently authoritative appearances in Carver's world, are not of the essence; they are merely props. In the context of recent American fiction, the reading of DeLillo's writing is an experience of overwhelming cultural density—these are novels that could not have been written before the mid-1960s. In this, their historical rigor, I suspect, lies their political outrage: the unprecedented degree to which they prevent their readers from gliding off into the comfortable sentiment that the real problems of the human race have always been about what they are today.

Don DeLillo

"Opposites," Chapter 10 of *Ratner's Star*

The abiding presence in Ratner's Star *(a novel loaded with cameo appearances by characters at once bizarre, funny, and scary) is fourteen-year-old Billy Twillig, winner of the first Nobel Prize in mathematics. The novel begins with Billy's trip to an unspecified "distant land," his destination Field Experiment Number One, a scientific institute where a coded radio signal has been received, apparently from another planet. It is thought that Billy might possess the mathematical wherewithal to decode the message, even though one mathematical giant has gone mad trying. In this chapter, Billy is on his way to a ceremony honoring Shazar Lazarus Ratner, a Nobel laureate in physics for whom a star has been named, the very star in whose vicinity the mysterious signal is thought to have originated. The thirty-two resident Nobel laureates are invited to the Great Hole—which Billy mishears as the Great Hall—along with Ratner's personal doctor, nurse, best friend, and a master of ceremonies who doubles as an organist. After a few opening paragraphs, where we find Billy in meditation on number, shape, and a sexy passage from his mentor's manuscript, the action begins.—F. L.*

He passed through twillig-shaped openings in the air, an infinite series of discrete convenient gateways.

Nobody seemed to know where the Great Hall was. He went to a nearby dining unit and checked the bulletin board ("advisory dispatch chart") for word of a torch-lighting ceremony. No word. No sign of Ratner's name. No directions to Great Hall. He read the lone note pinned there.

Vintage art films—8 millimeter
Sale or rent

1—"Two in a Tub"
2—"Aunt Polly's Banana Surprise"
3—"What the Butler Did"
4—"Volleyball Follies"
5—"Frenchy and the House Dick"

Contact O. Mohole
Maternity Suite

By appointment only

He walked along a semicircular corridor, asking directions in vain, met in fact with squinted eyes and little sniffles, everyone reacting to this entity the Great Hall in similar fashion, civilized pygmies asked to climb sequoia trees, something ancestral in their replies, a captive skepticism shading every face. Eventually he came to a moving walkway ("linear glide") and stepped on. He'd never ridden on one of the linear glides, although he'd seen them once or twice in different parts of the building. It was a pleasant experience. You simply stood there, holding on to the moving strap above your head. The strap, similar to the kind found in subways, was suspended from a flexible-strength wire that enabled you to pull it down to suit your particular stature.

Only moments earlier he'd imagined he was moving through air-gaps cut to his shape, an infinite number of distinct apertures. Now, on the linear glide, he felt he was passing through one continuous hole. Precisely his height and width. A custom perforation. Even a special opening to accommodate his raised right arm. He moved in a straight line through a dim midevening monochrome, a kind of interior dusk, abstract murals on either side. At one point a large figure, adumbral and shapeless, was superimposed on the geometry of walls and ceiling. Unerringly rendered shapes and amorphous overshadow. What was there about these surfaces that made the journey seem descendent and led him to believe he was breathing sheerest calculus? Strict precision strict. Down the line to dream the subliminal blend of number and function. Analysis rethought in arithmetical terms. Opposed positions. Whole numbers providing the substance for the continuous torsional spring of analysis. Atomism and flow. Down the line past history's black on white. Ideal of proof ideal.

Every semirecluse has his amaranthine woman. Imaginary love-lies-bleeding. "But in this case," Softly had written, "the woman was not only real but a mathematician as well. This is Sonja Kowalewski and we can only guess at the levels of intensity during those afternoons when she arrives at his home for lessons. Twenty years old to his fifty-five. Aristocratic and social, while he is accustomed to life in remote villages. To someone fixed in solitude she must have seemed a brighter presence than he could bear. She is brilliant, attractive, Moscow-born, an Eastern jade (it is suspected) determined to have her pick of the schoolmaster's gifts. So we speculate on the density of their meetings. The quality of the sunlight in his parlor. The tone of their discussions on power series and irrational numbers. The very clothes she wears. His face, while she listens. Her eyes, adventuring. Is it within the student's vested right to consume the preceptor's soul? He is a bachelor, remember, while she is married (in name at least). Another level worth exploring. To empty each other of possessions. To negate each other's artificial names. In his regard for logic, proof, exactitude and caution, he tries not to dwell on his own belief that death is payment for risks not taken, and pours himself a beer. And for her part—what? Does she have fantasies about mathematics? Does she imagine that in his attacks of vertigo he spins from room to room, a scientist trying to cope with holiness, or perhaps himself immune, a germ-carrier of ecstasy? She titles a mathematical memoir: *On the Rotation of a Solid Body About a Fixed Point*. They pass their afternoons and when she dies (surprise) he burns her letters." Of, pertaining to, or resembling the amaranth. An imaginary flower that never fades.

In the wall ahead was an archlike opening through which the linear glide continued to move. The hole was about as tall and wide as he was. He stepped off the glide just as it whispered through the darkened arch. Adjacent to this opening was a door with a black arrow painted on it. The arrow pointed down. He opened the door and went down a flight of old stone steps, cracked in many places. The lighting consisted of a makeshift network of low-watt bulbs strung along the ceiling. He came to the bottom of the vertical shaft around which the staircase had been constructed. There was a large jagged hole in one wall and next to the hole stood a man with a plastic torch in his hand, flames two feet high.

"I'm Evinrude," he said. "You're very, very late."

"Is this the ceremony?"

"They're working out size places and they want the smallest last. That's the only thing that saved you."

"But this is the ceremony for Ratner, right?"

"Just to make it official, I have to ask if you're a laureate."

"Yes."

"In what field?"

"Mathematics."

"Because only laureates are allowed beyond this point," Evinrude said.

"Zorgs. I won for zorgs."

"What's that?"

"A class of numbers."

"Out of curiosity, would I know what you were talking about if you described them further?"

"No."

"Can people do things with these numbers of yours?"

"The average person, forget about, but in his book-to-be, right where I'm up to now, Softly says zorgs in their own way hark back to the nineteenth-century redefinition of the ancient and semimystical idea of whole numbers forming the basis of all mathematics. They hark back, he says. Softly can be funny that way."

"Who or what is Softly?"

"Head of the School of Mathematics at the Center for the Refinement of Ideational Structures."

"Correct," Evinrude said.

The torch he held was very large and Billy hoped they wouldn't give him one to carry, particularly if the ceremony was scheduled to be a long one.

"What happens next?" he said.

"I ask you why you're late."

"Nobody could tell me how to get here. I asked everybody I saw and none of them ever even heard of the Great Hall. It's not that I didn't ask. They just never heard."

"No wonder they never heard of it," Evinrude said. "You gave them the wrong name. It's not the Great Hall. It's the Great Hole. Whoever told you Great Hall was guilty of a misnomer. This is the old part of Field Experiment Number One. The building was partly built on an existing structure. Not many people know that. The old structure was buried, and so instead of destroying it or bypassing it they incorporated the old part into what they were putting up, a buttress for the foundation, because of the archaeology involved. This is where we're standing now. The old part. The temple cave. They still haven't figured out how to make it disasterproof. A sudden noise or loud report could bring it all down."

"What's this about size places?"

"It's to get a dramatic effect with the torches."

"We all hold torches?"

"The laureates," Evinrude said. "All the laureates get a torch and go to their size places and then light the torch and hold it."

"Why are they having the ceremony down here?"

"Ratner's people."

"What kind of people?"

"The doctor, the nurse, the organist, the fella from the bearded sect. They insisted on having the ceremony in the Great Hole because of first of all there's the old gentleman's health to be considered and the air down here is the right kind of air and because of second of all there's a sense of the past in the Great Hole because of its being part of a venerable structure and there's that to be considered, awareness of past, respect for heritage. The laureates agreed. Those that were consulted."

"I wasn't consulted."

"You were very, very late. Maybe that's why you weren't consulted.

Ratner's people weren't late. They came thousands of miles but they got here on time."

"They weren't told Great Hall instead of Great Hole."

"Time to go in," Evinrude said. "Step lively, keep it moving, spread it out."

He dipped the torch and Billy stepped through the hole and walked down a flight of crooked stairs into a small dusty room with nothing in it but a bronze door and a stone bench. He sat on the bench and looked at the door. The particles in the air reminded him of chalk dust and he assumed all this powdery matter had simply floated off the walls and ceiling, further indications of the structure's fragility and age. The door opened, admitting a man wearing a mink fedora and a long black coat. His beard was white and untrimmed, reaching to his chest, and although its wispy attenuated ends made the boy think of surgical cotton sticking out of a box after a handful has been removed, he was sure on second glance that the beard was anything but soft, that its strands were coarse, firm and wiry, toughened by decades of misery and grit. The man's coat extended almost to his shoes. He approached the bench and Billy moved over to give him room to sit but the man stopped short of the bench, put his hands behind his back and leaned forward slightly, head inclined, lips beginning to move a few seconds before he actually said anything.

"The old gentleman wants you to present the roses."

"I thought you were the old gentleman."

"I'm Pitkin, who advises on the writings. I'm looking at the person he picked by hand to present him the roses face to face. He's one sweetheart of a human being. I advise him on the mystical writings. But if they forced it out of me with hot tongs, I'd tell them I learn more from Shazar Ratner than I could ever teach if I live to be—go ahead, name me a figure."

"A hundred."

"Name me higher."

"A hundred and fifty."

"Stop there," Pitkin said. "Many years ago he came back to his roots. Eastern Parkway. Strictness like you wouldn't believe. But the old gentleman he was tickled to get back."

"What kind of strictness?"

"The codes, the rules, the laws, the customs, the tablecloth, the silverware, the dishes."

"So then you're from Brooklyn, if your roots are Eastern Parkway. I'm surprised I never heard of the old gentleman, being from the metropolitan area myself."

"He's a living doll," Pitkin said. "After you present the roses he has a word or two he wants to whisper up to you. You're the youngest. He figures you'll be worth telling. The others he wouldn't give you two cents for the whole bunch. Science? He turned his back on science. Science made him a household word, a name in the sky, but he grew world-weary of it. He returned to the wellspring to drink. They assigned me then and there. I know the writings. Many years ago, long before a kid like you was even formed out of smelly mush in his mother's tubes, I committed the writings to memory. They don't know this, the other elders, because we're not supposed to memorize. It's considered cheating when you memorize. When you memorize you lose the inner meaning. But how else could a dumbbell like me become an elder? Name me a way and I'll do it. Just between us chickens I did a little cheating. So what's the damage? Show me who I harmed. Once in a while I sneak another look or two to refresh myself. But only once in a while and just to refresh. This I vow and you're my sworn witness who I'm looking at. If I'm lying, may both your eyes drip vengeful pus."

"Why my eyes?"

"Because that's the oath," Pitkin said. "I didn't word the oath. Go ask who worded it why your eyes."

"It must go way back, an oath like that, to when they believed in exact cruelty to each other's parts of the body. Eye for eye. Tooth for tooth."

"You know the writings?"

"Just something I heard."

"To where did the old gentleman return to drink?"

"He returned to the wellspring to drink."

"We all memorize. The memory is there, so where's the harm in using it? Here I depart from the other elders. The elders say interpret the writings. Find the inner meanings. Seek the sacred rays from the world of emanations. The writings say the same thing. But not everybody can interpret. It's hard for some people to interpret. You should pardon me but it's true. Pitkin memorizes. If you can name me one thing wrong with this that I haven't already figured out for myself, I'll take off all my clothes and walk naked through Crown Heights."

"I've heard of it."

"So show a little mercy to someone whose whole life has been awe, fear and kilt."

"Kilt?"

"Innocence and kilt."

"You mean guilt. Awe, fear and guilt. There, that makes sense. You said 'kilt.' But it's definitely pronounced guilt."

"A corrector I got in front of me. I need this from a peewee quiz kid? This kind of talk I need from someone that I don't even know if his little shvontzie got trimmed by the knife?"

"One second please."

"Inches away from a filthy urinator and I have to listen to my spelling corrected by some smart aleck in arithmetic?"

"I was brought up to wash everywhere."

"Filthy-impure, not filthy-dirty. Ritual filth, the worst kind. One thing I want to tell you even if it breaks my heart giving advice to a speller. A little advice free of charge straight from the mystical writings. You ready for this? Quiz kid, corrector, you want to be instructed from the writings or you want to go through life waving your shvontzie like a monkey?"

"I'm listening."

"Learn some awe and fear."

"Is that it?"

"White monkey, speller, keep your business out of other people's noses."

Billy began to imagine that under the beard and heavy dark clothes was a young fellow arrayed in the latest resort finery, a slick casual warm-up act who would end his comic routine by dressing up in shabby clothes, sticking on a beard and stepping out in Pitkin's skin to do some involuted patter about ghetto life in stone-age Brooklyn.

"What did I say you should learn?"

"Some awe and fear."

The bronze door opened and a doctor and nurse entered. The doctor held a huge syringe and the nurse was wheeling a device that consisted of a gallon bottle of colorless fluid and a thin black hose that extended from the bottle through a Pyrex vessel (filled with a semisolid material) and into a small clear cylindrical container. Paying no attention to the old man and boy, the doctor began to fill the syringe with fluid processed through the hose, vessel and tube. It was a complicated procedure and the doctor and nurse slapped at each other's hands, although with no animosity, whenever a faulty move was made.

"Some doctor," Pitkin whispered. "Only the worst cases he takes. If he sees you in the street having a heart attack, he walks right by. Tell him it's a tsetse fly in your lungs, if you're lucky he'll stop. He makes so much money you couldn't count that high. A house with grounds. Two big doors, front and back. A toaster that does four slices. His yacht he named it *Transurethral Prostatectomy*. Uses a colored nurse. See her? With the tube in her hand? Colored. Walk in any hospital right off the street and that's what you see. Uniforms, shoes, folded hats. Like anybody. Only colored. A total specialist, Dr. Bonwit. The old gentleman swears by him. Only because of Bonwit he came for the torches all this way. With Bonwit along he's willing to travel. Round trip we're paying. Ratner, Bonwit, Pitkin, the organ player, the colored nurse. We took up collections in the neighborhood. This is the respect people have for the name Ratner both before and after he turned his back."

"It's a back problem?"

"Turned his back on science."

"What's wrong with him then to make him have to travel with a doctor?"

"Not just a doctor please. A specialist. Never please say doctor to his face. You don't know this? What am I looking at here? How many kinds of genius did they tell me to watch out for? Pisher, where should you keep your business out of?"

"Other people's noses."

"A little awe and fear never hurt anybody."

"But what's the old gentleman suffering from?"

"Look it up," Pitkin said. "Turn to any page in the medical book and there he is. Swollen tooth sockets. Brown eye. Urinary leakage.

Hardening of the ducts. Hormone discolor. Blocked extremities. Seepage from the gums. The wind is bad. The lungs are on the verge. Bonwit gives the lungs two weeks. There's no breathing except shallow labored. The lungs, the lungs."

"What kind of wind?"

"Intestinal and digestive. Mixed wind. A little of each."

"What else?"

"The skin, the bones," Pitkin said.

"They must love him at Blue Cross."

"How are you behaving that I said you shouldn't behave like?"

"A white monkey."

"What am I looking at here?"

"A pisher."

"Moistness," Pitkin said. "His whole body is moist. The doctor, you should see him, night and day he works to keep it dry. Dedication at that price is worthless. You need heavy machines to keep a man alive. The face, the mouth."

Pitkin's lips continued to move and Billy wondered exactly how old this man Ratner must be if his advisor on the writings thought it suitable to refer to him as the old gentleman—an advisor with white hair growing out of his face at beard level and even above, crowding the eyes, and with lips that started moving before he spoke and did not stop until well after he was finished talking. Dr. Bonwit walked out now, syringe properly filled, and the nurse followed, wheeling the elaborate device.

"Is that for the old gentleman?"

"Nonclotting silicone," Pitkin said. "He doesn't like to see them fill up the needle, so they sneak around the nearest corner and do it there. Needles, who can look?"

"Didn't I hear something once about silicone that has to do with bigger breasts?"

"Watch with the language in front of an elder."

"Yes or no, are they injecting his breasts?"

"Get out from here."

"What for?"

"With language like that you address an elder?"

"I'm only asking."

"Get out from here."

"I do no wrong."

"They're injecting his face," Pitkin said. "His face collapsed coming over the ocean last night. A storm like nobody's business. Eagles on their hats they had to fly right into it. So now Bonwit builds up the face with a little shot. Poof, it fills right out. This is instant silicone, according to Bonwit, that fills you out, that coats the lining, that heats up the tissue and makes the moisture run off that's making trouble up and down the body. Good stuff. No clotting. He recommends."

"Not just for anybody."

"What can I say? He recommends. This is from his own words, Bonwit, that I memorized. With strictness like we got, who wouldn't memorize? This I ask. You're looking at an asker. If they put hot tongs on my body I might admit I could use another chance. Maybe with a second chance I could learn to interpret. Maybe it's less impossible than I think, dumbbell or not. But I'm asking who did I hurt but myself? An old man asks. True, I did a little cheating. I memorized here and there. I didn't look for the inner meanings. For years I'm sweating bullets over this thing. If they said I could have another chance I'd walk naked in the rush hour through a colored subway car. This I vow on a holy oath. If I'm lying, may you inherit a hotel with ten thousand rooms and be found dead in every room."

"These oaths are pretty dangerous to people just standing around listening."

"I didn't word them. They were worded five thousand years ago. You want to change the wording, go complain. Tell them Pitkin sent you. I'm in enough trouble with the cheating like a hot coal on my heart so I can't sleep at night, I might as well have that too, my name on a complaint by some pipsqueak speller from off the street. This is what happens with strictness. It has awe built in. The more you cheat, the greater the fear. Where's the impunity in this world?"

"Just don't start in with the vengeful pus."

"An oath is an oath."

"You don't have to use the worst ones."

"It's time to present the roses," Pitkin said.

They went through the bronze door, past the instant silicone apparatus and down several flights of stairs that seemed even older and more damaged than the stairs he'd descended earlier. He heard organ music below, a reverberating cavern-sized snore, and he followed Pitkin through a slit in the wall and out into the Great Hole, a vast underground chamber largely in a natural state (cool stone surfaces) but including remnants of ancient architecture (columns, half-walls, part of a platform) as well as elements of recent installation (fluorescent lighting and structural reinforcement). The lights were suspended from large portable appliances that resembled clothing racks. The organ, which was Endor's, the same neon pipe organ Billy had seen in the hobby room, was set on an outcropping of rock in a far corner. Aside from Pitkin, the only people he saw at the moment were the organist, now playing the kind of intermission music featured at hockey games, and the old gentleman's doctor, heading directly toward Pitkin. The two men exchanged a few words and then the bearded advisor disappeared into a dim hollow about thirty yards away. Listening to the organ, Billy recalled Evinrude's remark about a loud noise bringing down the entire Great Hole, if a hole could be thought of as something readily subject to being brought down.

"The old gent may or may not make it," Bonwit said. "One advantage is the air down here, crystal clear, a beautiful purifying agent for the biomembrane. Now here's how we'll work it. The laureates are in the antecave off the Great Hole and they're being instructed in torch manipulation. You don't join them until they file in and Sandow gives you a hand signal. Sandow's the man at the organ. After he gives the hand signal, the biomembrane is wheeled in by Pitkin and Georgette from that shadowy area with me leading the way. Then Sandow makes the opening remarks and the pigeons are released."

"When do I present the roses?"

"After the pigeons," Bonwit said.

"What's this biomembrane that's being wheeled in?"

"It's what keeps old Ratner alive. Ultrasterile biomedical membrane environment. This is the prototype model, fully operational but with still a few kinks. It's a total life-support system that grew out of the trace-element isolator used to keep lab animals germ-free. The old gentleman never leaves. This is the only nonhostile environment we could work out for him considering his state of deterioration. The bacterial count is zero. There are double airlocks for air current control. Pressure is regulated and there's automatic oxygen therapy when his system needs a jolt. It's even got a vapor duct to cut down the chance of self-infection. If he begins to fail, Georgette raises the shield and I crawl in and operate. The biomembrane is a self-sterilizing operating theater in miniature and it adapts to a post-operative therapy center, he should live so long, as the saying goes."

"Is Sandow a laureate?"

"Sandow is an organist," the doctor said.

"I was told laureates only. I can understand an MD and a nurse and even a person who reads from the writings. But if it's all laureates, why move that organ all the way down from where it was and include someone that didn't win? Except maybe he did win and only plays the organ on the side."

"Unless they give a Nobel Prize for pedaling, he didn't win. But it adds to the mood, an organ. I for one don't mind him around. It makes for more pomp, having an organ. 'LaMar T. Sandow at the keyboard.' Besides he's the old gent's lifelong friend. You want a friend to see you honored. I'm all for an organ at a function like this. It supplies a heady tone."

"What do you specialize in?"

"Everything," the doctor said.

Pitkin returned, bent and shuffling, a bouquet of white roses in his arms.

"The colored nurse told me to tell you the face filled out."

"Good," Bonwit said.

"I made believe I did a little reading. I gave a good show. It made him teary around the nose. Thick green nose-blow runs out of his eyes. From his nose you get nothing but water."

"What do *you* think of having an organ?" Bonwit said.

"We already got one. What, you want two?"

"Just want to know what you think. Fielding a few ideas."

"Why, somebody's against it?"

"That's right."

"Wait, let me guess."

"You want to give me the flowers?" Billy said.

"Against the organ, who could it be? Which person for his size makes the biggest corrections? Tell me if I'm warm if I move toward the speller."

"It belongs to Endor. They should have left it where it was."

Sandow broke off the intermission music and began playing a triumphal march. Pitkin handed Billy the flowers and went back to the dark corner, this time accompanied by Dr. Bonwit. The laureates started filing in, thirty-one of them, in size places. Multicolored neon, flashing intermittently, pulsed through the clear tubing that extended well above the organ. The torches carried by the laureates were as large as the one Evinrude had used to light the way into the original jagged hole. Although still unlit, the torches were being held as if each one were about to cough forth an assortment of fresh lava; that is, the laureates kept the plastic devices well away from their bodies, every head averted. They seemed to march accompanied by a terrible belief in their own potential for self-immolation. It passed methodically down the line, a bland handshake, freezing them to their processional drag-step.

The small parade came to a halt as Sandow lifted his hands from the keyboard and spun himself to the end of the bench, looking directly at Billy. Echoes of the organ music collided high above the floor of the Great Hole. Sandow tapped his right hand twice on the inside of his left thigh. This, it turned out, was only the first of two signals and he followed it with a little wiggle of the thumb. Billy, with the flowers, took his place at the front of the line. He realized now that the first hand signal had been meant for him (get in line) and the second for the doctor, the nurse and Pitkin (wheel in the biomembrane), for at this moment a massive transparent tank came into view. Its basic shape was simple: a cylinder on wheels, a blunt-nosed torpedo set lengthwise on a metal undercasing to which were fixed four scooter-sized tires. Dr. Bonwit walked ahead of the biomembrane, kicking small stones out of the way, and behind it were Pitkin and the nurse, pushing. Everywhere on the ten-foot-long tank were complex monitoring devices and all sorts of gauges, tubes and switches. It was by far the most elaborate health mechanism Billy had ever seen and he stood on his toes to get a look at Ratner himself but the angle wasn't favorable just then. What he could see, clearly, were a half-dozen large bright sponsor decals and stickers on both sides of the biomembrane and even on the blunt front end. Corporate names, brand names, slogans and symbols:

MAINLINE FILTRONIC
Tank & Filter Maintenance

STERILMASTER PEERLESS AIR CURTAINING
"The breath you take is the life we save"

BIZENE POLYTHENE COATING
UDGA inspected and approved

WALKER-ATKINSON METALIZED UNDERSURFACES
From the folks at Uniplex Syntel

EVALITE CHROME PANELING
The glamour name in surgical supplies

DREAMAWAY
Bed linen, mattress and frame
A division of OmCo Research
"Building a model world"

Sandow stood before the organ on the natural rock shelf and waited for the bearded man and the nurse to stop wheeling. When they did, all was quiet except for an underground stream nearby and the last sobbing echo of the triumphal march barely reaching them from a distant surface of the huge cavern. Sandow, a balding thickset man, wore a sort of Oriental smile, a pained look subtly altered by decades of erosion.

"I'd like to open my remarks by reaffirming my friendship with the old gentleman despite going our separate ways more than twenty-five years ago due to clashing ideologies, which explains my presence here, symbolic of a coming together, a let's-join-hands-type-thing, and what a setting it is, ladies and gentlemen, a basilica if I may use that word in a nonsectarian sense of earthen rock and the relics of an unknown civilization these many feet down to light our torches in tribute to this gentle soul of science, who, when we were young men, he and I, espoused all there was to espouse in those benighted days of the principles of scientific humanism, including, as I recall, individual freedom, democracy for all peoples, a ban on nationalism and war, no waiting for a theistic deity to do what we ourselves could do as enlightened men and women joined in our humanistic convictions, the right to get divorced; but who, as I understand it, has now returned to the ideas and things from which so many of us were so eager to flee, proving, I suppose, that there's a certain longevity to benightedness, and I won't take up the time here providing you with a list of this great ex-scientist's current convictions beyond mentioning the secret power of the alphabet, the unnamable name, the literal contraction of the superdivinity, fear of sperm demons; so to enlarge on an earlier statement this is not only a coming together but a going away in a way, for having come to science and humanism, so has he gone, and in lieu of an eternal flame, which I had hoped to borrow for the occasion, we are here to light our torches to Shazar Lazarus Ratner, reasoning what better way to honor this man, this scientific giant, than to have the Nobelists light their torches from an eternal flame, which I'd wanted to get flown in from one of the nations in or near the cradle of civilization, simply borrowing the flame and returning it after the ceremony and they could bill us at their convenience but I was wary of pressure groups and I foresaw the remark from someone in such a group saying 'cradle of *whose* civilization,' for there is always this prejudice against Western civilization having its own cradle and calling it *the* cradle when other peoples have their own ideas of where the cradle is and even whether or not there is a cradle as we employ the term, being merely self-descriptive and not, I don't think, intending to pre-empt, none of which, as I thank you for your time and attention, has any bearing on the pigeons."

Apparently reacting to a prearranged word or phrase, one of the laureates stepped out of the line and approached a crate that was set beneath the natural stage where the organ was located.

"The pigeons," Sandow said. "Let us release the pigeons. The releasing of the pigeons, ladies and gentlemen."

The man raised the top of the box and about fifty pigeons came shaking out, like a series of knots unraveling on a single line, and flew toward the top of the cavern, veering just before they got there into an opening in the rock wall, merely a whisper now.

"The presenting of the roses," Sandow said. "The boy steps up to the great medico-engineering feat and symbolically presents the roses."

Billy strode to the tank and was lifted in the air by Dr. Bonwit and held standing on the curved surface of the transparent shield. Below, he saw the small figure of Ratner, pillowed in deep white. The doctor stood on one side of the tank, the nurse on the other, and together they supported Billy as he displayed the flowers for the benefit of the old gentleman.

"Ratner sees the roses," Sandow said. "The old gentleman acknowledges the floral bouquet."

The doctor and nurse lowered Billy to a straddling position on the tank. Bonwit turned a dial, activating a chambered device set into the clear shield directly over Ratner's face and about a foot from Billy's crotch. Immediately a bit of static was emitted from the interior of the biomembrane, apparently the sound of Ratner breathing through the bacteria-filtered talk chamber.

"The boy prepares to listen to the circulated words," Sandow said.

Bonwit took the flowers and inserted them in a sort of scabbard at the side of the biomembrane. Without the bouquet Billy was able to settle into a more comfortable straddling position. On his back Ratner looked directly into the boy's face. In a gesture of respect the latter leaned forward, trying to indicate his eagerness to hear the old gentleman's remarks. He was in fact neither eager nor respectful but the occasion seemed to demand gestures. Ratner wore a black beret and a long fringed prayer shawl that covered him from shoulders to feet.

"The old man speaks to the boy," Sandow said. "Sunk in misery and disease he speaks actual words to the little fellow on the tank."

The small ancient face was glazed like artificial fruit. The beret, however, gave the old man a semblance of heroic bearing. His arms were crossed on his chest, baby fists curled. What Pitkin had referred to as nose-blow was indeed being discharged from Ratner's eyes. Fortunately just a trickle. Far corner of each eye. Slowly the withered lips parted and the old man spoke.

"The universe, what is it?"

"I don't know."

"It began with a point. The point expanded so that darkness took up the left, light the right. This was the beginning of distinctions. But before expansion, there was contraction. There had to be room for the universe to fit. So the *en-sof* contracted. This made room. The creator, also known as G-dash-d, then made the point of pure energy that became the universe. In science this is what they call the big bang. Except for my money it's not a case of big bang versus steady state. It's a case of big bang versus little bang. I vote for little. Matter was so dense it could barely explode. The explosion barely got out. This was the beginning if you're speaking as a scientist. The fireball got bigger, the temperature fell, the galaxies began to form. But it almost never made it. There was such density. Matter was packed in like sardines. When it finally exploded, you almost couldn't hear it. This is science. As a scientist my preference is definitely little bang. As a whole man I believe in the contraction of the *en-sof* to make room for the point."

Billy raised his head and looked toward the laureates standing in line with their unlighted torches.

"He votes for little bang," he said. "The noise was muffled."

Then he crouched over the biomembrane as Ratner prepared to speak once again.

"The *en-sof* is the unknowable. The hidden. The that-which-is-not-there. The neither-cause-nor-effect. The G-dash-d beyond G-dash-d. The limitless. The not-only-unutterable-but-by-definition-inconceivable. Yet it emanates. It reveals itself through its attributes, the *sefiroth*. G-dash-d is the first of the ten sefirothic emanations of the *en-sof*. Without the *en-sof*'s withdrawal or contraction, there could be no point, no cosmic beginning, no universe, no G-dash-d. I learned this not long after I looked through my first telescope growing up as a boy in Brooklyn. But I failed to understand at that time."

Ratner paused here, apparently to regain his strength, and Billy glanced toward the others and made another capsule report, as he assumed they wished him to do, having traveled from every part of the world to be here for the ceremony.

"No universe without contraction. Grew up in Brooklyn, a boy, nonbelieving."

He turned his attention to Ratner once more. The lacquered face was unevenly puffy. Where teeth were missing, the inflamed sockets had bulged to the point of convexity, leaving a mouth divided between shaky teeth and burnt-out gummy nubs. Finally the old man's voice resembled a wind-up toy's, metallic and unreal, but Billy didn't know whether this was the result of his physical condition or the purifying action of the electronic talk chamber.

"We come from the stars," Ratner said. "Our chemicals, our atoms, these were first made in the centers of old stars that exploded and spread their remains across the sky eventually to come together as the sun we know and the planet we inhabit. I started out with binoculars, viewing the sky. It seemed remarkable to a boy like me, underfed and pale, with a small mental vista, that there was something bigger than Brooklyn. In those days of no television, the stars could be awesome to a boy, the way they swarmed, thin as I was, growing up, with binoculars. Later I got a telescope, my first, bought from a junk dealer, with a tripod, borrowed, and I stuck it out the window, top floor, and gazed for hours. Star fields, clusters, the moon. I read books, I learned, I gazed. Knowledge made me punch my fists against the walls in awe and shame. Our atoms were formed in the dense interiors of supergiant stars billions of years ago. Stars millions of times more luminous than our sun. They broke down and decayed and began to cool. Atoms from these stars are in our bones and nervous systems. We're stellar cinders, you and me. We come from the beginning or near the beginning. In our brain is the echo of the little bang. This is science, poeticized here and there, and this you can compare with the kabbalistic belief that every person has a sun inside him, a radiant burst of energy. Try to reach a mystical state without radiant energy and see what happens."

"Secondhand telescope," Billy said to the others. "Gazed at the stars and learned we're made of them. Pale and thin for his age."

"When I go into mystical states," Ratner said, "I pass beyond the opposites of the world and experience only the union of these opposites in a radiant burst of energy. I call it a burst. What else can I call it? You shouldn't think it's really a burst. Everything in the universe works on the theory of opposites. To see what it looks like outside the universe, you have to go into a trance or two. According to Pitkin, G-dash-d could live anywhere. He doesn't need the universe. He could set up headquarters east or west of the universe and not miss a thing. But this is Pitkin. A rare attempt to interpret. The mystical writings. The mystical oral traditions. The mystical interpretations, oral and written. These exist beneath the main body of thought and thinking. You don't go into a trance reading the everyday writings. The hidden texts, try *them*. The untranslated manuscripts. The oral word."

Billy looked at the laureates, then shrugged from his position atop the shield.

"Written, oral," Ratner said. "Black, white. Male, female. Let's hear you name some more."

"Day, night."

"Very good."

"Plus, minus."

"Even better," Ratner said. "Remember, all things are present in all other things. Each in its opposite."

Billy turned and shrugged once more.

"I gazed constantly, learning, a young man, top floor still, gaining weight. Finally I realized a portable telescope no longer suited my needs and aspirations. I married a woman whose father had a house with a backyard. I thought here I could build what I truly needed, a ten-inch reflector with rotating dome. So with his permission and blessing we moved into his house."

"In the desert, I bet, for the clear air."

"In Pittsburgh," Ratner said. "There we lived and built. Halvah helped me, my wife, grinding the mirror, assembling the mount, measuring and cutting wood, sending away for instructions, pasting and hammering. I started to accumulate academic degrees, to go beyond amateur ranking. All that reading, it was paying off. I continued to gaze. It was awful, Pittsburgh, in those days. Smoke, soot, particles of every description. There was a steel mill two blocks away. I had to gaze between shifts. Many times Halvah's father tried to read to me from the writings. I paid no attention, acquiring my degrees, corresponding with leading minds in the sciences and technologies. He would hum as he read, a sound of piety, fear and shame. Smoke came pouring over the backyard. Thick black ash fell all over the dome. I had to stand on a chair and sweep off the top with a broom. I gazed whenever possible, I ate the cooking, I corresponded with the leading minds. Sometimes I punched the bedroom door, plentifully replete as I was with knowledge of the physical world. My father-in-law hummed, Fish, my father-in-law. I asked Halvah what kind of writings these were that her father never ceased to read from. I said Halvah what writings are these? I inquired of her what manner of writings her father so incessantly read. The mystical writings, she said. I resilvered the mirror, these being the days before widespread aluminum. He tried to give me instructions, Fish, in the secrecy of things, the hiddenness, the buried nature. Did I listen or did I sit in my dome, rotating, gazing, an occasional belch from the food?"

Billy reported to the others: "Telescope in a dome in the backyard. Marriage to the man's daughter owning the house. Science pays off. He gazes between shifts."

The metallic lilt of Ratner's voice, when again he spoke, seemed to possess an extra shading, a suggestion of querulous tremor.

"You know what you remind me of?"

"What?"

"Somebody who's giving only one side of the story," the old man said. "Don't think I can't hear that you're reporting only science, leaving out the mystical content, which they could use a little exposure to, those laureates with their half a million Swedish kronor. It was less in my day. And don't think I didn't notice all that shrugging when I was saying black-white, male-female, a little bit of everything present in its opposite. Because I noticed."

"Some things are hard to summarize."

"Give the whole picture," Ratner said.

"I'll do better."

"If you want to repeat, repeat both sides."

"From now on you'll see improvement."

"How many sefirothic emanations did the *en-sof* emanate?"

"Ten," Billy said.

"In words, what can we say about the *en-sof*?"

"I don't know."

"Something or nothing?"

"Nothing."

"There is always something secret to be discovered," Ratner said. "A hidden essence. A truth beneath the truth. What is the true name of G-dash-d? How many levels of unspeakability must we penetrate before we arrive at the true name, the name of names? Once we arrive at the true name, how many pronunciations must we utter before we come to the secret, the hidden, the true pronunciation? On what allotted day of the year, and by which of the holiest of scholars, will the secret pronunciation of the name of names be permitted to be passed on to the worthiest of the initiates? And how passed on? Over water, in darkness, naked, by whispers? I sat in my dome, rotating, knowing nothing of this. Nor of the need to exercise the greatest caution in all aspects of this matter. Substitution, abbreviation, blank spaces, utter silence. The alphabet, the integers. Triangles, circles, squares. Indirection, numerology, acronyms, sighs. Not according to Pitkin, however. If you listen to him, everything means exactly what it says. Not one ounce of deviation. Interpretation isn't one of his strong points, Pitkin. He's not so good, Pitkin, when it comes to interpreting."

Ratner's toy voice hissed and crackled through the chambered slot. The laureates were silent, standing in size places. Pitkin sat nearby on a large stone, silent, one hand covering most of his face, the mink fedora well back on his head, legs crossed and white flesh showing between the top of his black socks and his hitched-up trousers. The doctor and nurse were silent, respectfully set back about ten yards from the biomembrane, one on each side. Sandow was sitting on the edge of the organ bench, silent. Somewhere beneath them the hidden stream moved over smooth rock, making a faint smacking sound. From the boy's viewpoint the decals on either side of the tank appeared to be lettered in reverse. He looked closely at the old gentleman, tiny inside his prayer shawl, face gleaming with polymerized sweat.

"Go into your own bottom parts," Ratner said. "Here you find the contradictions joined and harmonized. This is a good place to look for the secrets you didn't even know existed. If you think I'm lying, knock once on top of the tank."

"I do not knock."

"The writings have a substructure, a secret element of the divine. Kabbalists delving into esoteric combinations of letters widened the meaning of particular texts. I allowed this much to flow from Fish's lips, progressing as a man, winning prizes in the sciences, sharing the marriage bed with my Halvah, stinky feet or not, ashes raining down. The way Fish hummed as he read. It began to get to me. What is there in these writings, I asked myself, that this man should hum? A noise of shame, fear and humiliation, my Halvah's father's humming. I refitted the tracks under the dome so it could rotate more smoothly. I learned physics to go with astrophysics. Radio astronomy to match my astronomy. I punched the walls with knowledge. Halvah gave birth, a baby, born screaming. The only nonmystical state where the opposites are joined is infancy. So perfect they often die, babies, without cause. What's your opinion?"

"I was an incubator baby."

"Then you know what it's like, living in a tank. Look who I am. Someone whose air is cleaned every four hours. A face that collapses at the slightest provocation. Climb in for a minute. Come, lift the shield. I want to whisper in your ear."

Pretending he hadn't heard these last few words, Billy looked away to make his report.

"The mystical humming of his father-in-law. A child is born. Punching the walls. The dome rotates with added smoothness."

Reluctantly he turned once again to the figure in the biomembrane.

"Don't look down your nose at esoterica," Ratner said. "If you know the right combination of letters, you can make anything. This is the secret power of the alphabet. Meaningless sounds, abstract symbols, they have the power of creation. This is why the various parts of the mystical writings are not in proper order. Knowing the order, you could make your own world from just reading the writings. Everything is built from the twenty-two letter elements. The alphabet itself is both male and female. Creation depends on an anagram."

"It's hard to picture."

"We have acrostics too."

"Do you have numbers?"

"Is Mickey a mouse?" Ratner said. "Of course we have numbers. The emanations of the *en-sof* are numbers. The ten *sefiroth* are numerical operations that determine the course of the universe. Constant and variable. The *sefiroth* are both. I could go into sefirothic geometry but you don't have the awe for that, being mathematical. *Sefiroth* comes from the infinitive 'to count.' The power of counting, of finger-numbers, of one-to-ten. We also have gematria, which you probably heard about, assigning numerical value to each letter of the alphabet. I won't even tell you about the hidden relationships between words that we discover in this way. It would be too much of a feast to set before someone who isn't ready for it, a lifelong eater of peanuts, by which I refer to myself as viewed in the face of Fish's revelations, gazing, a man, backyard, night upon night, galaxies and nebulas, my head filled with NGC numbers. The steel mill went on strike. I gazed like a madman. You couldn't get me out of the dome with threats to my child. I decided to study the sun. Adjustments, new equipment, unsilvered mirror, precautions. The sun is a frightening thing to view through a telescope, solar wedge or no solar wedge. I thought ahead to the helium flash. The final expansion. Having come from the stars, we are returned. The sun within us, the source of all mystical bursts, is perfectly counterbalanced by the physical sun that presses outward, swallowing up the orbits of the nearest planets."

Beneath the beret, Ratner's face sagged a bit. The lustrous muscles went slack and there was a suggestion of reinforced flesh about to melt.

"Picture this," he said. "From that great unstable period, the sun collapses drastically. It becomes the same size as the former earth. Now we're right inside it, mongrelized with three other planets, compacted down to a whiff of gas. The sun proceeds to cool, white dwarf, red dwarf, black dwarf, a dead star, dark black. No energy, no light, no heat, no twinkle. The end."

"Can I get off now?"

"We come from supergiant solar bodies, great hot ionized objects, and we end in the center of a dead black sphere. We're part star, you and me. Our beginning and end are made in the stars. Light, dark. High, low. Big, little. Go ahead, take it from there."

"East, west."

"Up," Ratner said.

"Down."

"In."

"Out."

"Give me a few, to test my fading powers."

"Love."

"Hate," Ratner said.

"Innocence."

"Kilt."

"Very good," Billy said after a thoughtful pause.

The old man lay back, panting gently. A few minutes passed. Finally he stirred himself.

"When the strike ended I went back to gazing by night. I studied eclipsing stars, flare stars, variables of every kind, reading star catalogues in my spare time, memorizing star tables, taking the cooking into the dome with me, a real fanatic. Also I feared the sight of Fish, always with the writings in his hand. He took books and folios into the toilet with him and stayed for hours. We could hear the humming from his bedroom half the night. He pushed his armchair into a corner and sat with his back to the room. This kind of transcendence I feared, a scientist, still young, pledged to the observable, welcomed into organizations, reaching a peak of knowledge, Pittsburgh, the backyard, my own dome, handmade, that rotated. The night sky was sensational. I made charts and calculations, identifying novalike variables, Cepheids, cool and hot stars, egg-shaped doubles. The child developed putative diarrhea, terrible, a living diaper. Did I realize I was being punished for knowledge without piety or did I sit in the observatory, scanning, light from the universe entering my eye?"

"Looks like trouble's coming," Billy said to those assembled in the Great Hole. "He fears this person Fish who's always in the toilet reading. The kid is sick. A question is asked about piety and sitting."

"Come in and browse," Ratner said. "I know a few words I want to whisper in your ear. Come, pay a visit. Bonwit does it all the time, the doctor, holding his breath. A thing he denies doing to make me feel better. Come, let me whisper."

"I can hear you from right here."

"Pay a dying man a visit."

"I'll catch something. The shield might jam behind me and then where am I? I can hold my breath just so long."

"Browse a while."

"Put yourself in my place," the boy said. "What if the shield jams while I'm in there and then you die? What happens then? I'm probably taking a chance just sitting up here. All they told me was the flowers. Present the flowers."

"So this Fish," Ratner said. "This in-law Fish of mine. My Halvah's father. He begins to get to me with a remark passed at dinner about the hidden source of the mystical writings, doctrines and traditions. A secret beginning in the Orient. All this esoterica. Born in the East. Moving as if by stealth to other parts of the world. Always this obscurity. This secret element. I'll tell you an interesting piece of news. If you think I'm making it up, tap once on the shield. A dying man has no shadow. First heard from Fish. The person about to die lacks all shadow. Knock once if I'm lying."

"I don't understand the question."

"You know what you remind me of?"

"What?"

"A golem," Ratner said.

"What's that?"

"An artificial person."

"No such thing."

"According to instructions in the secret manuscripts, you get a little earth, run some water over it and then recite the letters of the alphabet in esoteric combinations with the four consonants of the t-dash-t-r-dash-g-r-dash-m-m-dash-t-dash-n. From this you get a golem."

"I'm almost ready to knock once."

"Light from the universe entered my eye," Ratner said. "I am in the dome, gazing, an ordinary night, through the eyepiece, open clusters, rich fields, my name being mentioned in the journals, this and that prize coming my way, a signer of petitions, the arts, the sciences, the humanisms, our child still in diapers, a tragedy, making watery excess thirty times a day, my Halvah up to her wrists in baby-do. Suddenly what do I see? A thing beyond naming. Not a thing at all. A state. I am falling into a state. Radiance everywhere. An experience. I am having an experience."

Breaking the long silence that followed, Billy spoke to the others.

"An ordinary night in the dome, getting famous, he starts to see something. The in-law Fish is winning."

Ratner's left thumb quivered slightly.

"There's nothing more I can say. I lived my life. Good, evil. Aphelion, perihelion. Hungry, full. Since then I have often fallen into states, passing beyond the opposites of the world. What use was a telescope after this? I had the states. Every experience was a new experience. It's something you don't get used to. Fish instructed me. In time I went back to my original roots, Eastern Parkway, the dispersed of Judah. We prospered as a family, learning fear, shame, piety and awe, my mind no longer filled to satiation with knowledge of the physical universe. Being pious I felt no need to punch the walls. They kept in touch with me, the leading minds, still an award or two, invitations every week. Only one I accepted, to visit Palomar, the two-hundred-inch reflector. I sat in the observer's cage right inside the telescope. Just the cage was bigger than my whole dome. I looked at some galaxies in detail. Nice, I liked it. When I climbed out they told me they had a special honor. A star. They gave a star my name."

"Falling into states," Billy said to the others. "Back to Brooklyn, the walls no longer punched. He visits Palomar. A star is named."

"Lift the shield and climb in," Ratner said. "I know some words to whisper. Come, take time. Make the sacrifice. A dying man needs visits. Be a sport for once in your life."

"Infectious danger."

"Hold your breath and lift out the shield. Take time. It's a worthwhile whisper or I wouldn't ask."

"I'm scared in plain English."

"We're all scared," Ratner said. "Who isn't scared? You, me, the laureates. Terror is everywhere. This I learned from the writings. Fish, humming, gave me his folios to take back to Brooklyn. Pitkin advises every day on the terror around us. Take demons, for example. You wouldn't think there's a connection between demons and the sperm in your testicles. The terror of onanism is that bodiless demons are able to make bodies for themselves from the spilled seed. Look at a drop of semen under a microscope and see how amazed you become at the concentration of life in that small area, the darting swarm, a phenomenon irresistible to demons. To be onanistic is to make children for the demonic element. You become the father of evil spirits. How can the pious and the G-dash-d-fearing campaign against such things? It's not easy, believe me. Nothing in the writings is easy. If I give the impression I abandoned science for the easy life, knock once. In returning to my roots I entered a world of strict mystery. A lot of loose ends, true. But great strictness in the numerology, the permutations, the legends, the symbolism, the esoteric combinations of letters, the compiling of substitutes for the ineffable name, the secrets of golem-making. In words, what can be said about the mystical state I entered while looking through the telescope in the dome in Pittsburgh, the yard covered with soot, double shifts at the mill?"

"Nothing."

"The first man was a golem before he gave names to things," Ratner said. "He was unformed matter waiting for a soul. Golem-making is laden with danger. What else can I say to a person who reminds me of one?"

The old gentleman's face appeared to be collapsing. Clear matter was being discharged from his pores as the face itself began to settle. This degenerative action was such that even the beret was affected. It slid forward a bit and to one side, coming to rest at a sharp angle over Ratner's left eye, much more rakish than the occasion seemed to warrant. His voice, running down, was a mechanized caw, barely a trace remaining of the desperate melodies of Brooklyn. He raised his right hand slightly.

"What is this but a place?" he said. "Nothing more than a place. We're both here in this place, occupying space. Everywhere is a place. All places share this quality. Is there any real difference between going to a gorgeous mountain resort with beautiful high thin waterfalls so delicate and ribbonlike they don't even splash when they hit bottom—waterfalls that *plash;* is this so different from sitting in a kitchen with bumpy linoleum and grease on the wall behind the stove across the street from a gravel pit? What are we talking about? Two places, that's all. There's nowhere you can go that isn't a place. So what's such a difference? If you can understand this idea, you'll never be unhappy. Think of the word 'place.' A sun deck with views of gorgeous mountains. A tiny dark kitchen. These share the most important of all things anything can share. They are places. The word 'place' applies in both cases. In this sense, how do we distinguish between them? How do we say one is better or worse than the other? They are equal in the most absolute of ways. Grasp this truth, sonny, and you'll never be sad."

Billy felt himself being lifted in the air. It was Dr. Bonwit, removing him from the biomembrane and setting him on the floor. Although he wasn't sure he liked all this lifting, he was glad to be off the tank. Observing size places he returned to the front of the line. Pitkin approached the tank, put his ear to the chambered slot and then departed. As Bonwit and the nurse busied themselves at the cart that held the silicone preparation, Sandow rose from the organ bench.

"Let us light the torches," he said. "The lighting of the ceremonial torches. The torch-lighting commences, ladies and gentlemen."

Holding a lighted candle, Pitkin stood now at the base of the natural stage. As Sandow called their names, the laureates proceeded in alphabetical order to touch the wicks of their torches to Pitkin's candle-flame. Then each returned to the line. As he waited for his name to be called Billy began to get nervous. He didn't know why; lighting a torch would be easy compared to straddling a biomembrane and being invited inside. Yet his nervousness grew. He actually feared the sound of his name being called. Person after person was summoned and the tension accumulated. He'd never experienced anything like this. He began to doubt that he'd be able to respond when his name was finally called. It made no sense. There was nothing to fear. It was just his name being spoken aloud as part of a series of names. His distress increased as Sandow reached the M's. What did it mean? His name had been called hundreds of times in a dozen places. Routinely he'd acknowledged it. It was his name, wasn't it, and he was the person who answered, right? He felt pressure building, a tightness in his chest and throat. Sandow got closer to T. There was no clearly defined threat and yet the pressure built. He'd faced worse threats with relative poise. From LoQuadro and the void core to Endor's hole's hole to Grbk and his nipples to Mohole's big greenie. Through all these nonspecific threats he had endured if not prevailed. The current threat, if it even qualified as such, was in a different category, he felt. The others, vague as they were, definitely qualified as threats. This one went too deep to be defined. (Existenz.) Maybe there was no word or phrase that quite described the tenuous nature of being. (Oblivio obliviorum.) To exist was to have being or actuality. To have life; live. To continue to live. To be present under certain circumstances or in a specified place. (Nihil ex nihilo.) Maybe he would not occur when his name was called. It wasn't merely a question of not being there to answer or of not being able to respond because of the pressure in his chest. Maybe he would not *occur*. (Nada de nadiensis.) The calling of his name might pre-empt him. The name itself might assimilate his specific presence.

"Twillig."

He realized he had no torch. No one had given him a torch. Nevertheless he walked over to Pitkin, not knowing what else to do and finding it a reasonably easy procedure. To counteract an intangible threat to one's sense of existence it may be necessary only to take a step from here to there. He looked up into the long coarse beard, feeling the sense of constriction begin to leave his body. Pitkin remained motionless, the candle burning at eye level.

"I have no torch."

"Well put," the advisor said. "You could make a career uttering truths."

"What happens next?"

"The old gentleman told me to tell you something even though you were in such a hurry you couldn't take time to pay a visit before the face collapsed and they had to inject. It was so serious they filled the needle right in front of him. That serious I never saw it. But he took time to give me a message, face or no face, even though a certain person I'm looking at was too much of a smarty pants to climb inside. He told me whisper to the golem in his ear."

After a pause, Pitkin's lips began to move. However, no sound emerged.

"What did he tell you to whisper?"

The lips paused a second time. When they moved now, however, words were soon to follow.

"The universe is the name of G-dash-d. All of us. Everything. Here, there, everywhere. Time and space. The whole universe. It all adds up to the true name of G-dash-d."

Another laureate's name was called and the man advanced to light his torch. Pitkin's lips were still moving. Billy moved out of the way as the remaining two or three people responded to Sandow's roll call. Finally all the laureates were back in line, this time with lighted torches. Sandow took his place at the keyboard and began playing a profound lament, the neon pulsing through the clear pipes in slow motion. Pitkin, still holding the candle, moved toward Billy in an earnestly furtive manner, sideways, inch by inch, eyes straight ahead, feet not lifted from the ground.

"For once in my life I talk without looking," he said. "You who I looked at before, hair-splitter, I'm only talking this time, making sure you're reminded not to fidget. Arithmetic monkey, keep your knuckles off the ground. One squirm and out you go goodbye. Even watch with the way you breathe. Never through the nose. You who I'm talking to."

"I understand you're growing a beard," Billy said.

Swiftly, with no excess motion, Dr. Bonwit had put on a surgical mask, raised the shield, climbed into the tank and administered the facial injection, hunched over Ratner's shrunken form. Now he and the nurse wheeled the biomembrane toward a man-made opening beyond which, Billy assumed, an elevator waited. Pitkin followed them, his feet alternately gliding and bumping over the ground. Finally the biomembrane, its sponsor decals gleaming, disappeared into the opening, followed first by Pitkin and then, as the music reached a despondent coda, by the laureates in single file, their lighted torches casting shadow-tremors on the walls. This left Sandow, who climbed down from the stage and hurried out of the Great Hole.

This in turn left Billy, still shaken by the awareness that his own specific presence could seem so insubstantial, so nearly imaginary, a condition easily threatened by a one-word utterance. Pessimistic echoes were still diminishing as he headed through the opening. He came to a tall gate fastened across a shaft that was broad enough to hold a freight elevator. The elevator had already departed, however, leaving only the nurse behind, Georgette Bottomley, a slender figure dressed in white.

"They could fit all those people in one elevator?" Billy said. "Plus the tank too?"

"Plus the tank too but not plus Georgette."

"No room for one more?"

"I don't mind telling you I'm peeved off about that. Whenever doctor wants to get in his clientele's good graces, it means nurse have to wait. All my professional life I've been standing aside for the parade to go by. There's a chain of priority, you got to understand. This time it was doctor first, patient second, Nobel Prize winners third, rhythm section fourth, old man with beard fifth, Georgette in her accustomized place bringing up the rear. I'm good and peeved. I'll say it again."

"Where are you from?"

"United States."

"Whereabouts?"

"Hundred Thirty-eighth Street."

"I've heard of it."

"Ever been there?"

"Never been there. Just heard of it."

"Good and peeved," she said. "All my life I did without. I launched my professional career so I could stop doing without. Doctor has a house with grounds. I always know when he's trying to impress somebody, because that's when he tells me to step off an elevator or get out of a moving vehicle. Business, industry and the corporation. Nothing under an executive vice-president gets into that office. We run checks so nobody can falsify their title. Doctor looks up their fannies and tells them they're doing just fine. When we get their waste specimen reports back from the lab, he calls them up and says fine, doing fine, keep it up. If they're out of town on business, he wires them about their specimens. Nice, fine, beautiful. He gives them encouragement. He praises their specimens. Oldest trick in the world but it always works."

"I guess that's how you get a house with grounds."

"Always I'm the one's got to make room, understand. But no point you and me swinging the heavy gloves. We got a long flight ahead. It's doctor and the beard I'm peeved off at."

"I'm not going back."

"Mean to tell me you're staying here?"

"I guess so."

"You standing there and telling me plane or no plane you are not hot-trotting your body away from this locale?"

"I stay until somebody says leave, I guess. Nobody's said anything as far as I know. I guess I stay."

"That fazes me. It really does. That fazes my whole composure."

"You think it's that bad here?"

"It's not a question of bad," Georgette said. "An accident is bad, which I've been at a hundred before I went into private practice. This place is no accident, no. But it's got such separate parts, seems like to me. Maybe it's just too new. All I know is one thing doesn't lead to another the way it should. I'm glad I'm going. I just wish this elevator had a button I could push so a light come on and we get out of here fast. See, that's what I mean about one thing not leading to another. Whenever you have an elevator with no button to call it with, that's when you wake up in the middle of the night with the menses cramps."

The freight elevator descended and kept right on going. Through the gate they watched it pass their level. A few minutes later they heard it coming up. When it stopped finally, Evinrude was aboard. He still carried the torch he'd been holding when Billy had encountered him in the vicinity of the jagged hole. This time the torch was unlighted. Georgette unlatched the gate and they stepped into the elevator. Evinrude lifted a projecting handle, starting them upward. He gave the two passengers no more than a grudging nod before directing his attention to the floor between his feet. After a long climb he depressed the lever and the elevator came to a stop.

"You, the nurse, you step off. The boy stays until we reach his stop. Stand back for the moving gate, watch your step stepping off, walk don't run."

They ascended again, two of them, moving in remarkably smooth fashion considering the fact that this was a freight elevator and not the smaller vibrationless kind. "And so irrational numbers were defined as convergent sequences of rationals," the manuscript had said. "The deft manipulation of such polar extremes, with resulting approximate values, may drive the purely logical observer to seal himself in a brickwork privy as a means of perverse defense against the cries of 'poetic truth' that so often accompany sequential definitions and (to cross the mathematical brink this once, and briefly) approximations of any kind." Evinrude stopped the elevator, opened the gate and led Billy into a gigantic storeroom full of equipment.

"This is where we expect them to surface," he said.

"Who?"

"The pigeons."

"The ones released in the ceremony?"

"They flew through a hole in solid rock and from there either back out again or into a ventilation duct that leads up eventually into this storeroom. If they flew back out into the Great Hole, that's not so bad. If they're in here or en route to in here, that means trouble."

"Didn't anyone know this would happen?"

"They weren't supposed to release pigeons," Evinrude said. "The subject was raised at a briefing. It was determined no pigeons. We drew up guidelines. We went to great lengths. But they released anyway, so now we have to retrieve. I happen to hate pigeons. I can't stand being anywhere near them. But it's my job to retrieve so I'll just have to submerse my feelings and go do it. All this because somebody ignored the guidelines."

"Pitkin, I bet."

"The duct's over that way."

"Why do I have to be here?"

"I need someone to help me deal with the pigeons. I didn't have the wherewithal emotionally to ask someone my own age. Besides, children know how to deal with animals. Adults have grown too far from their origins to be able to confront animals on a nonpet basis. The duct comes out of the wall behind that long row of tables."

They pushed through a dozen stacks of shipping containers. Deal with the pigeons, the man had just said. To Billy this sounded as though either a massacre or a bargaining session was in store. Evinrude still carried the unlighted torch, a circumstance suggesting massacre.

"So you do mathematics."

"I'm the one."

"The very word strikes fear into my heart," Evinrude said.

"Mathematics?"

"It goes back to early schooling. The muffled terror of those gray mornings getting out of bed and going to school and opening up a mathematics textbook with its strange language and letters for numbers and theorems to memorize. I didn't mind any other subject. But math struck terror. Everything about it. The sound of the words. The diagrams and formulas. The look of the book. Sometimes I find it hard to believe that humans actually do mathematics, considering what's involved. It's like a branch of learning in outer space."

As they got closer to the ventilation duct, Evinrude carefully inspected the floor as well as every item of equipment within reach.

"I don't think they're here," he said. "Because I'll tell you why. Wherever pigeons are, pretty soon the shithing starts."

"The what?"

"Pigeons are known for their shith."

"You mean 'shit,' don't you?"

"Did I say it wrong?"

"Definitely."

"There's not something called bullshith?"

"There's no *h* at the end. There's just one *h* and it's near the beginning."

"I should be standing here frankly amazed. I should but I'm not. Because I'll tell you why. All my life I've been making little mistakes like that. 'Shith' is just one example. I guess I learned it wrong."

"Where did you grow up?"

"In the outskirts," Evinrude said. "With a volunteer family. I had no parentage of my own. I think this led to oversights in my upbringing. Little gaps here and there. I'm weak in some areas. No doubt about it."

"Shit is universal no matter which language. Use my spelling and I guarantee you're safe."

They reached the duct. Evinrude flicked a switch, reversing the air current.

"If they were on their way this way they can forget it because once the air is flowing the other way the only thing they can do is relax and be carried back to the Great Hole. They're on their way down. We got here in time. They haven't surfaced. I definitely think that entitles us to something."

A single pigeon stood about sixty feet to Evinrude's right. Billy pointed it out to him. The pigeon began to approach, taking little pink-footed grip-steps. Evinrude held his torch out away from his body, then placed it gently on the ground, as though signifying his peaceful intentions.

"Why isn't it flying?" he said. "I can accept their presence in the air. When they walk I hate them. I just want to crumple."

"Then let's leave."

"Why isn't it afraid? It's walking right at us. I hate the way the head goes back and forth. They're full of disease in case you didn't know. Look at the funny steps it takes. They're very famous for disease. Watch out for your nervous system in particular."

"I'm going," Billy said. "Goodbye."

"I consider myself terrified. I'm consciously trying to inundate my feelings but so far no luck at all. I am really scared. I can hardly bear to look at its little head gliding forward and back, forward and back. I hate the way it walks, don't you? Those scabby little feet. It's definitely headed this way in case you had hopes."

"I'm running," Billy said. "If I were you, I'd do the same. Come on. Let's go. Goodbye."

"I don't know how to run."

"Come on, hurry."

"I never learned," Evinrude said.

"Everybody knows how to run. It's easy. You just move your legs and then you're running. The brain sends a message to your legs and all of a sudden you're running. If you don't hurry up about it, I'm leaving. Just move your legs fast. Get your brain to send the message. Everybody can run. It's not hard. Try it and see what happens."

The pigeon took several more pink steps.

"It's not hard if you know how," Evinrude said. "I don't happen to know how. The subject of running is foreign to me. As a child I wasn't taught how to run and I've never been able to pick it up on my own. It's something I've always envied in other people, this marvelous ability to run."

Anthony DeCurtis

"An Outsider in This Society": An Interview with Don DeLillo

It began like this. In May of 1988 a friend of mine in the publicity department at Viking called and said that Don DeLillo's new novel, *Libra*, about the assassination of President Kennedy, would be published soon, and that, uncharacteristically, DeLillo might be willing to do some interviews. Because DeLillo had written a piece about the assassination for *Rolling Stone* in 1983, my friend thought *Rolling Stone* was one magazine DeLillo might talk to.

I was delighted. I asked him to send along the galleys for the novel, and said I'd bring it up with the magazine's executive editor. The galleys arrived with a note that read, in part, "As I told you over the phone, DeLillo has been very reluctant to give interviews in the past. But with the right person, and with the proper format (one restricting itself mostly to the book itself, and to the life and times of Lee Harvey Oswald), DeLillo might be agreeable. A few biographical details won't hurt, but he's wary of the full treatment."

Everyone at *Rolling Stone* went wild over the book. I wrote my friend that we were willing to do the interview on more or less whatever terms DeLillo stated. He passed our request along to DeLillo. DeLillo turned us down.

I talked to my friend. Would it help if I wrote a letter directly to DeLillo—that is, addressed to DeLillo by name, delivered to my friend to pass along to DeLillo—telling him what the interview would be like and explaining a little bit about myself? It might.

I spent a couple of hours writing the letter. It included earnest sentences like, "In addition to being a senior writer at *Rolling Stone,* I hold a Ph.D. in contemporary fiction from Indiana University, and I'm very familiar with all your novels." It also included a paragraph summary of how I thought *Libra* related to his earlier books, which, with true journalistic economy, I later plumbed for the introduction I wrote for the interview when it eventually ran in *Rolling Stone*.

As I wrote the letter, I was both haunted and inhibited by the references to journalists in DeLillo's books. It was hard, at least in my own mind, not to sound like one of his characters. I consciously used the term "full-length interview" in the letter, rather than the first term that came to mind—"major piece"—because of a specific passage in which the filmmaker in *The Names* speaks about writers: "You know how I am about privacy. I'd hate to think you came here to do a story on me. A major piece, as they say. Full of insights. The man and his work. . . . The filmmaker on location. The filmmaker in seclusion. Major pieces. They're always major pieces."

Writing for *Rolling Stone* presented complexities along that line as well. The magazine that gives DeLillo's novel *Running Dog* its title bears some resemblance to *Rolling Stone*. And, as someone who writes primarily about rock 'n roll, I've always loved the passage in *Great Jones Street,* in which a television reporter from ABC shows up at the apartment of Bucky Wunderlick, rock star in self-exile, to ask for an interview:

> "Who are you?"
> "ABC," he said.
> "Forget it."
> "Nothing big or elaborate. An abbreviated interview. Your tele-

vised comments on topics of interest. Won't take ten minutes. We're all set up downstairs. Ten minutes. You've got my word, Bucky. The word of a personal admirer."

"Positively never."

"I haven't done this kind of massive research since I've been in the glamour end of the business," the reporter pleads—a plea ("I'm very familiar with all your novels") that touches the heart of an ex-academic now at play in the fields of popular culture.

Anyway, I gave the letter to my friend and went on vacation. It was late June by this time. When I returned around July 4th there was a message on my answering machine from my friend. "Don liked your letter," he declared. (Student eternal, I confess to thrilling at the words.) Don—suddenly, now, he was Don—was more interested in doing the interview; he would call me—himself!—to discuss it further. If all this sounds protracted and unnecessarily complicated, you've never tried to get an interview with Sting, David Byrne, or George Harrison.

One afternoon a few days later, the phone rang at work: "This is Don DeLillo." The questions were simple and friendly: "How do you go about doing one of these things?" (We meet someplace quiet and talk for about two hours with a tape recorder running.) "Do you do much editing?" (Yes, for reasons of space and because a lively spoken conversation does not necessarily translate directly into a lively printed interview. [For the record, all material of interest that was edited out of the interview as it appeared in *Rolling Stone* for reasons of space has been restored for this version.]) "Where do you want to do this?" (Wherever you like that's quiet.) We arranged to meet at his house a few weeks later.

The train ride from midtown Manhattan to the picture-book Westchester suburb where DeLillo lives offers a capsule view of virtually the entire spectrum of American life. After leaving Grand Central Station, the train comes up from underground at Ninety-sixth Street on Manhattan's East Side, rolls serenely through Harlem, then crosses the Harlem River and enters the devastated landscape of the South Bronx. The journey continues through the North Bronx, the working-class neighborhood where DeLillo, whose parents were Italian immigrants, grew up and attended college at Fordham University. Finally, the train passes into Westchester's leafy environs.

At DeLillo's station, the author and his wife, Barbara Bennett, were waiting. The sun was blazing. A crushing August heat. Like the train trip, which links the quotidian splendor and the nightmarish underside of the American dream, the brutal weather seemed appropriate. "This is the last comfortable moment you'll have for a while," DeLillo said with a smile as he got in the car. "The car is air-conditioned, but the house isn't." Bennett, who was driving, jokingly suggested that we do the interview in the car, or perhaps at a local bar. When I told the couple about the hard time I had recently interviewing a musician who was frustratingly inarticulate and far more adept at talking around questions than answering them, DeLillo turned around and assured me, "I plan to be exactly that way myself."

One of the major voices in American fiction for nearly two decades, DeLillo, who is now fifty-one, said he rarely grants interviews because he lacks "the necessary self-importance." "I'm just not a public man," he said. "I'd rather write my books in private and then send them out into the world to discover their own public life.

"*Libra* is easier to talk about than my previous books," he continued. "The obvious reason is it's grounded in reality and there are real people to discuss. Even someone who hasn't read the book can respond at least in a limited way to any discussion of people like Lee Oswald or Jack Ruby. It is firmer material. I'm always reluctant to get into abstract discussions, which I admit my earlier novels tended to lean toward. I wrote them, but I don't necessarily enjoy talking about them."

Still, *Libra*—DeLillo's ninth novel—is more of a culmination than a departure. DeLillo's first novel, *Americana*, which appeared in 1971, ends in Dealey Plaza, in Dallas, the site of the Kennedy assassination, and references to the slaying turn up in several of his other books. The piece DeLillo wrote for *Rolling Stone* in 1983, "American Blood," effectively serves as a précis for *Libra*.

Moreover, rather than advancing yet another "theory" of the assassination, *Libra* simply carries forward the themes of violence and conspiracy that have come to define DeLillo's fiction. "This is a work of the imagination," he writes in the author's note that concludes the book. "While drawing from the historical record, I've made no attempt to furnish factual answers to any questions raised by the assassination." Instead, he hopes the novel will provide "a way of thinking about the assassination without being constrained by half-facts or overwhelmed by possibilities, by the tide of speculation that widens with the years."

In *Libra*, DeLillo describes the murder of the President as "the seven seconds that broke the back of the American century." But this cataclysm differs only in scale from the killings that shatter complacent, enclosed lives in *Players* (1977), *Running Dog* (1978), and *The Names* (1982). Similarly, the college football player who is the main character in *End Zone* (1972) and the rock-star hero of *Great Jones Street* (1973) both achieve an alienation that rivals the emotional state DeLillo sees in Lee Harvey Oswald. Apocalyptic events profound in their impact and uncertain in their ultimate meaning shadow *Ratner's Star* (1976) and *White Noise* (1985), just as the assassination does the world of *Libra*—and our world, a quarter of a century after it occurred.

The interview took place in DeLillo's backyard; afterward we went off to a diner on the town square—a village center DeLillo approvingly described as "like something out of the fifties"—for a late lunch of burgers, fries, and Cokes. In his yard, DeLillo sat on a lawn chair and sipped iced tea. Fortunately, the yard was shady, and the sky clouded over a bit. Even so, the heat, the humidity, the lush green of the grounds and the eerie din of cicadas gave the scene an almost tropical feel. DeLillo—wiry and intense, wearing jeans and a plaid shirt open at the collar, speaking with deliberate slowness in a gripping monotone—seemed the image of a modern-day Kurtz, a literary explorer of the heart of darkness comfortably at home in the suburbs of America.

DECURTIS: The Kennedy assassination seems perfectly in line with the concerns of your fiction. Do you feel you could have invented it if it hadn't happened?

DELILLO: Maybe it invented me. Certainly, when it happened, I was not a fully formed writer; I had only published some short stories in small quarterlies. As I was working on *Libra*, it occurred to me that a lot of tendencies in my first eight novels seemed to be collecting around the dark center of the assassination. So it's possible I wouldn't have become the kind of writer I am if it weren't for the assassination. Certainly when it happened I had no feeling that it was part of the small universe of my work, because my work, as I say, was completely undeveloped at that point.

DeCurtis: What kind of impact did the assassination have on you?

DeLillo: It had a strong impact, as it obviously did for everyone. As the years have flowed away from that point, I think we've all come to feel that what's been missing over these past twenty-five years is a sense of a manageable reality. Much of that feeling can be traced to that one moment in Dallas. We seem much more aware of elements like randomness and ambiguity and chaos since then.

A character in the novel describes the assassination as "an aberration in the heartland of the real." We still haven't reached any consensus on the specifics of the crime: the number of gunmen, the number of shots, the location of the shots, the number of wounds in the President's body—the list goes on and on. Beyond this confusion of data, people have developed a sense that history has been secretly manipulated. Documents lost and destroyed. Official records sealed for fifty or seventy-five years. A number of suggestive murders and suicides involving people who were connected to the events of November 22nd. So from the initial impact of the visceral shock, I think we've developed a much more deeply unsettled feeling about our grip on reality.

DeCurtis: You have been interested for a long time in the media, which certainly played a major role in the national experience of the assassination. Television had just made its impact on politics in the 1960 election, and then for the week following the murder, it seemed that everyone was watching television, seeing Jack Ruby's murder of Lee Harvey Oswald and then Kennedy's funeral. It's as if the power of the media in our culture hadn't been fully felt until that point.

DeLillo: It's strange that the power of television was utilized to its fullest, perhaps for the first time, as it pertained to a violent event. Not only a violent, but, of course, an extraordinarily significant event. This has become part of our consciousness. We've developed almost a sense of performance as it applies to televised events. And I think some of the people who are essential to such events—particularly violent events and particularly people like Arthur Bremer and John Hinckley—are simply carrying their performing selves out of the wings and into the theater. Such young men have a sense of the way in which their acts will be perceived by the rest of us, even as they commit the acts. So there is a deeply self-referential element in our lives that wasn't there before.

DeCurtis: The inevitable question: Where were you when John Kennedy was shot?

DeLillo: I was eating lunch with two friends in a restaurant on the west side of Manhattan and actually heard about the shooting at a bank a little later. I overheard a bank teller telling a customer that the President had been shot in Dallas. And my first curious reaction was, "I didn't even know he was in Dallas." Obviously it was totally beside the point. But the small surprise then, of course, yielded to the enormous shock of what these words meant. I didn't watch very much television that weekend. I didn't watch much of the funeral. I think I have a kind of natural antipathy to formal events of that kind. But certainly a sense of death seemed to permeate everything for the next four or five days.

DeCurtis: You refer to the assassination at various points in novels prior to *Libra*, and of course you wrote an essay about the assassination for *Rolling Stone* in 1983. What finally made you feel that you had to pursue it as the subject of a novel?

DeLillo: I didn't start thinking about it as a major subject until the early part of this decade. When I did the 1983 piece in *Rolling Stone*, I began to realize how enormously wide-reaching the material was and how much more deeply I would have to search before I could begin to do justice to it. Because I'm a novelist, I guess I defined "justice" in terms of a much more full-bodied work than the nonfiction piece I had done, and so I began to think seriously about a novel.

Possibly a motivating element was the fact that Oswald and I lived within six or seven blocks of each other in the Bronx. I didn't know this until I did the research for the *Rolling Stone* piece. He and his mother, Marguerite, traveled to New York in '52 or early '53, because her oldest son was stationed at Ellis Island with the Coast Guard.

They got in the car and drove all the way to New York and eventually settled in the Bronx. Oswald lived very near the Bronx Zoo. I guess he was thirteen and I was sixteen at the time. I suppose this gave me a personal nudge toward the material.

Turning it into fiction brought a number of issues to the surface. If I make an extended argument in the book it's not that the assassination necessarily happened this way. The argument is that this is an interesting way to write fiction about a significant event that happens to have these general contours and these agreed-upon characters. It's my feeling that readers will accept or reject my own variations on the story based on whether these things work as fiction, not whether they coincide with the reader's own theories or the reader's own memories. So this is the path I had to drive through common memory and common history to fiction.

DECURTIS: Did it seem odd that some reviews evaluated your theory of the assassination almost as if it were fact and not fiction?

DELILLO: Inevitably some people reviewed the assassination itself, instead of a piece of work which is obviously fiction. My own feeling at the very beginning was that I had to do justice to historical likelihood. In other words, I chose what I consider the most obvious possibility: that the assassination was the work of anti-Castro elements. I could perhaps have written the same book with a completely different assassination scenario. I wanted to be obvious in this case because I didn't want novelistic invention to become the heart of the book. I wanted a clear historical center on which I could work my fictional variations.

DECURTIS: Apart from the personal reason you mentioned, why did you choose to tell the story from Oswald's point of view?

DELILLO: I think I have an idea of what it's like to be an outsider in this society. Oswald was clearly an outsider, although he fought against his exclusion. I had a very haunting sense of what kind of life he led and what kind of person he was. I experienced it when I saw the places where he lived in New Orleans and in Dallas and in Fort Worth. I had a very clear sense of a man living on the margins of society. He was the kind of person we think we know until we delve more deeply. Who would have expected someone like that to defect to the Soviet Union? He started reading socialist writing when he was fifteen; then, as soon as he became old enough, joined the Marines. This element of self-contradiction seemed to exemplify his life. There seemed to be a pattern of self-argument.

When he returned from the Soviet Union, he devised a list of answers to possible questions he'd be asked by the authorities upon disembarking. One set of answers could be characterized as the replies of a simple tourist who just happened to have spent two-and-a-half years at the heart of the Soviet Union and is delighted to be returning to his home country. The other set of answers was full of defiance and anger at the inequities of life in capitalist society. It carried a strong sense of his refusal to explain why he left this country to settle in Russia. These mutually hostile elements seemed always to be part of Oswald's life, and, I think, separate him slightly from the general run of malcontents and disaffected people.

DECURTIS: It's almost as if Oswald embodied a postmodern notion of character in which the self isn't fixed and you assume or discard traits as the mood strikes you.

DELILLO: Someone who knew Oswald referred to him as an actor in real life, and I do think there is a sense in which he was watching himself perform. I tried to insert this element into *Libra* on a number of occasions.

I think Oswald anticipates men like Hinckley and Bremer. His attempt to kill General Edwin Walker was a strictly political act: Walker was a right-wing figure, and Oswald was, of course, pro-Castro. But Oswald's attempt on Kennedy was more complicated. I think it was based on elements outside politics and, as someone in the novel says, outside history—things like dreams and coincidences and even the movement or the configuration of the stars, which is one reason the book is called *Libra*. The rage and frustration he had felt for twenty-four years, plus the enormous coincidence that the motorcade would be passing the building where he worked—these are the things that combined to drive Oswald toward attempting to kill the President. So in this second murder attempt I think he presages the acts of all of the subsequent disaffected young men who seem to approach their assassination attempts out of a backdrop of dreams and personal fantasy much more than politics.

DECURTIS: You quote Oswald's statement about wanting to be a fiction writer, and you describe him as having lived a life in small rooms, which is a phrase similar to ones you've used to describe your life as a writer. Do you see Oswald as an author of some kind?

DELILLO: Well, he did make that statement in his application for the Albert Schweitzer College. He did say he wanted to be a writer. He wanted to write "short stories on contemporary American life"—and this, of course, is a striking remark coming from someone like him. There's no evidence that he ever wrote any fiction; none apparently survived if he did. But I think the recurring motif in the book of men in small rooms refers to Oswald much more as an outsider than as a writer. I think he had a strong identification with people like Trotsky and Castro, who spent long periods in prison. I think he felt that with enough perseverance and enough determination these men would survive their incarcerations and eventually be swept by history right out of the room. Out of the room and out of the *self*. To merge with history is to escape the self. I think Oswald knew this. He said as much in a letter to his brother. It is the epigraph [to *Libra*]: "Happiness is taking part in the struggle, where there is no borderline between one's own personal world, and the world in general."

I think we can take Oswald's life as the attempt to find that place. But he never could. He never lost sight of the borderline. He never was able to merge with the world in general or with history in particular. His life in small rooms is the antithesis of the life America seems to promise its citizens: the life of consumer fulfillment. And I think it's interesting that a man like Oswald would return to this country from Russia with a woman who, of course and understandably, was completely amazed by this world of American consumer promise. I think it must have caused an enormous tension in his life. Her desire to become more fully a part of this paradise she'd been hearing about all her life and his ambivalent feelings about being a husband who provides for his family and at the same time being a leftist who finds an element of distaste in consumer fulfillment. In one of his apartments in Dallas he actually worked in a room almost the size of a closet. This seemed almost the kind of negative culmination of a certain stream that was running through my own work of men finding themselves alone in small rooms. And here is a man, and not even a man I invented, a real man who finds himself in a closet-sized room planning the murder of General Walker.

DeCurtis: You read the Warren Commission Report and traveled quite a bit. Did you do other research for *Libra*?

DeLillo: I looked at films and listened to tapes. Hearing Oswald's voice and his mother's voice was extremely interesting. Particularly interesting was a tape of an appearance Oswald made on the radio in New Orleans in the summer of 1963. He sounds like a socialist candidate for office. He was extremely articulate and extremely clever in escaping difficult questions. Listening to this man and then reading the things he had earlier written in his so-called historic diary, which is enormously chaotic and almost childlike, again seemed to point to a man who was a living self-contradiction. Nothing I had earlier known about Oswald led me to think that he could sound so intelligent and articulate as he did on this radio program.

The movie I looked at is a compilation of amateur footage taken that day in Dallas, and it covers a period from the time the President's plane landed in Dallas until the assassination itself. It's extremely crude footage, but all the more powerful because of it. I suppose the most powerful moment is also the most ambiguous. We see the shot that kills the President, but it seems to be surrounded in chaos and in shadow and in blurs. The strongest feeling I took away from that moment is the feeling that the shot came from the front and not from the rear. Of course, if that's true, there had to be more than one assassin. In fact, it's hard to escape that feeling. The other strange moment, I suppose, is when dozens and dozens of people are seen shortly after the shooting running up a set of stairs that proceeds right toward the grassy knoll and toward the stockade fence which separated Dealey Plaza from a parking lot. I hadn't read in any earlier accounts that there had been such an exodus from the scene, and seeing it was shocking because it seemed to indicate that people were running in the direction they thought the shots had come from, not just four or five people, but possibly as many as fifty. And it's just another of those mysteries that hovers over the single moment of death.

DeCurtis: At one point you describe the Warren Commission Report, which is twenty-six volumes long, as the novel that James Joyce might have written if he had moved to Iowa City and lived to be a hundred.

DELILLO: I asked myself what Joyce could possibly do after *Finnegans Wake*, and this was the answer. It's an amazing document. The first fifteen volumes are devoted to testimony and the last eleven volumes to exhibits, and together we have a masterwork of trivia ranging from Jack Ruby's mother's dental records to photographs of knotted string. What was valuable to me most specifically was the testimony of dozens and dozens of people who talk not only about their connection to the assassination itself but about their jobs, their marriages, their children. This testimony provided an extraordinary window on life in the fifties and sixties and, beyond that, gave me a sense of people's speech patterns, whether they were private detectives from New Orleans or railroad workers from Fort Worth. I'm sure that without those twenty-six volumes I would have written a very different novel and probably a much less interesting one.

DECURTIS: How long did it take to write *Libra*?

DELILLO: A little over three years. The only time I had to do this much research was in writing *Ratner's Star*. But I found doing this novel much more invigorating, I think because the reading I had to do dealt with real people and not with science and mathematics and astronomy and so on. And for the same reason I'm sure the experience of writing this novel will stay with me much longer. In fact, I'm certain I'll never quite get rid of these characters and this story. They'll always be part of my life.

DECURTIS: What was your writing regimen once you started working on the book?

DELILLO: Well this book is unusual in my own experience because I worked two sessions a day at the typewriter, and this is the first time I've ever done that for an extended period. I worked in the morning, roughly from nine to one, and then again in early evening for about an hour and a half. I couldn't do all the research, all the reading, in one extended stretch and then begin to write the novel, because there was simply too much reading to do. So I had to space it chronologically. This meant that often I worked much of the day at the typewriter and then spent the night or part of the night trying to catch up. One week I'd be exploring the Bay of Pigs, the next week the Italian mafia and the next week the Yuri Nosenko affair and the next week the U-2 incident. So I felt that I had to write nearly twice as much in a given day just to keep up.

DECURTIS: Given the complexity of the subject, was there any point that constituted a breakthrough for you?

DELILLO: Once I found Oswald's voice—and by voice I mean not just the way he spoke to people but his inner structure, his consciousness, the sound of his thinking—I began to feel that I was nearly home free. It's interesting that once you find the right rhythm for your sentences, you may be well on your way to finding the character himself. And once I came upon a kind of abrupt, broken rhythm both in dialogue and in narration, I felt this was the prose counterpart to not only Oswald's inner life but Jack Ruby's as well. And other characters too. So the prose itself began to suggest not the path the novel would take but the deepest motivation of the characters who originated this prose in a sense.

DECURTIS: The title *Libra* seems to reflect the concern in your novels with the occult and superstitions of various kinds. What fascinates you about those nonrational systems?

DELILLO: I think my work has always been informed by mystery; the final answer, if there is one at all, is outside the book. My books are open-ended. I would say that mystery in general rather than the occult is something that weaves in and out of my work. I can't tell you where it came from or what it leads to. Possibly it is the natural product of a Catholic upbringing.

Libra was Oswald's sign, and because Libra refers to the scales, it seemed appropriate to a man who harbored contradictions and who could tilt either way.

DECURTIS: Did you consider other titles?

DELILLO: The first title I considered was the one I used for the *Rolling Stone* piece, "American Blood." As the months passed, I think the only other title that interested me as I went along was "Texas School Book," which seemed to have a sort of double resonance. It was, of course, the Texas School Book Depository where Oswald worked, and the notion of schoolbooks seemed relevant to his life and his struggle. But finally when I hit upon this notion of coincidence and dream and intuition and the possible impact of astrology on the way men act; I thought that Libra, being Oswald's sign, would be the one title that summarized what's inside the book.

DECURTIS: Did you select the photo of Oswald that's on the cover?

DELILLO: I asked Viking to consider using it, yes. It seems that picture would be one of the central artifacts of Oswald's life. He is holding a rifle, carrying a revolver at his hip and holding in his free hand copies of *The Militant* and *The Worker*, two left-wing journals he regularly read. He's dressed in black. He's almost the poor man's James Dean in that picture, and there's definitely an idea of the performing self. He told his wife that he wanted her to take this picture so that their daughter may one day know what kind of person her father was.

DECURTIS: In the author's note at the end of *Libra*, you say the novel might serve as a kind of refuge for readers. There is an implication that searching for a "solution" to the mysteries of the assassination, as the CIA historian Nicholas Branch does in the book, leads inevitably to a mental and spiritual dead end. What does fiction offer people that history denies to them?

DELILLO: Branch feels overwhelmed by the massive data he has to deal with. He feels the path is changing as he writes. He despairs of being able to complete a coherent account of this extraordinarily complex event. I think the fiction writer tries to redeem this despair. Stories can be a consolation—at least in theory. The novelist can try to leap across the barrier of fact, and the reader is willing to take that leap with him as long as there's a kind of redemptive truth waiting on the other side, a sense that we've arrived at a resolution.

I think fiction rescues history from its confusions. It can do this in the somewhat superficial way of filling in blank spaces. But it also can operate in a deeper way: providing the balance and rhythm we don't experience in our daily lives, in our real lives. So the novel which is within history can also operate outside it—correcting, clearing up and, perhaps most important of all, finding rhythms and symmetries that we simply don't encounter elsewhere. If *Ratner's Star* is, in part, a way to embody what it is all about, that is, if it's a book of harmonies and symmetries, because mathematics is a search for a sense of order in our lives, then I think *Libra* is, in a curious way, related to *Ratner's Star*, because it attempts to provide a hint of order in the midst of all the randomness.

DECURTIS: Do you see the book as related in any way to other novels about public events, like Norman Mailer's *The Executioner's Song*, which is about the execution of Gary Gilmore, or Robert Coover's *The Public Burning*, about the Rosenbergs?

DELILLO: I haven't thought about *Libra* in terms of other novels at all—including the so-called nonfiction novels, like *In Cold Blood* or *The Armies of the Night*. It doesn't seem to me to be part of the same current of contemporary fiction. I think of it as a novel. And as I was trying to explain earlier, I think that the book is an exploration of what variations we might take on an actual event rather than an argument that this is what really happened in Dallas in November of 1963 and in the months before and in the years that have followed.

DECURTIS: From a certain vantage point, your books can almost be taken as a systematic look at various aspects of American life: the Kennedy assassination; rock music in *Great Jones Street*; science and mathematics in *Ratner's Star*; football in *End Zone*. Do you proceed in that methodical a fashion?

DELILLO: No, not at all. That notion breaks down rather easily if you analyze it. *Americana* is not about any one area of our experience. *End Zone* wasn't about football. It's a fairly elusive novel. It seems to me to be about extreme places and extreme states of mind, more than anything else. Certainly there is very little about rock music in *Great Jones Street*, although the hero is a musician. The interesting thing about that particular character is that he seems to be at a crossroad between murder and suicide. For me, that defines the period between 1965 and 1975, say, and I thought it was best exemplified in a rock-music star. *Ratner's Star* is not about mathematics as such. I've never attempted to embark on a systematic exploration of American experience. I take the ideas as they come.

DECURTIS: On the other hand, some specific American realities have a draw for you.

DELILLO: Certainly there are themes that recur. Perhaps a sense of secret patterns in our lives. A sense of ambiguity. Certainly the violence of contemporary life is a motif. I see contemporary violence as a kind of sardonic response to the promise of consumer fulfillment in America. Again we come back to these men in small rooms who can't get out and who have to organize their desperation and their loneliness, who have to give it a destiny and who often end up doing this through violent means. I see this desperation against the backdrop of brightly colored packages and products and consumer happiness and every promise that American life makes day by day and minute by minute everywhere we go.

DeCurtis: In *The Names*, which is principally set in Greece, you speak about the way Americans abroad especially seem to feel the imminence of violence.

DeLillo: I do believe that Americans living abroad feel a self-consciousness that they don't feel when they are at home. They become students of themselves. They see themselves as the people around them see them, as Americans with a capital A. Because being American is a sensitive thing in so many parts of the world, the American response to violence, to terror, in places like the Middle East and Greece is often a response tinged with inevitability, almost with apology. We're just waiting for it to happen to us. It becomes part of a sophisticated form of humor that people exchange almost as a matter of course. The humor of political dread.

DeCurtis: Humor plays an important role in your novels. Do you see it as providing relief from the grimness of some of your subjects?

DeLillo: I don't think the humor is intended to counteract the fear. It's almost part of it. We ourselves may almost instantaneously use humor to offset a particular moment of discomfort or fear, but this reflex is so deeply woven into the original fear that they almost become the same thing.

DeCurtis: Your first novel, *Americana*, was published when you were about thirty-five, which is rather late. Did you think of yourself as a writer before that?

DeLillo: *Americana* took a long time to write because I had to keep interrupting it to earn a living, which I was doing at that time by writing free-lance, mostly advertising material. It also took a long time because I didn't know what I was doing. I was about two years into the novel when I realized I was a writer—not because I thought the novel would even be published but because sentence by sentence and paragraph by paragraph I was beginning to see that I had abilities I hadn't demonstrated in earlier work, that is, in short stories I'd written when I was younger. I had a feeling that I could not solve the structural problems in *Americana*, but it didn't disturb me. Once I realized that I was good enough to be a professional writer, I simply kept going in the somewhat blind belief that nature would eventually take its course.

I think I started work on *End Zone* just weeks after I finished *Americana*. The long-drawn-out, somewhat aimless experience of writing *Americana* was immediately replaced by a quick burst of carefully directed activity. I did *End Zone* in about one-fourth the time it had taken me to write *Americana*.

DECURTIS: At what point were you able to earn your living as a fiction writer?

DELILLO: Starting with *End Zone*, I stopped doing every other kind of writing.

DECURTIS: Movies frequently come up in your work. When did they become significant for you?

DELILLO: I began to understand the force that movies could have emotionally and intellectually in what I consider the great era of the European films: Godard, Antonioni, Fellini, Bergman. And American directors as well—Kubrick and Howard Hawks and others.

DECURTIS: What did you find inspirational about those directors?

DELILLO: Well, they seem to fracture reality. They find mystery in commonplace moments. They find humor in even the gravest political acts. They seem to find an art and a seriousness which I think was completely unexpected and which had once been the province of literature alone. So that a popular art was suddenly seen as a serious art. And this was interesting and inspiring.

DECURTIS: Both *The Names* and *Ratner's Star* are pretty exacting texts. Is the difficulty of those books part of a commitment you feel you need to demand from readers?

DELILLO: From this perspective I can see that the reader would have to earn his way into *Ratner's Star*, but this was not something I'd been trying to do. I did not have a clear sense of how difficult this book might turn out to be. I just followed my idea chapter by chapter and character by character. It seems to me that *Ratner's Star* is a book which is almost all structure. The structure of the book *is* the book. The characters are intentionally flattened and cartoonlike. I was trying to build a novel which was not only about mathematics to some extent but which itself would become a piece of mathematics.

It would be a book which embodied pattern and order and harmony, which is one of the traditional goals of pure mathematics.

In *The Names*, I spent a lot of time searching for the kind of sun-cut precision I found in Greek light and in the Greek landscape. I wanted a prose which would have the clarity and the accuracy which the natural environment at its best in that part of the world seems to inspire in our own senses. I mean, there were periods in Greece when I tasted and saw and heard with much more sharpness and clarity than I'd ever done before or since. And I wanted to discover a sentence, a way of writing sentences that would be the prose counterpart to that clarity—that sensuous clarity of the Aegean experience. Those were my conscious goals in those two books.

DECURTIS: It's rather uncommon for contemporary writers not to give readings or teach. Why don't you do those things?

DELILLO: Well, the simplest answer is the true one: I never liked school. Why go back now? I simply never wanted to teach. I never felt I had anything worth saying to students. I felt that whatever value my work has is something of a mystery to me. Although I could discuss with limited success what devices I've used to build certain structures in my books, I wouldn't know how to help other writers fulfill their own visions. And besides I'm lazy.

DECURTIS: Do you have a sense, because of the extreme issues raised in your work, that one part of your readership is drawn from the fringes of American society?

DELILLO: Yeah, one segment of my readership is marginal, but beyond that I find it hard to analyze the mail I get and make any conclusions as to what kind of readers I have. Certainly, *White Noise* found a lot of women readers, and I don't think too many women had been reading my books before that. So I really can't generalize. In the past I got a lot of letters from people who seemed slightly unbalanced. This hasn't been happening for the past three or four years. It seems that the eighties have been somewhat more sane than the seventies, based on my own limited experience of measuring letters from readers. I've reached no conclusion about the kind of readers I have based on the mail I get. There are all sorts.

DECURTIS: In *The Names* and some of your other books, language itself seems to be one of your subjects. That self-referential quality parallels a lot of theoretical work being done in philosophy and literary criticism these days. Do you read much writing of that kind?

DELILLO: No, I don't. It is just my sense that we live in a kind of circular or near-circular system and that there are an increasing number of rings which keep intersecting at some point, whether you're using a plastic card to draw money out of your account at an automatic teller machine or thinking about the movement of planetary bodies. I mean, these systems all seem to interact to me. But I view all this in the most general terms, and I have no idea what kind of scientific studies are taking place. The secrets within systems, I suppose, are things that have informed my work. But they're almost secrets of consciousness, or ways in which consciousness is replicated in the natural world.

DECURTIS: There also seems to be a fascination with euphemism and jargon in your books; for example, the poisonous cloud of gas that creates an environmental disaster in *White Noise* is repeatedly referred to as the "airborne toxic event."

DELILLO: It's a language that almost holds off reality while at the same time trying to fit it into a formal pattern. The interesting thing about jargon is that if it lives long enough, it stops being jargon and becomes part of natural speech, and we all find ourselves using it. I think we might all be disposed to use phrases like "time frame," which, when it was first used during the Watergate investigation, had an almost evil aura to it, because it was uttered by men we had learned to distrust so deeply.

I don't think of language in a theoretical way. I approach it at street level. That is, I listen carefully to the way people speak. And I find that the closer a writer comes to portraying actual speech, the more stylized it seems on the page, so that the reader may well conclude that this is a formal experiment in dialogue instead of a simple transcription, which it actually is. When I started writing *Players*, my idea was to fill the novel with the kind of intimate, casual, off-the-cuff speech between close friends or husbands and wives. This was the whole point of the book as far as I was concerned. But somehow I got sidetracked almost immediately and found myself describing a murder on the floor of the stock exchange, and of course from that point the book took a completely different direction. Nevertheless, in

Players, I think there is still a sense of speech as it actually falls from the lips of people. And I did that again in *Libra*. In this case I wasn't translating spoken speech as much as the printed speech of people who testified before the Warren Commission. Marguerite Oswald has an extremely unique way of speaking, and I didn't have to invent this at all. I simply had to read it and then remake it, rehear it for the purposes of the particular passage I was writing.

DeCurtis: Often your characters are criticized for being unrealistic—children who speak like adults or, as in *Ratner's Star*, characters whose consciousnesses seem at points to blur one into the other. How do you view your characters?

DeLillo: Probably *Libra* is the exception to my work in that I tried a little harder to connect motivation with action. This is because there is an official record—if not of motivation, at least of action on the part of so many characters in the book. So it had to make a certain amount of sense, and what sense was missing I tried to supply. For example, why did Oswald shoot President Kennedy? I don't think anyone knows, but in the book I've attempted to fill in that gap, although not at all in a specific way.

There's no short answer to the question. You either find yourself entering a character's life and consciousness or you don't, and in much modern fiction I don't think you are required to, either as a writer or a reader. Many modern characters have a flattened existence—purposely—and many modern characters exist precisely nowhere. There isn't a strong sense of place in much modern writing. Again, this is where I differ from what we could call the mainstream. I do feel a need and a drive to paint a kind of thick surface around my characters. I think all my novels have a strong sense of place.

But in contemporary writing in general, there's a strong sense that the world of Beckett and Kafka has redescended on contemporary America, because characters seem to live in a theoretical environment rather than a real one. I haven't felt that I'm part of that. I've always had a grounding in the real world, whatever esoteric flights I might indulge in from time to time.

DeCurtis: There seems to be a fondness in your writing, particularly in *White Noise*, for what might be described as the trappings of suburban middle-class existence, to the point where one of the characters describes the supermarket as a sacred place.

DELILLO: I would call it a sense of the importance of daily life and of ordinary moments. In *White Noise*, in particular, I tried to find a kind of radiance in dailiness. Sometimes this radiance can be almost frightening. Other times it can be almost holy or sacred. Is it really there? Well, yes. You know, I don't believe as Murray Jay Siskind does in *White Noise* that the supermarket is a form of Tibetan lamasery. But there is something there that we tend to miss.

Imagine someone from the third world who has never set foot in a place like that suddenly transported to an A&P in Chagrin Falls, Ohio. Wouldn't he be elated or frightened? Wouldn't he sense that something transcending is about to happen to him in the midst of all this brightness? So I think that's something that has been in the background of my work: a sense of something extraordinary hovering just beyond our touch and just beyond our vision.

DECURTIS: Hitler and the Holocaust have repeatedly been addressed in your books. In *Running Dog*, a pornographic movie allegedly filmed in Hitler's bunker determines a good deal of the novel's plot. In *White Noise*, university professor Jack Gladney attempts to calm his obsessive fear of death through his work in the Department of Hitler Studies.

DELILLO: In his case, Gladney finds a perverse form of protection. The damage caused by Hitler was so enormous that Gladney feels he can disappear inside it and that his own puny dread will be overwhelmed by the vastness, the monstrosity of Hitler himself. He feels that Hitler is not only bigger than life, as we say of many famous figures, but bigger than death. Our sense of fear—we avoid it because we feel it so deeply, so there is an intense conflict at work. I brought this conflict to the surface in the shape of Jack Gladney.

I think it is something we all feel, something we almost never talk about, something that is *almost* there. I tried to relate it in *White Noise* to this other sense of transcendence that lies just beyond our touch. This extraordinary wonder of things is somehow related to the extraordinary dread, to the death fear we try to keep beneath the surface of our perceptions.

DeCurtis: What was the idea in *Running Dog* of locating the pornographic movie in Hitler's bunker?

DeLillo: Well, this made it an object of ultimate desirability and ultimate dread, simply because it connected to Hitler. When the Hitler diaries "surfaced," in quotes, in the early eighties, there was even a more beserk reaction to them than there was to this film in *Running Dog*. If anything, I was slightly innocent about my sense of what would happen if such an object emerged. What I was really getting at in *Running Dog* was a sense of the terrible acquisitiveness in which we live, coupled with a final indifference to the object. After all the mad attempts to acquire the thing, everyone suddenly decides that, well, maybe we really don't care about this so much anyway. This was something I felt characterized our lives at the time the book was written, in the mid to late seventies. I think this was part of American consciousness then.

DeCurtis: What about the fascination with children in your books?

DeLillo: Well, I think we feel, perhaps superstitiously, that children have a direct route to, have direct contact to the kind of natural truth that eludes us as adults. In *The Names* the father is transported by what he sees as a kind of deeper truth underlying the language his son uses in writing his stories. He sees misspellings and misused words as reflecting a kind of reality that he as an adult couldn't possibly grasp. And I think he relates this to the practice of speaking in tongues, which itself is what we might call an alternate reality. It's a fabricated language which seems to have a certain pattern to it. It isn't just gibberish. It isn't language, but it isn't gibberish either. And I think this is the way Axton felt about his own son's writing. And I think this is the way we feel about children in general. There is something they know but can't tell us. Or there is something they remember which we've forgotten.

Glossolalia or speaking in tongues, you know, could be viewed as a higher form of infantile babbling. It's babbling which seems to mean something, and this is intriguing.

DeCurtis: *Ratner's Star*, which has a child as its central character, seems to juxtapose the intense rationality of science with a variety of mystical experiences, like speaking in tongues.

DeLillo: Well, *Ratner's Star* is almost a study of opposites, yes.

Only because I think anyone who studies the history of mathematics finds that the link between the strictest scientific logic and other mysticism seems to exist. I mean, this is something any true scientist might tend to deny, but so many mathematicians, in earlier centuries anyway, were mystical about numbers, about the movements of heavenly bodies and so forth, while at the same time being accomplished scientists. And this strange connection of opposites found its way into *Ratner's Star*. I think modern physicists seem to be moving toward nearly mystical explanations of the ways in which elements in the subatomic world and in the galaxy operate. There seems to be something happening.

DECURTIS: You've been denounced as a member of the paranoid left. Do you have a sense of your books as political?

DELILLO: No, I don't. Politics plays a part in some of my books, but this is usually because the characters are political. I don't have a political theory or doctrine that I'm espousing. *Libra* obviously is saturated with politics, of necessity. Certainly the left-wing theories of Oswald do not coincide with my own. I don't have a program. I follow characters where they take me and I don't know what I can say beyond that.

DECURTIS: How do you assess your own works? Are there specific ones that you feel are your best or your favorites?

DELILLO: My feeling is that the novels I've written in the 1980s —*The Names, White Noise,* and *Libra*—are stronger books than the six novels I published in the seventies. This may be what every writer feels about more recent works. But I think the three novels I've written in this decade were more deeply motivated and required a stronger sense of commitment than some of the books I wrote earlier, like, for example, *Running Dog* and possibly *Great Jones Street,* which I think I set out to write because I had become anxious about the amount of time that had passed since I finished my previous book and I wanted to get back to work. I think one of the things I've learned through experience is that it isn't enough to want to get back to work. The other thing I've learned is that no amount of experience can prevent you from making a major mistake. I think it can help you avoid small mistakes. But the potential for a completely misconceived book still exists.

DECURTIS: There's something of an apocalyptic feel about your books, an intimation that our world is moving toward greater randomness and dissolution, or maybe even cataclysm. Do you see this process as irreversible?

DELILLO: It could change tomorrow. This is the shape my books take because this is the reality I see. This reality has become part of all our lives over the past twenty-five years. I don't know how we can deny it.

I don't think *Libra* is a paranoid book at all. I think it's a clear-sighted, reasonable piece of work which takes into account the enormous paranoia which has ensued from the assassination. I can say the same thing about some of my other books. They're *about* movements or feelings in the air and in the culture around us, without necessarily being *part* of the particular movement. I mean, what I sense is suspicion and distrust and fear, and so, of course, these things inform my books. It's my idea of myself as a writer—perhaps mistaken—that I enter these worlds as a completely rational person who is simply taking what he senses all around him and using it as material.

DECURTIS: You've spoken of the redemptive quality of fiction. Do you see your books as offering an alternative to the dark reality you detect?

DELILLO: Well, strictly in theory, art is one of the consolation prizes we receive for having lived in a difficult and sometimes chaotic world. We seek pattern in art that eludes us in natural experience. This isn't to say that art has to be comforting; obviously, it can be deeply disturbing. But nothing in *Libra* can begin to approach the level of disquiet and dread characterized by the assassination itself.

Daniel Aaron

How to Read Don DeLillo

He sits on a stair in a hallway and gazes unsmiling into the camera, his expression severe and suspicious. He looks alert and intense and unrelaxed, almost prim. Coatless, open-collared, sleeves rolled, he might be an intellectual apartment house super with a hidden past (some refugee from graduate school? a lapsed priest?) wary of interrogators.*

Who is Don DeLillo? He's rather skimpy with his interviews, shuns the milieu and company of literary gossip-mongers ("privacy" is a theme in *Great Jones Street*) and doesn't say much about himself or his social origins or family upbringing. No one character in any of his nine novels can confidently be said to speak for him. He is in all of them and none of them, diffused in the eddies of his inventions.

DeLillo is the son of Italian immigrants and a graduate of Fordham University. I think it's worth noting that nothing in his novels suggests a suppressed "Italian foundation";

*Photograph of Don DeLillo, *Rolling Stone* (17 November 1988).

hardly a vibration betrays an ethnic consciousness. His name could just as well be Don Smith or Don Brown. His ethnic past doesn't serve for him as an "intoxicant of the imagination" (Allen Tate's phrase) in the way New England Puritanism did for Hawthorne and Emily Dickinson or the experience of being Jewish did for several generations of Jewish writers. DeLillo can be very funny, but unlike black and Jewish writers who have sucked humor from their humiliations, there's nothing particularly "ethnic" about his dark comedy unless we imagine that traces of the uneasy alien or of ethnic marginality are discernible in his brand of grotesque parody, his resistance to the American consensus, and his sympathy and respect for the maimed, the disfigured, and the excluded people in his novels.

DeLillo's presumably Roman Catholic upbringing rarely surfaces in his books although his accounts of the spiritual and carnal excesses of his seekers, prodigies, terrorists, spies, academicians, gangsters, entrepreneurs can be read as the musings of a crypto-Christian and profane moralist who finds his most rewarding subject matter in the precincts of a fallen world. The sexual episodes in his novels, of which there are a good many, are at once "explicit" and lust-chilling. He charts the curves, angles, declivities of entangled bodies with a topographical exactness, but the lovemaking itself is usually a joyless and unrevelatory business.

He promises but holds back. The signs, sounds, signals his characters think they see or hear or feel defy reason and intuition. These unexplained phenomena, whether presented in the language of scientists or cranks, seem to hint of a religious disposition or at least a hankering for transcendent answers, but DeLillo never takes the reader into his confidence, leaves few if any clues to point to his philosophy, social views, habits, and tastes. He is a withholder, a mystifier, a man without a handle and like the trickster mushroom of Emily Dickinson's poem—surreptitious, circumspect, and supple—he keeps popping up in unexpected places.

Impressions of DeLillo: I see him as an Ear, an Eye, a Nose, a Camera, a Tape Recorder, a Sound Track; as a Fact-and-Word Collector; as a restless and speculative artist utilizing ideas to counterpoint the action of his narratives; as a popular culture specialist and possessor of a considerable stock of disparate information, some of it pretty esoteric stuff acquired very likely by purposeful reading, a lot of it simply the by-product of astute observation and bemused interest in what goes on about him. His vocabulary is large and rich, and he names things exactly.

I see something of him in his own creation, Dr. Pepper, the "aw-thentic genius" in *Great Jones Street*, authority on "crisis sociology," dope-master and brain mechanic, wheeler-dealer of the elicit, changeable as Proteus, blending into his surroundings so completely that he can become anonymous, given to a "tightfisted humor," and blessed with the "gift of putting distance between himself and his applauders." In his fictive world, DeLillo, like Dr. Pepper, has "lived among dangerous men, worked in hazardous circumstances."

Here are a few key topics that keep erupting in the thoughts and conversations of his characters and in the mini-essays interspersed throughout his novels.

Catastrophe: (Under this rubric I include destruction in all its varied manifestations—plain murder and assassination, the Holocaust, nuclear explosions, toxic pollution, etcetera.)

Gary Harkness, of *End Zone*, playing lethal football for Logos College in West Texas, is both "seriously depressed" and fascinated by the prospect of nuclear war. He is addicted to doomsday statistics and impressed by "the rationality of irrationality," by the verbal magic that can impersonalize killing on a cosmic scale through the employment of "words and phrases like thermal hurricanes, overkill, circular error probability, post-attack environment, stark deterrence, dose-rate contours, kill-ration, spasm war." (To paraphrase a remark in *Ratner's Star*, the more extreme the danger, the more abstract the vocabulary to describe it: euphemism is tantamount to terror.) The pleasure Gary takes in reading the beautiful language of destruction is "almost sensual," he unhappily concludes. Is he mad? Do others share his feelings?

Yes they do. Heinrich Gladney in *White Noise*, one of DeLillo's formidably informed adolescents, also savors with "some kind of out-of-the-world elation" the mechanisms and logistics of disaster. And so does his father, Jack Gladney, DeLillo's narrator and founder of the department of Hitler studies at College-on-the-Hill. Friday evenings find the Gladney family riveted to the TV set silently watching "floods, earthquakes, mud slides, erupting volcanoes." Their appetite for lava and burning villages is insatiable; every cataclysm makes them "wish for something bigger, grander, more sweeping." This yearning, Jack's knowing friends tell him, is perfectly natural and normal. Disasters focus our attention. We need them and depend upon them so long as they occur elsewhere.

DeLillo's presentation of his catastrophists' eerie tastes is witty and unsolemn, and it's not always easy to tell when (like one of his pop-cult experts) he is being playful "in a pulverizing way" and when he's being seriously apocalyptic. For me he is most himself as the sociologist of crisis, pondering the ways in which the raw facts of natural and man-made disasters are processed into theory and insinuated in the public mind.

Conspiracy: "This is the age of conspiracy," says Moll Robbins (*Running Dog*), the age of "connections, links, secret relationships." The magazine she writes for fans popular belief in international conspiracies and "fantastic assassination schemes." In the era of Watergate and Dallas when "every stark fact" is layered in ambiguity, faith in conspiracy theory can be very comforting: a stay against chaos and a support for an "ordering instinct."

DeLillo has thought a lot about conspiracies and kindred operations (military and industrial espionage, secret plans and schemes, covert criminal and terrorist activities) that flourish in a technological climate. His archetypal plot is a mystery whose generally inconclusive solution depends on the deciphering of clues—a name, word, number, code. The protagonists are usually troubled intelligent persons already poised to kick over the traces and susceptible to intrigue. He sets them tunneling deeper and deeper toward some unreachable solution or explanation, then shows them to be players in a game manipulated by unknowable forces. As they press beyond confining boundaries in quest of spiritual independence and self-recognition, they are likely to fall into the chaos they had hoped to shape and correlate. At bottom they are only integers in a vast information network created and controlled by "banks, insurance companies, credit organizations, tax examiners, passport offices, reporting services, police agencies, intelligence gatherers." Only the real men of power in finance, government, and the military speak and comprehend "the true underground idiom," and they are the beneficiaries of a technology they can't control, shadowy figures doubly dangerous because they are ignorant of their ignorance.

More palpable are their technicians and agents who gather and condense multifarious data for the masters. Such a person is Rowser (*The Names*), specialist on "money, politics, and force" and fact-gatherer for a subsidiary of "the point," a $2 billion conglomerate. Rowser's "Group" sells risk insurance to multinationals whose executives have become ransom targets for kidnappers and terrorists in the Middle East. Calamities *per se*—"meltdowns, runaway viruses," and the like—have for him only an actuarial significance, yet if oblivious of "deep and unseen" things, he is physically affected by the atmosphere of fear so pervasive in DeLillo's downward and deathward-pointing novels.

Landscape: DeLillo's fictional landscape isn't confined to the United States. Greece is the setting for *The Names*, a novel which besides its many other virtues is a remarkable piece of travel writing. *Ratner's Star* takes place at a dreamlike superscience complex in some distant nameless territory. Mostly, however, he favors American cities (New York, Dallas, Washington, among others), terminals of fear whose "casual savagery" and "fatal beauty" seem to energize his imagination. From these centers of infection, urban sickness filters into the hinterlands. A good deal goes on in office buildings, warehouses, dingy flats, and bars, but his camera eye ranges as well over suburbia and small towns and stretches of highway. He is never supercilious or smart-alecky about places and regions (his social satire when he indulges it is muted, sly) and he is particularly sensitive to supermarkets and to motels situated beyond the limits of "large and reduplicating" cities.

His supermarket is a magical and sexy place. Inside the "great omniscient door," sliding and closing unbidden, are aisles of plenty, a lotusland, a temple of fecundity where fruits are always in season. David Bell, the narrator of *Americana*, observes the checkout girls moving "their hips against the cash registers." In *White Noise*, Murray Jay Siskind likens the supermarket to a Tibetan heaven, "well-lighted . . . sealed off . . . self-contained." To Siskind who has spent his life "in small steamy delicatessens with slanted display cabinets full of trays that hold soft wet lumpy matter in pale colors," the "large and clean and modern" cornucopia is a revelation full of "psychic data" ready for analysis. But his friend Jack Gladney hears a disturbing undercurrent: "The toneless systems, the jangle and skid of carts, the loudspeaker and coffee-making machines, the cries of children. And over it all, or under it all, a dull and unlocatable roar, as of some form of swarming life just outside the range of human apprehension."

Motels provoke in DeLillo an even more complex and discordant response. No one, with the possible exception of Nabokov, has written so eloquently and penetratingly about them. For DeLillo the motel is "a powerfully abstract" invention—hermetic, temporary, and bland. As in these descriptions from *Americana*, he wonderfully catches motelness: chill damp sheets, the "steady and almost unendurable whispering of ventilation," the "too many hangers in the closet, as if the management were trying to compensate for a secret insufficiency too grievous to be imagined." And yet the motel room is "in the heart of every man," an idea of deliverance from chaos, a kind of depersonalization chamber in which the sojourner can achieve "mathematical integrity" and merge with other transients who occupy similar cells all over the world. Such a state would be unattainable in the "all too personal" borrowed apartment or fleabag. Only in the motel "flows the dream of the confluence of travel and sex."

America: After the publication of *Libra*, one prominent reviewer called DeLillo a literary vandal and a bad citizen, another declared him to be a self-proclaimed outsider who holds an "ostentatiously gloomy view of American life and culture" and loathes American society. Had he confined his "paranoid" visions and "lurid imaginings" to science fiction, say, and eschewed "real people and important events," his tediously predictable "politics" wouldn't matter much. But in serving up suppositions and half-truths about a momentous national tragedy, he has committed a mischievous act.

Such charges are similar to those made several years ago against Gore Vidal's *Abraham Lincoln, A Novel* and revive old questions that touch on the legitimacy of certain kinds of historical fiction, the social responsibilities of writers, and definitions of literary transgression. Historical truth, Vidal insisted, is "what is best imagined," particularly when it's based on "the disagreed as well as agreed-upon facts." Literature (I quote a remark attributed to Carlos Fuentes) is "what history conceals, forgets, or mutilates." I think this comes close to DeLillo's view of the matter. *Libra* draws "from the historical record," he advises his readers, while making "no claim to literal truth," but he affirms the novelist's privilege to alter and embellish.

This isn't the occasion to debate the charge that he has traduced "an ethic of literature" by taking liberties with historical facts and flouting "the judicious weighing of possibilities." The accusation, however, does have a bearing on the depiction of him as a "leftist" suffering from "ideological virulence," a flag-burner whose vision of America is unmitigatedly bleak and sinister. The simplest reply to such an allegation would be to say that how writers see and describe their country is their own business and that nay-saying isn't unconstitutional. Then one might want to add that the conception of DeLillo as a surly revolutionary is based on a partial or superficial reading of his books and misrepresents his position.

Given his diffidence toward his readers, and the games and puzzles he confronts them with, and given his inclination to dress his ideas in masquerade, it's no wonder that he has been misjudged. "The writer is working against the age," he told an interviewer in 1983, "and so he feels some satisfaction in not being widely read. He is diminished by an audience." Furthermore, DeLillo has taken pains to separate himself from his characters. He neither likes nor dislikes them, he says; he recognizes them and reports their attitudes, leaving it up to the reader to decide the degree to which he shares or rejects their sentiments. (I think he does care about their ideas, although he is professedly indifferent to them as "persons," and he isn't always so detached as he claims to be.)

Yet it so happens that a good many speakers in his novels from *Americana* to *Libra* roundly and eloquently savage American society and culture. In brief, their collective indictment might be summed up as follows: the country is "totally engulfed by all the so-called worst elements of our national life and character." It is populated with lonely, bored, empty, fearful people inured to abominations and complicit, whether they realize it or not, in the destruction of what they ostensibly revere—including the treasured beliefs and artifacts of the past. Perceived from abroad, America signifies ignorant, blind, and contemptuous corporate power, "the whole enormous rot and glut and glare" of its popular culture spreading across the world like a cancer. It is "big business, big army and big government all visiting each other in company planes for the sole purpose of playing golf and talking money."

This hyperbolical indictment is usually voiced by wacky or disintegrating personalities launched on obsessional quests. They may serve as vents for DeLillo's own vagrant meditations, but there's no reason to assume that in unequivocally rejecting an "Amerika" devoid of "beauty, dignity, order, proportion," they are invariably speaking for him. DeLillo is no ideological Jeremiah. He thrives on "blaring" social imperfections and is fascinated by the one-dimensional, ruthless half-men, the single-minded system planners and management consultants and nuclear strategists who exhibit "distinctly modern" characteristics. The blackened America in which they flourish is less a historical place, a people with a history, than it is a premonition, a clue to the puzzle of what's to come, and a target of a universal grievance. America in DeLillo's fiction is objectified in the accents and tones of American language. It's a real place with its own colors and textures, not like the allegorical or abstracted settings of Kafka and Beckett. "Fiction without a sense of real place," he tells an interviewer, "is automatically a fiction of estrangement." Contrary to the accusations of his detractors, he is no more estranged from America than the best of his predecessors and contemporaries. (American literature, politicians need constantly to be reminded, abounds with marginal men and women, savage misanthropes, avid experimenters, all dissatisfied and restless.)

Essays and Set Pieces: DeLillo's characters might be likened to actors in a traveling theatrical company, ready at any moment to harangue, comment, speculate, and improvise, yet they stick to their scripts and seem to have no real autonomy, no continuing presence or independent life once they have delivered their lines, spoken their monologues, and disappeared into the wings. Whoever or wherever they are, they speak in the voice of the author, if not necessarily for him, and tend to be smart as well as fluent. While not exactly playing interchangeable roles, a number of them could easily blend into any one of DeLillo's nine novels, for they are more than mere fictional inventions: they are emanations of Don DeLillo.

Some readers may find his novels too talky and become fatigued by the plethora of opinions his speakers all too willingly offer and by the recondite lore that wells up in their talk. (David Bell, in *Americana*, concedes that one of his "main faults was a tendency to get blinded by the neon of an idea, never reaching truly inside of it.") Others, like me, will be charmed and instructed by their comico-serious chatter. DeLillo can be boring at times, and occasionally he overwrites, strains too hard; but how quick his speakers are to spot the extraordinary in the commonplace, how sensitive to shades and nuances, sounds and colors, and how perceptively they read the language of movement and gesture:

A woman spied on by a lustful adolescent through half-closed blinds, "ironing with the smooth movements of a lioness caressing her cubs."

Another woman observed cutting a hedge, "her arms beating somewhat like a bird discovering flight."

A rock musician "strait-jacketed in crushed velvet" who somehow "managed to invest the simple act of sniffling with an element of the gravest accusation."

A hospital scene: "People crossed the hall like wandering souls, holding their urine aloft in pale beakers."

A sound heard in an old house: "the indolent sermon of a saw on wood."

A detail: "He opened the trailer door and watched them get out, two men showing the stiff weighted movements of long-distance drivers."

An observation: "Collings had the spare build, the leanness and fitness of an older man who wants you to know he is determined to outlive you."

"I have reached the point," one of DeLillo's characters in *Americana* announces, "where the coining of aphorism seems a very worthy substitute for good company or madness." Whether or not DeLillo is speaking for himself here, his novels are studded with aphoristic comment on such matters as living defensively ("the central theme of our age"); on death ("an unknotting of consciousness in a space of *n* dimensions"); on digital clocks (they tell time "too bluntly" and are hard to connect with homely quotidian events); on the "solitary trance of power" released in the act of sighting down the barrel of a gun; on growing old quietly after the shock of reaching forty; on sunsets ("A sunset is the story of the world's day); on self-deprecation as a form of ego and aggression ("a wanting to be noticed even for one's flaws").

Concise observations of this sort can lengthen into little essays. In *Great Jones Street,* Bucky Wunderlick reflects for a paragraph on how a disconnected telephone, "deprived of its sources, becomes in time an intriguing piece of sculpture. The business transacted is more than numbed within the phone's limp ganglia; it is made eternally irrelevant. Beyond the reach of shrill necessities the dead phone disinters another source of power. The fact that it will not speak (although made to speak, made for no other reason) enables us to see it in a new way, as an object rather than an instrument, an object possessing a kind of historical mystery. The phone has made a descent to total dumbness, and so becomes beautiful."

The narrator in *The Names* soliloquizes on the tourist as an escapist from accountability: "Tourism is the march of stupidity. You're expected to be stupid. The entire mechanism of the host country is geared to the travelers acting stupidly. You walk around dazed, squinting into fold-out maps. You don't know how to talk to people, how to get anywhere, what the money means, what time it is, what to eat or how to eat. . . . Together with thousands, you are granted immunities and broad freedoms. You are an army of fools, wearing bright polyesters, riding camels, taking pictures of each other, haggard, dysenteric, thirsty. There is nothing to think about but the next shapeless event."

DeLillo's set pieces are longer than his essayettes and more studiedly keyed to the novels' moods and themes. They might be described as strategic pauses in the action, as literary arias. Some examples:

In *Americana,* an artfully composed recollection of deadly summers in a small town. The lyricism of the narrator's language oddly contrasts with his intimations of impending terror ("The menace of the history of quiet lives") especially strong on Sundays when the "neat white churches stand in groves of sunlight," and it seems to him "as though the torpor of Christianity itself is spread over the land."

In *Great Jones Street,* a failed pornographer, happy to be free from his mechanical labors ("Every pornographic work brings us closer to

Fascism") describes his "terminal fantasy." During the day he writes, sustained by tomato juice, saltines, and Budweiser beer, but at night he prowls the building in which he lives, armed with a magic shotgun and a "giant machete" and escorted by two vicious German shepherds. The fantasy culminates with the slaughter of eight invaders, a scene of "choreographed movie violence," and making bonfires of the bodies in the street. But a new fantasy has supplanted the old: writing "terminal fiction" after the financial system goes kaput, not for money or fame but to let survivors know what they've survived. (That might be a DeLillo fantasy too.)

The ramblings and inspired messages of the possessed heard over the airways: like the rant of Tom Thumb Goodloe (*Americana*), "the midnight evangelist": "If you can't pronounce a man's name, that man is a stranger. . . . Keeryst Jesus was not a stranger in his own land. He spoke the lingo. He ate the grub. He felt right at home." Like the voice of the announcer Doo-Wop "churning with gastric power." Like the pleased and excited expostulations of Dr. Pepper (*Great Jones Street*), friend of all the legendary nuts and con-persons and a legend in his own right, who wants "to tap untapped fields of energy" and control "biorhythms from the basic frequencies of the universe." (He isn't all that far removed from the Nobel Prize scientists in *Ratner's Star* or from sundry of DeLillo's listeners who hear messages in glossolalia.)

The crazies move comfortably and confidently in their grooves, unlike, for example, Sherwood Anderson's sad grotesques. Their obsessions, far from bottling them up, have liberated them, made them coherent, shaved their lives down to a point, eliminated doubt. Whether they know it or not, they have joined the company of the twice-born and are en route to some ultimate epiphany. The coach in *End Zone* finds his zone of tranquility in the center of a football scrimmage. His career is the parody of a saint's: renunciation of self, spiritual preparation "in an inner world of determination and silence," and finally the blessed conviction that "pain is part of the harmony of the nervous system." Earl Mudger, professional American soldier and organizer of a rogue intelligence apparatus in *Running Dog*, is a variation of the type of terrible simplifier, "honed" (to use one of DeLillo's favorite words) to the sharpness of the knives he makes in his workshop for the good of his soul, a model of controlled violence and a sensitive monster.

Writers, monsters of another sort, are interested in obsession, DeLillo is quoted as saying, "because it involves a centering and a narrowing down, an intense convergence." "Convergence" he often associates with a historical event, "the angle at which realities meet." (Compare with Emerson's "the veracity of angles.") The obsessed are intense. They have a special integrity for him, are "already on the page," so to speak. Thus DeLillo sees obsession as a state "close to the natural condition of a novelist at work" and an obsessed person as "an automatic piece of fiction."

Pure mathematics is also an obsession, at least as it is defined by Billy Twillig, the young math genius in *Ratner's Star,* and akin in its aims and discipline to DeLillo's literary aesthetic. That is to say, it is simple, severe, and intense, balances "inevitability" with surprise, disdains the "slack" and the "trivial," strives for "precision as a language," pursues "connective patterns and significant form," and offers "manifold freedom in the very strictness it persistently upholds." The narrative line in DeLillo's novels is not consecutive, and logical connections aren't heavily underscored, but his books have their story forms, their own musical structures. They can be read as fables of the artist's breakthrough, after attendant tortures, into a realm of order in which all hitherto discordant things fall into place as past and present conflate.

I quote from W. H. Auden's *The Double Man*: "The situation of our time / Surrounds us like a baffling crime." Detective DeLillo sifts the clues, tries to make sense out of the babble. "Plot" in his novels is the imposition of a design. Plots, like mathematics, make sense. The fiction writer's impulse to "restructure reality" becomes more urgent the messier the world is or seems to be. His tools are words; he uses them to reorder disorder and "to know himself through language." Words are open sesames to secret caves.

The most recent DeLillo novel, *Libra,* one way or another subsumes most of the themes, topics, mannerisms, slants, attitudes, and styles of the previous eight, but it differs from them in several interesting respects. *Libra* makes greater concessions to reader expectations: its principal characters are less flattened; it moves by a logic that is more inexorable than the logic in the early works, although the order and continuity may only be a consequence of DeLillo's choosing to harness the action of the novel to historical persons and events. But if *Libra* is more sequential than his earlier novels and moves more relentlessly toward an inevitable resolution, hedged by the "facts" of history, it reflects like them his preoccupation with the meaning of chaos and order, conspiracy and buried revelation.

The kinship between the cast of *Libra* and DeLillo's other free-floating actors isn't hard to detect. No borderline divides their personal worlds from "the world in general." Hitler, Trotsky, Dallas, New Orleans, the Mafia, the CIA, Lee Harvey Oswald—the mix of "players" who inhabit "a world within a world" and form "a daisy chain of terror, suspicion and secret wish"—all these are in DeLillo's pre-*Libra* books. It's as though, unbeknownst to himself, he was always nosing toward the most dramatic of his historical scenarios. Subways figure in the educations of both Billy Twillig and Oswald. The creepy David Ferrie finds thoughts of bombs heart-lifting (as do, to their dismay, Gary Harkness and Jack Gladney), and he dreams of living in a hole—as one of the scientists in *Ratner's Star* actually does.

And *Libra* in a masterly and assured fashion recapitulates other familiar DeLillo themes:

Technology and human values: the human cost of exposure to vast spy systems, the literal and symbolic transgressions of U-2 planes, electronic devices, "orbiting sensors" and the like that, as an ex-CIA operative puts it, drain conviction out of us, "make us vague and pliant." Clandestine intelligence gathering by government agencies, and the selecting and processing by corporations of "all the secret knowledge of the world," acquire "an almost dreamy sense of connection to each other."

Language and secrecy: Libra further explores the metaphysics of codes and cryptonyms, the power of secrecy. DeLillo's nest of plotters acts on the principle espoused by the cultist leader in *The Names*: "When the name is itself secret, the power and influence are magnified. The secret name is a way of escaping the world." Secrecy engenders "a special language," the key to which lies in a locked safe or in the bowels of a buried computer.

The aesthetics of conspiracy: "A conspiracy is the perfect working of a scheme . . . everything that ordinary life is not. It's the inside game, cold, sure, undistracted, forever closed off to us. We are the flawed ones, the innocents, trying to make some rough sense of the daily jostle. Conspiracies have a logic and a daring beyond our reach. All conspiracies are the same taut story of men who find coherence in some criminal act."

The analogy between the conspirator and the writer is instructive. A perfect conspiracy matches Poe's formula for a short story in which each part and word must fit into "one pre-established design." Henry James's artist-conspirator cuts through the "inclusion and confusion" of "clumsy Life" (what DeLillo calls the "daily jostle"), selects and discriminates "in search of the hard latent *value*." *Libra*, among other things, is a literary exercise on the subject of conspiracy, and the conspirators themselves are characters in a larger plot whose involutions they are unaware of.

Win Everett, the initiator of the original plot-plan, thinks of himself as a kind of supernovelist. After all, he has really invented Lee Oswald before the drifter comes into the plotters' focus. Oswald is the incarnation of a hypothetical construct, an idea materialized into "a name, a face, a bodily frame," or, to use a writer's phrase, into "plain text." The next stage in Everett's procedure is to "show the secret symmetries in a nondescript life," but he's troubled by the possibility that the plot he has concocted, and Oswald's destined part in it, may follow a logic of its own and go awry. In his version, the President is to be spared. All the same, he knows "that the idea of death is woven into the nature of every plot," and that "a narrative plot" is "no less than a conspiracy of armed men" prepared to disregard the author's injunctions. Everett is thrust aside by the forces he had fondly hoped to direct as precisely as a surgeon uses a laser beam in a tricky operation.

Nicholas Branch is assigned the task of piecing together the fragments left in the wake of the Kennedy assassination. This would seem to be an easier task than Everett's, since Everett is ignorant of the counterplot at work inside his own, and is unable to anticipate accident and chance. Branch has only to organize and assess the evidence of a finished episode. Yet the historian finds himself bogged down in the "fact-rubble of the investigations" that increases in volume as the event itself recedes in time. It is premature, he decides, to turn his "notes into coherent history," and it will remain premature so long as new data and new theories keep altering the slippery story. He must perforce turn artist, think imaginatively, and arbitrarily impose a design on the muddle.

Don DeLillo is a writer of fiction, not a historian, but like Nicholas Branch his mind's eye fixes on the shadowy connections professional historians usually fail to see or dismiss as baseless supposition. All of his novels breathe a kind of historical essence. They catch what he has described as the "movements or feelings in the air and the culture around us" and (I should add) the reverberations from below. I like to read him for many reasons: for his intelligence and wit, his range of reference, vocabulary, energy, and inventiveness, and not the least for the varieties of styles in which he couches his portentous bulletins to the world.

Hal Crowther

Clinging to the Rock: A Novelist's Choices in the New Mediocracy

A writer's reputation is sometimes enhanced, even made and sustained, by the proper enemies. Ferocious attacks by the Victorian rearguard helped to bring Dreiser, Faulkner, and Joyce the attention they deserved. It's been argued that Faulkner, without the notoriety generated by Temple Drake and Popeye's dreadful corncob, would have left the stage as a curiosity and a cult writer, to be discovered by another generation. The trick is to catch your natural enemies on the decline, a decline as obvious to literary historians as the decline of the bluestocking in the early decades of the twentieth century. It strikes me that Don DeLillo may be recorded, and profit by being recorded, as the last serious novelist denounced by the American media establishment while it still acknowledged the existence of literature, or indeed of anything that wasn't created by, for, or in conjunction with television.

To those of us who make a living as journalists, that peculiar pair of attacks on DeLillo that Frank Lentricchia examined in *Raritan*, and elaborates in his introduction to this book, will appear as a significant benchmark in the corruption of our profession. They amount to something rather different from the predictable crankiness of reactionaries who have read something that goes contrary to their prejudice. Consider, again, the language of the extraordinary column by George Will that brands DeLillo's *Libra*, a fictional life of Lee Harvey Oswald, "an act of literary vandalism and bad citizenship." *Libra* "is valuable," writes the Reagan apologist turned literary critic, "only as a reminder of the toll that ideological virulence takes on literary talent." Will goes on to label DeLillo "a study in credulity regarding the crudities of the American left" and "a talented writer whose talent is subordinated to, and obviated by, puerile political stances." Will's piece is full of angry, defensive formulations: "ideologists of the left weave indictments of America"; "the loathing some intellectuals feel for American society." In conclusion he dismisses the novelist (with a reference to Eliot, the kind of erudite affectation that has become his trademark) as "a bad influence."

For readers of the *Washington Post* who might have missed the party line on *Libra* because they can no longer stomach George Will, there was a second gunman waiting on the book page. Will's *Post* colleague and coreligionist Jonathan Yardley chimed in with a venomously negative review of DeLillo's novel, a ponderous diatribe that ground to a halt, almost sputtering, with the words "beneath contempt." Yardley, too, lumps *Libra* with "the ideological fiction of the left" and waves it off as "a slight variation upon what the paranoid left has feasted on for a quarter-century." DeLillo's craft, he says, is "the evanescent craft of pamphleteering rather than the durable art of fiction."

It pains any journalist to concede that these are formidable enemies. Will is the dogged and now somewhat dog-eared partisan, of Himalayan self-importance, who relished and traded on his friendship with Nancy Reagan. Yardley is one of those eager egos of letters, lacking the stature and the cheek to peddle an actual autobiography, who has written one of those "closet" autobiographies disguised as a tribute to a member of his family—in his case, a father who was a small-time snob, even less noteworthy than his son. If I recall correctly, each of them holds the mandatory Pulitzer Prize for criticism or commentary that goes to everyone who occupies the right chair at the right newspaper long enough for his turn to come around. Such credibility as they enjoy may rest entirely on these prizes, which the *Post*'s own Janet Cooke did so much to devalue when she carried one off for a series that was purer fiction than anything yet written by Don DeLillo. But by current standards they manage to pass for mandarins, these two, and it might be wishful thinking to dismiss this matched set of punitive essays as partisan petulance—or as coincidence. The language is inappropriately virulent, it seems to me, and inappropriately political.

It's the language of *Izvestia*, and pre-perestroika *Izvestia* at that. It's the language of official censure and rebuke, the language an authoritarian government uses against citizens who refuse to eat what their government serves them. In terms of Huxley's *Brave New World*, it's the voice that says, "Take your soma, comrade, and shut up." And since the only thing the author of *Libra* has refused to swallow is the Warren Commission Report, his denunciation as a left-wing pamphleteer seems to herald a new literary McCarthyism.

"It takes a steady adult nerve to stare unblinkingly at the fact that history can be jarred sideways by an act that signifies nothing but an addled individual's inner turmoil," asserts George Will, who appears to accept the "lone, crazed gunman" theory as part of his patriotic duty. But it takes "a study in credulity" indeed, and an astonishing capacity for denial, to embrace the conclusions of the Warren Report and ignore the mountain of circumstantial evidence that contradicts them. I wasn't aware that anyone serious had partaken of this indigestible mass of indirection and obfuscation, even at the *Washington Post*. In *Libra* one of DeLillo's characters calls the Warren Report "the megaton novel James Joyce would have written if he'd moved to Iowa City and lived to be 100."

To offend Joe McCarthy, at the very least you had to speak well of Joe Stalin; now all you have to do is speak ill of America or any of its official creations. When did it become "bad citizenship" to exhibit the same skepticism that was almost universal at the time the Warren Report was released? When did such language begin to appear under prominent bylines in power papers like the *Post*? Readers of *Libra* will find little trace of "the paranoid left" and no clear ideological twist of any sort, just a novelist's attempt to offer a psychologically plausible alternative to the see-no-evil evasions of the official historians who chose to treat Oswald as if he had landed in Dallas aboard a UFO. To choose judiciously from the many bizarre characters and events connected to the life and death of Lee Harvey Oswald—for the purpose of constructing a fiction—is hardly the same thing as subscribing to, much less promoting, one of the conspiracy theories in all its Byzantine splendor. No doubt DeLillo believes that conspiracy theory in general merits more attention than the Warren Report, and so do I.

The target of DeLillo's indignation is America's official attempt to disown its native sons, not only Lee Harvey Oswald but by extension John Fitzgerald Kennedy as well. By sticking them in a cheap morality play—the Prince of Camelot and the sniveling psychopath—we banish them both from history. *Libra* puts them back in, with a vengeance. It's my guess that DeLillo approached this novel with more political intentions, with more finger pointing in mind. As he learned more about his subject, I suspect he became more committed to the justice of restoring Oswald to his rightful context.

To attempt to tell the psychological truth about Oswald and Kennedy is to attempt to tell the truth about the society that produced them. No doubt there are many who find DeLillo's particular truths unwelcome ("I see contemporary violence as a kind of sardonic response to the promise of consumer fulfillment in America," he tells *Rolling Stone*), and many who feel that the questions raised in *Libra* should be posted against trespassing by artists and wise guys. But when did telling the truth about America become the same thing as attacking it from the left? I can't muster quite enough left-wing paranoia to accuse the *Post* and its award-winning wordsmiths of operating as enforcers for state-supported mythology—though it must be noted that *Post* editor Benjamin Bradlee was virtually a member of the Kennedy family and that loyalty to the Camelot legend, official canon, King James Version, could be regarded as one of the central loyalties of his life.

The paranoia seems to lie with the media establishment. There are several ways to account for the extreme overreaction to *Libra* and the public censure of its author, who is not a public man. But none of them are convincing unless you understand the recent history of the media—the rapid taming and trivialization of what was once an interesting and obstreperous free press. Required reading for anyone who presumes to comment on the media is Ben Bagdikian's *The Media Monopoly*, which explains that about three quarters of all the newspapers, TV stations, magazines, cable companies, book publishers, film studios, radio stations, networks, and film and video distributors in this country are owned by approximately two dozen conglomerates. Mergers reduced the number of media overlords by nearly a dozen while Bagdikian was preparing a second edition of his book. He predicts that the twenty-first century will begin with about fifteen board chairmen in a position to dictate everything that an American reads, sees, or hears.

It's significant that this remarkable book by Bagdikian, formerly an editor at the *Washington Post*, was published by none of the major conglomerate-controlled houses (including those affiliated with the *Post*), but by Beacon Press, an independent outfit operated by the Unitarian Universalist Church. Even more frightening than the small number of controlling interests is the system of interlocking directorships that binds them all together, and binds them to a hundred other industries including weapons, chemicals, and defense contracts of all varieties. Bagdikian documents any number of terrible decisions that have already been influenced by these conflicts of interest, and predicts much worse when the corporate religion of the Bottom Line has entirely obliterated the feisty skepticism and anti-establishment belligerence of the Old Guard.

Volumes have been written, and many more remain to be written, exposing the toxic effects of television on the profession of journalism. I sounded some alarms in the seventies when I was writing media criticism, at different times, for *Newsweek*, *The Humanist*, and the *Buffalo Evening News*. But I could never have predicted shows like *Geraldo* or even ABC's *PrimeTime Live*, where television's thin line between information and entertainment has vanished entirely. After avoiding almost all television for a decade I bring an alien's innocence to the changes I find, and I'm continually astonished. On *PrimeTime Live* I found the network's two most conspicuous and high-priced *journalists*, Sam Donaldson and Diane Sawyer, working in a tabloid format that owes less to *60 Minutes* than to *Lifestyles of the Rich and Famous*. Donaldson, the one-time bulldog of the White House press corps, was doing a bad imitation of Mike Wallace—an embarrassing imitation—on the clownish baseball tycoon George Steinbrenner. Sawyer, for her part, was fawning over the irrepressible Cher, whose latest video shows her wagging her middle-aged, surgically enhanced bare bottom—and that's *bare*—at a shipload of make-believe sailors.

I punched the remote-control switch and found Barbara Walters taking viewers on a tour of the palatially ridiculous home of retired ex-singer Phyllis McGuire, a mobster's widow. Nearly every question Walters asked involved some other celebrity, some name the audience was supposed to recognize. I interviewed Barbara Walters when she was the tough reporter who had clawed her way up the ladder at NBC News, when her ambition was to become the first female Walter Cronkite, and she seemed very likely to achieve it.

The cult of celebrity consumed her years ago, along with her vocation. There's something dreadfully wrong when we're compelled to pity the people we're supposed to envy, the handful who've achieved the most visible and lucrative jobs our profession has to offer. Today's TV journalists work their way up to the big money and get to do the garbage. From the Pentagon to the Common Market to Cher's behind. The networks manufacture their own celebrities in the callous hit-and-miss factory of prime-time entertainment and then generate another category of celebrities to discuss them and interview them on magazine shows and talk shows. The categories fuse after a while, and the audience loses the distinction between interviewer and interviewee, between news and gossip, between information and performance. Everyone is a star. On daytime game shows, the nomenclature for the toothy fellows in charge has evolved from "announcer" to "emcee" to "host" to "star." Hollywood has more stars than heaven now, but few of them produce any heat or light. They're regarded as interchangeable by the executives who pay them. The "star" of the game show *Wheel of Fortune* recently made the jump to a network talk show, where he can fawn over Cher just like Diane Sawyer.

Television's celebrity mill runs the supermarket tabloids and dominates the mass-market slicks, not just the insufferable *People* but the fat pretentious ones like *Esquire* and *Vanity Fair.* Its newspaper subsidiary is *USA Today,* which recently featured, above its front-page headline, a strip announcing that the loud, obese TV comedienne of the moment had published an autobiography that described her first sexual experience. *USA Today,* whose inside sections are marked Money, Sports, and Life, in that order, is considered the face of the future by all the smart money still invested in newspapers. Ralph Ingersoll II, the Colonel Sanders of tabloids, is challenging the St. Louis *Post-Dispatch* with a new daily so derivative of the industry's darling that pages from *USA Today* are taped on the walls next to signs reading "Your Guide to Excellence." Bill Kovach hastened his departure as editor of the Atlanta *Journal-Constitution* when he took offense at management's suggestions that he should pay more attention to *USA Today*. The publishers hired a *USA Today* editor shortly after Kovach resigned.

USA Today has become the American publisher's Bible, and his prophet is its founder Allen Neuharth. Among the things Neuharth learned during his years as president of the Gannett chain, besides the cutthroat corporate stratagems he boasts about in his autobiography, *Confessions of an S.O.B.,* was that readers have no patience with depth reporting or news analysis, or much of anything that can't be packaged in a few punchy sentences. Since the skills that produce depth reporting and thoughtful analysis are about 90 percent of the difference between a professional journalist and a typist, Neuharth doesn't leave the profession much room to maneuver. His disciple Ingersoll openly disparages investigation and analysis, and boasts that his papers are "top-heavy with editors."

Neuharth also learned that newspaper readers would rather tell you what they think than listen to what you think, and that they prefer editorial comment in predictable, carefully labeled packages so they never have to suffer the discomfort of reading something they don't agree with. So his papers are packed with reader polls and what I call "ping-pong," ideological racket games pitting one cast-iron extremist against another. This sport has proven so popular, editors now take it on faith that no individual is objective or perceptive enough to provide sufficient balance under one byline. No Walter Lippmanns need apply.

On TV and in the new tabloids opinion is a team sport, often played without a referee to mediate or clarify. The final, I should say terminal result of this travesty is that team players designated as journalists lose sight of the fading distinction between opinion and propaganda, and propagandists masquerading as journalists pass unchallenged. Players shuttle back and forth between the media and political appointments: George Will made his first appearance in the retinue of a conservative politician; Diane Sawyer worked in the Nixon White House. An establishment syndicate solicited my column a couple of years ago and then wrote back that they were sorry, but the openings in their lineup had been filled by Jeane Kirkpatrick and Lee Iacocca. I don't sell cars or bully third world ambassadors, but everybody writes a column. The worst crimes against journalistic practice and privilege have been committed by right-wing fanatic Patrick Buchanan, who has played columnist for twenty years between speech writing and public relations assignments for Republican presidents. Buchanan was recently censured by other right-wingers for a column that disdained disarmament and expressed nostalgia for the Cold War and the fascist dictators American boys like him had learned to love.

Without context, without intelligent perspective, the news is just noise—*White Noise*, as Don DeLillo identified it in the novel that won the American Book Award. Without a single voice or source it can trust, with nothing but mirrors of its own ignorance and prejudice, the public has begun to display serious confusion. Those polls Neuharth loves show that most Americans approve of George Bush, but place no faith whatever in his promises or his programs. A small majority believes that abortion is murder, and a large majority believes that this "murder" should remain legal. The media establishment, attuned to its audience more intimately than ever before, is receiving information of even poorer quality than the information it dispenses. Garbage in, garbage out, as I understand someone said about computers. The very covenant of communication implied in every democracy is breaking down. We live in what I call a mediocracy.

There isn't much comfort to be had. *The Closing of the American Mind* was an effective alarmist title, but the book doesn't express half the alarm I feel when I contemplate the media dominated by network hucksters and disciples of Al Neuharth. When journalists lose their independence and authority, when they're writing less to inform us than to distract us and deflect our anxiety, language itself begins to shrivel and die.

Into this Village of Ruined Language, patrolled by hired guns and company goons, rides the last free agent, the last free lance—the novelist with literary credentials (the only other free agents are poets, who are insufficiently read, and "gonzo" journalists, who are insufficiently edited). Journalism looks like a ghost town from a distance, but DeLillo finds Posted at the city limits an ugly pair of watchdogs, surgically altered to pass White House inspection but still bad-tempered as hell. DeLillo is the natural enemy of the language-shrinkers, a pilgrim from another era who believes that language is holy, that it should be hard and exacting like the old religions. Perhaps no metaphor in fiction expresses the writer's faith in language—in The Word—more gracefully than this passage from *The Names* (1982), in the voice of an American archaeologist named Brademas:

> "I've been thinking of Rawlinson, the Englishman who wanted to copy the inscriptions on the Behistun Rock. The languages were Old Persian, Elamite and Babylonian. Maneuvering on ladders from the first group to the second, he nearly fell to his death. This inspired him to use a Kurdish boy to copy the Babylonian set, which was the least accessible. The boy inched across a rock mass that had only the faintest indentations he might use for finger-grips. Fingers and toes. Maybe he used the letters themselves. I'd like to believe so. This is how he proceeded, clinging to the rock, passing below the great bas-relief of Darius facing a group of rebels in chains. A sheer drop. But he made it, miraculously. . . . What kind of story is this and why have I been thinking about it lately?"

No less passionate is the testimony of the novel's protagonist, James Axton, describing his first visit to the Parthenon:

> No one seems to be alone. This is a place to enter in crowds, seek company and talk. Everyone is talking. I move past the scaffolding and walk down the steps, hearing one language after another,

> rich, harsh, mysterious, strong. This is what we bring to the temple, not prayer or chant or slaughtered rams. Our offering is language.

The man who wrote these passages sounds like a Messiah born to rid us of George Will and Jonathan Yardley and all the eunuchs of the media who use language to disinfect, sterilize, bowdlerize reality before it reaches us. But I don't think they've read enough of DeLillo's fiction to grasp that, to appreciate the passion for precise systems that produced *Ratner's Star,* or the withering contempt, crystallized in *White Noise,* for the processed tabloid babble in which the American vulgate is drowning. I don't think they recognize their nemesis. I think they simply caught him poaching. Like any sentry who falls asleep at his Post, a George Will hates the man who picked up his rifle and assumed his watch—a novelist of all people. Will is a fool—I honestly believe that Will and Yardley are fools and bad journalists, if not necessarily bad men—but not such a fool that he doesn't sense his failure.

At the *Post* they love to talk about Watergate, but they don't want to talk about Dallas. Establishment journalists know in their guts that they chickened out on the biggest story of their time and left it to fringe players and exhumers of Elvis. *Libra* caught them by surprise and opened all the old wounds. Previous volumes on the assassination, fictional and conjectural, were produced by writers of less talent and stature. DeLillo's best-seller, a dead-earnest work of fiction by the harshest reckoning—only Yardley could stoop to call it deliberate exploitation—created an unprecedented consciousness of the enormous vacuum in our comprehension where the press used to earn its keep. Lee Harvey Oswald is a symbol of their decline. As *Libra* makes clear, and as Lentricchia points out, Oswald was a creature of the media like no other, an actor who conceived his life through a television screen and watched his own death on a television monitor. Even his name was a media creation. He was just Lee Oswald before he shot Kennedy. The media created and devoured Lee Harvey Oswald, but they never stopped to think about him. It took a novelist to do that.

So I suspect that DeLillo was pilloried at the *Post* because he wrote what its reporters should have written a generation ago, and because it reminded them of their increasing impotence and subservience to the politicians who used to fear them. What is shocking about the attack is the weird false dignity and the identification with official authority, and the indiscriminate application, entirely unjustified, of witch-hunter's words like "left-wing."

These questions are critical to a journalist. What's more intriguing to a reader or scholar is whether Don DeLillo is conscious of picking up a torch that journalists dropped, of reclaiming territory that journalism abandoned. Or how conscious, anyway. A conventional way of discussing DeLillo is in postmodern terms like "the paranoid novelist" whose characters resemble figures in Thomas Pynchon and even in Kafka. This works better for some of his books than for others, but *Libra* is a clear departure. And there's every indication that DeLillo was well aware he was taking on a new set of literary responsibilities along with a new set of enemies. For one thing, he began to separate himself from the postmodern mindset:

> In contemporary writing in general, there's a strong sense that the world of Beckett and Kafka has descended on contemporary America, because characters seem to live in a theoretical environment rather than in a real one. I haven't felt that I'm part of that. I've always had a grounding in the real world, whatever esoteric flights I might indulge in from time to time.

In another quote from the same *Rolling Stone* interview, DeLillo explicitly accepts a responsibility to history and its bewildered victims—and strays uncomfortably close to unfashionable writer-as-conscience theories, with more than an echo of John Gardner's "moral fiction."

> . . . I think the fiction writer tries to redeem this despair. Stories can be a consolation—at least in theory. The novelist can try to leap across the barrier of fact, and the reader is willing to take that leap with him as long as there's a kind of redemptive truth waiting on the other side, a sense that we've arrived at a resolution.
>
> I think fiction rescues history from its confusions. It can do this in the somewhat superficial way of filling in blank spaces.

> But it can also operate in a deeper way: providing the balance and rhythm we don't experience in our daily lives, in our real lives.

That's a far cry from the cutting edge of literary theory in the eighties. And his most recent fiction bears witness to a shift in the novelist's self-image. A representative DeLillo novel like *Great Jones Street* or *Players* creates empathy with a recognizably human protagonist menaced by irrational forces. "Paranoid" is a fair adjective —the danger is neither supernatural nor familiar, but in the nature of long shadows cast by things we know and half-know. In *White Noise*, DeLillo's greatest critical success, the menace is much more specific. It's American, it's up-to-the-minute, it seems to have jumped from the pages of the nearest supermarket tabloid. The situations it creates and the characters who face them are sometimes hysterically funny. *White Noise* is satire, greeted by critics with references to Jonathan Swift. It's some of the best satire written by a living American—and maybe some of the last. Writers are having a problem with satire, as I tried to point out when I reviewed *White Noise* four years ago:

> DeLillo is a satirist who can't write fast enough to avoid journalism. He tries to outrun reality, to stay far enough ahead of it, to look back with a safe lead, but it keeps gaining on him. For an ideal reading, keep a newspaper folded on one side of the book and a supermarket tabloid on the other, and cross-reference.

Tom Wolfe said the same thing in a newsmagazine interview, with a credit to Philip Roth:

> Roth said that we live in an age in which the imagination of the novelist is helpless before what he knows he will read in tomorrow's newspaper. And it's true. No one can dream up the things that pop up in the papers every day.

DeLillo might have been listening, because *Libra* is no satire, unless you have the darkest streak of humor since Céline's. It's no attempt to outrun a tabloid American reality that seems more and more like the work of a paranoid postmodern novelist. What strikes readers first about *Libra* is that they know nothing about this Lee Harvey Oswald, in spite of all the times they've read and spoken his name. They appreciate DeLillo's homework. The same reaction helped to make a best-seller of Tom Wolfe's *Bonfire of the Vanities*. In spite of all the photographs, all the articles in *Vanity Fair* and *People* and the *Village Voice*, no one knew anything about the social intricacies of Manhattan and the forces that make it work and fail to work. No one knew what to think about the city, as a unity, until they read Wolfe's book. You get no sense of it in the *New York Times*, as you get no sense of postmodern Washington from reading the *Post*. Even with enough freedom, what journalists have enough distance from their subject?

Many of the virtues of *Bonfire* are journalistic virtues, and so are many of the virtues of *Libra* (the same virtues I found in *The Executioner's Song*, which, in spite of my perhaps too herd-inspired misgivings about Norman Mailer, I liked very much). It is Wolfe, unwittingly, who offers the most eloquent justification for what DeLillo is trying to do in his novel. Describing his own work, Wolfe says, "It's the idea of the novelist putting the individual in the setting of society at large and realizing the pressure society exerts on the individual. This is something that has been lost over the past 40 years in the American novel."

It's a fine irony to find Wolfe and DeLillo plowing the same or at least adjacent literary fields. It represents a complete reversal on Wolfe's famous New Journalism manifesto, in which he accused novelists of abandoning history and human society ("the social tableau, manners and morals, the whole business of 'the way we live now,' in Trollope's phrase") for fantasy and introspection. "The novelist, in this reading, dropped the family jewels, leaving the (new) journalists to pick them up and pocket them for themselves," Joseph Epstein writes in his essay on *Bonfire*.

No doubt DeLillo, with his paranoid postmodern label, would have been one of Wolfe's favorite targets, one of the fools who dropped the jewels. Twenty years later it's the journalists who've dropped the family jewels, or offered them to the surgeon's knife; we hear very little of the New Journalism and see very little of the old; and Wolfe and DeLillo are both writing corrosive, disturbing fiction about things people need to know—like themselves. Wolfe found that journalism didn't give him quite enough freedom. Perhaps DeLillo found that the fiction he'd been writing didn't give him quite enough of a stake in a culture that was fighting for its life and losing. When Anthony DeCurtis asks him about the "apocalyptic feel" of his books, "an intimation that our world is moving toward greater randomness and dissolution, or maybe even cataclysm," DeLillo answers: "This is the shape my books take because this is the reality I see. This reality has become part of all our lives over the past twenty-five years. I don't know how we can deny it."

For such candor DeLillo has been dismissed as a giddy left-winger. For a certain hauteur and respect for style, and for violating the fashionable taboo against criticism of any and all organized minorities, Wolfe has been attacked as a reactionary. And yet their latest novels have filled up the same vacuum and challenged some of the same orthodoxies. DeLillo will never say with Wolfe, "I'm a journalist at heart; even as a novelist, I'm first of all a journalist. I think all novels should be journalism to start, and if you can ascend from that plateau to some marvelous altitude, terrific." But Wolfe has named the game, hasn't he? And DeLillo goes at least half as far when he says, "It's my idea of myself as a writer—perhaps mistaken—that I enter these worlds as a completely rational person who is simply taking what he senses all around him and using it as material."

Joseph Epstein, in his essay on Wolfe in *The New Criterion* (1988), steers me toward a good excuse for preferring DeLillo, as I do:

> Novelists who refrain from making use of such material because they consider it merely journalistic are very great fools. But the serious novel, while including all this, goes beyond it. The difference, ultimately, between the novelist and the journalist is that the real subject of the novel is the truth of the human heart.

According to this criterion, Epstein found *Bonfire of the Vanities* short of the mark as a novel. I don't think he'd find *Libra* short on the same scale. It is, oddly, a book with a large heart as well as a dark heart. It's easier for a novelist to assume a journalist's responsibilities than for a journalist to develop an accomplished novelist's capacities. Tom Wolfe would never have written, as DeLillo writes in *The Names*, again in the voice of Brademas:

> In this century the writer has carried on a conversation with madness. We might almost say of the 20th-century writer that he aspires to madness. Some have made it, of course, and they hold special places in our regard. To a writer, madness is a final distillation of self, a final editing down. It's the drowning out of false voices.

Maybe that's the voice the false voices were hearing when they sent the SWAT team from the *Post* to eliminate Don DeLillo. It's a voice they don't hear in the newsroom or over their headphones. It's one thing to be flogged and contradicted by the southerner in the cream-colored suit; at least he's one of them, sort of. But this gloomy Italian from the Bronx sounds dangerous.

The decline in the influence and independence of the individual journalist and the individual newspaper shouldn't be confused with any decline in the power of the media to censor and harm us. That power only increases as the media product is trivialized and standardized, and as maverick voices are silenced. And of course the peevish patriots of the *Post* are gentlemen and scholars compared with the illiterate rabble that's already superseding them, in the livery of Al Neuharth and Ralph Ingersoll.

My favorite alarmist is NYU's Neil Postman, the Paul Revere of communications, who calls himself "a media ecologist." In his most important book, *Amusing Ourselves to Death*, Postman argues that it's Huxley's *Brave New World*, rather than Orwell's *1984*, that provides the relevant myth for the decline and fall of America.

> In the Huxleyan prophecy, Big Brother does not watch us, by his choice. We watch him, by ours. There is no need for wardens or gates or Ministries of Truth. When a population becomes distracted by trivia, when cultural life is redefined as a perpetual round of entertainments, when serious public conversation becomes a form of baby-talk, when, in short, a people become an audience and their public business a vaudeville act, then a nation finds itself at risk; culture-death is a clear possibility.

Postman might have added, "when all communication has commercial intent, when anything disturbing is left-wing, when the President participates in the faking of a drug bust for TV cameras, when a network news crew is caught using actors to recreate an incident they never could have filmed. . . ." Living in such a society is very much like inching across the rock face by fingerholds, but the language we have left won't support our weight. Cultural paralysis is well advanced when none of the custodians of our public reality will interpret it or respect it, or even insist upon it; when no one but writers of fiction are interested in the facts.

In *White Noise*, DeLillo has already imagined a grim near-future where all culture is shtick and all language is like the drone of insects and machines. In the words of the narrator, Jack Gladney, "I have reached an age, an age of unreliable menace. The world is full of abandoned meanings."

That's a terrible, an apocalyptic lament. But instead of merely proclaiming his grief at the Wailing Wall of literature, Don DeLillo has chosen with *Libra* to reinhabit some of those abandoned meanings. It's no mean ambition for a novelist. If they aren't intimidated by the enemies he made, other artists might do well to follow his example.

John A. McClure

Postmodern Romance: Don DeLillo and the Age of Conspiracy

Don DeLillo crafts his fictions out of the forms of popular romance: out of the espionage thriller, the imperial adventure novel, the western, science fiction, even the genre of occult adventure. He may conduct us, in one novel, across several genres: *Running Dog* begins as a spy story, turns, as one of the characters remarks, into a western, and ends on a note of New Age adventure, with the introduction of a figure out of Castaneda's Don Juan books. Contemporary literary theory invites us to see in such minglings the project of pastiche: a play across forms uninflected with any impulse to criticism or reanimation. But DeLillo is not simply playful; there's a logic to the transitions he orchestrates, an urgency to the shiftings and sortings, a critical edge to his appropriations. He is engaged in tracing a kind of history of romance: challenging the modernist notion that global secularization and "rationalization" would make its production impossible; showing how these very processes produce new sources for romance. And he is interested in exploring the power of the new formulas, the nature of their appeal. But in the end he insists, against the manifest fact of his own fascination, that the deepest rewards of romance are not to be found in the roles and regions where the white male culture of America now locates them: in espionage and conspiracy. And he gestures, albeit tentatively, beyond these realms into regions where romance might yet find the resources it needs to be reborn in something like adequate form.

DeLillo portrays romance as a rich and protean mode that constantly adapts itself to changing historical conditions, returning again and again to the drama of the historical moment for the "raw materials"—the human models and settings and ideologies—it requires to construct its stories of quest and contest, radical alterity, divine or demonic otherness. One requirement of romance is a world plausibly permeated with mysterious forces, with magical or sacred or occult powers. But as Western society became increasingly secularized and rationalized, romance tended increasingly to locate this world on the great imperial frontiers: Africa, Asia, Latin America, and the American West. These "marginal" zones were imaginatively exploited both by writers of popular adventure fiction and by writers of high romance, novelists like Joseph Conrad, E. M. Forster, Malcolm Lowry, and Graham Greene. They were represented as places where the conditions of romance still obtained, where one could enjoy adventures unavailable in a world of law and order, achieve goals out of reach in a class-bound society, experience emotional and sensual intensities prohibited in a world of carefully regulated responses, and enjoy experiences of the sacred, the demonic, and the sublime unavailable in a utilitarian, scientific, and secular world.

The search for raw materials that preoccupies DeLillo is made necessary by the global elimination of such premodern places, the penetration of capitalism into all the enclaves once available for imaginative exploitation in romance. The moderns anticipated this moment with dread, and their relation to the imperialism that made its coming inevitable was a vexed one. On the one hand, they drew on the records and experiences of actual imperial adventurers to create their tales of exotic adventure, lend plausibility to their representations of magical and miraculous events; on the other, they recognized that the existence of these reports and reporters spelled doom for the exotic lives and exotic places they depicted. Even as they exploited the materials of romance made available by imperial penetration of premodern cultures, they projected a Weberian future in which the rationalizing spirit of the West would produce a universal disenchantment of the world. Conrad's Marlow reminisces wistfully, at the beginning of *Heart of Darkness*, over the time not so long ago when the map of Africa, now filled in, was "a blank space of delightful mystery —a white patch for a boy to dream gloriously over." In a similar vein, a character in Virginia Woolf's *The Voyage Out* condemns British imperialism, not for exploiting and impoverishing the peoples of Latin America, but for "robbing a whole continent of mystery." And in Conan Doyle's *The Lost World*, a character declares regretfully that "the big blank spaces in the map are being filled in, and there's no room for romance anywhere."

A passage deleted from the final version of *Heart of Darkness* provides a somewhat more detailed version of this narrative of disenchantment. At the beginning of the novel, as Marlow and his friends sit on their sailboat waiting for the tide to turn, a "big steamer," undeterred by such natural forces, comes down the channel. She is, we are told,

> bound to the uttermost ends of the earth and timed to the day, to the very hour with nothing unknown in her path [,] no mystery on her way, nothing but a few coaling stations. She went full-speed, noisily . . . timed from port to port, to the very hour. And the earth suddenly seemed shrunk to the size of a pea spinning in the heart of an immense darkness.

The steamboat, a symbol of triumphant technology, shrinks the world, displacing a terrestrial darkness which is at once threatening and satisfying, and rendering experience all too predictable. Its disenchanting passage might even be said to sponsor, emblematically anyway, Marlow's countervoyage up the Congo, a voyage which seems designed to reconstitute the world, put the darkness back where it belongs, at its heart. And Marlow's journey is but one of many by which modernists typically orchestrate a temporary escape from disenchantment into the so-called "dark places of the world."

The postmodern period begins, according to Fredric Jameson, at the moment when these places are abolished: The "prodigious expansion of capital into hitherto uncommodified areas," Jameson writes in *New Left Review* (1984), "eliminates the enclaves of precapitalist organization it had hitherto tolerated and exploited in a tributary way." The result is the "purer capitalism of our own times" and the eradication of those cultures and professions from which the modernists extracted romance. To hear a modernist's response to this act of foreclosure, we need only turn to John Berger, who declares, in *The Look of Things*, that the eradication of the precapitalist sanctuaries of the Western imagination has made the world uninhabitable. "The intolerability of the world," he writes, "is, in a certain sense, an historical achievement. The world was not intolerable so long as God existed, so long as there was the ghost of a pre-existent order, so long as large tracts of the world were unknown."

DeLillo refuses to make this modernist judgment his point of departure. Instead, while modernists such as Berger continue to seek out remnants of the premodern among vestigial communities, DeLillo focuses his attention on sites within capitalism, and discovers there the materials of new forms of romance. It's true, he suggests, that capitalism has penetrated everywhere, but its globalization has not resulted in global rationalization and Weber's iron cage. It seems instead to have sponsored a profound reversal: the emergence of zones and forces like those that imperial expansion has erased: jungle-like techno-tangles; dangerous, unknown "tribes"; secret cults with their own codes and ceremonies, vast conspiracies. "This is the age of conspiracy," says a character in *Running Dog*, with the mixture of wonder and revulsion that is everywhere in DeLillo's work. This is "the age of connections, links, secret relationships." These zones and forces—the various computer circuits, multinational business networks, espionage agencies, private armies, and unconventional political players—make a mockery of collective desires for democracy and social justice. But at the same time they assuage collective fears of a totally domesticated and transparent world, and become substitutes, in the popular imagination, for earlier sources of mystery, adventure, and empowerment. Thus the espionage thriller, with its vision of a world riven by clashes between vast conspiratorial forces, replaces the imperial adventure story and its American subform, the western, as the most popular mode of (masculine) romance. And conspiracy theory, on which the thriller is based, replaces religion as a means of mapping the world without disenchanting it, robbing it of its mystery. For conspiracy theory explains the world, as religion does, without elucidating it, by positing the existence of hidden forces which permeate and transcend the realm of ordinary life. It offers us satisfactions similar to those offered by religions and religiously inflected romance: both the satisfaction of living among secrets, in a mysterious world, and the satisfaction of gaining access to secrets, being "in the know," a member of some esoteric order of magicians or warriors.

In *Players*, DeLillo's early venture in the conspiracy thriller, espionage networks provide certain satisfactions which used to be found only in the non-Western world. Now, it's "everywhere, isn't it?"

> Mazes. . . . Intricate techniques. Our big problem in the past, as a nation, was that we didn't give our government credit for being the totally entangling force that it was. They were even more evil than we'd imagined. More evil and much more interesting. Assassination, blackmail, torture, enormous improbable intrigues. All these convolutions and relationships. . . . Behind every stark fact we encounter layers of ambiguity . . . multiple interpretations.

The secret government has replaced Conrad's labyrinthine Congo and satanic Congolese, who taught Marlow "the fascination of the abomination," as the site of evil and interest, the darkly enchanted Elsewhere of our dreams. Indeed, DeLillo suggests, it is now "the secret dream of the white collar" to escape into that world,

> to place a call from a public booth in the middle of the night. Calling some government bureau, some official department, right, of the government. "I have information about so-and-so." Or, even better, to be visited, to have them come to you. "You might be able to deliver a microdot letter, sir, on your visit to wherever," if that's how they do things. "You might be willing to provide a recruiter with cover on your payroll, sir." Imagine how sexy that can be for the true-blue businessman or professor. What an

> incredible nighttime thrill. The appeal of mazes and intricate techniques. The suggestion of a double life. "Fantastic, sign me up, I'll do it."

The familiar has become fantastic, the public institutions of a rationalizing age have metastasized into sinister but alluring webs of mystery.

In another novel about Americans drawn into the secret world of espionage, *Running Dog*, DeLillo shows even more explicitly that in spite of modernist fears, the social world has not been rendered totally "readable" by science and technology. Max Weber equated rationalization not with "an increased and general knowledge of the condition under which one lives," but with the "belief that if one but wished one *could* learn [about] it at any time," that "there are no mysterious incalculable forces that come into play." But in DeLillo's America this process has been suspended, even reversed: "it's the presence alone, the very fact, the superabundance of technology. . . . Just the fact that these things exist at this widespread level. The process machines, the scanners, the sorters. . . . What enormous weight. What complex programs. And there's no one to explain it to us." We have been cast back into mystery by the very forces—scientific, rationalizing—that threatened or promised enlightenment.

DeLillo relates this reversal to the history of romance in *The Names*, his novel about an American based in Athens who does "risk analysis" of Asian and African nations for an American corporation. James Axton and his friends like to see themselves as playing out roles in an old-fashioned colonial romance: "It is like the Empire," says one character. "Opportunity, adventure, sunsets, dusty death." But their self-consciousness betrays an awareness that the roles they imagine themselves playing are no longer available in a world divided into nations and crisscrossed with air routes, telecommunications networks, and shipping lanes. Has the world become the "withered pea" of Conrad's nightmare? This view of things is emphatically denied:

> "They keep telling us it's getting smaller all the time. But it's not, is it? Whatever we learn about it makes it bigger. Whatever we do to complicate things makes it bigger. It's all a complication. It's one big tangled thing. . . . Modern communications

> don't shrink the world, they make it bigger. Faster planes make it bigger. They give us more, they connect more things. . . . The world is so big and complicated."

In other words, the instruments that many modernists saw as adversaries of sublimity and enchantment turn out to be producing them: the great steamer which threatens to rob Conrad's world of its satisfying strangeness is in effect celebrated by DeLillo—and not just in *The Names* but throughout his work—as the unwitting agent of a fascinating new intricacy.

In *The Names,* James Axton goes looking for mystery where the modernists found it, in the exotic countries he studies as a risk analyst for his employer, and in the mysterious cult of assassins he studies as a sideline. He likes to see himself as a colonial adventurer. But in the end he discovers that the most dramatic mysteries are *behind* him, in the corporate world he takes for granted, and in Athens, the seat of Western civilization. He has been working all along, it seems, not for a private company but for the CIA; he has been pursued not by exotic cultists but by Greek nationalists. Caught up in his nostalgia for outmoded forms of romance, he has failed to recognize that he is playing a leading part in a contemporary adventure story, a tale of conspiracy and terrorism. The drama of rationalization ends—or at least can be seen as ending—with a literal deus ex machina in which a zone of enchantment emerges out of the machinery of the modern. "Elsewhere," which was mapped geographically in the popular imagination of the modernist era, is now mapped geologically, as the subterranean segment of a global political and economic circuitry, the world of conspiracy. And romance, which once had to depend on distant premodern places for its raw materials, now finds them at the heart of the postmodern metropolis.

The age of conspiracy offers us, by way of satisfactions, new forms of intricacy, entanglement, and complication, a new jungle with its own "fibrous beauty." It offers us the opportunity to be thrilled by the power, the impenetrability, and the almost demonic malevolence of new systems. It even offers, to the lover of sacred and esoteric language, a new "poetry," the "technical idiom" of new systems of communication and control, "number-words and coinages [that] had the inviolate grace of a strict meter of chant." To the more daring, it offers the possibility of actual participation in the new cults and combat units, the "nighttime thrill" of a double life. To the rest of us, the readers of the fictitious *Running Dog* magazine or the real *Running Dog*, it offers the pleasure of vicarious participation in these adventures, momentary escape from our all-too-predictable lives. It rescues us, in other words, from the modernist nightmare of an entire world reduced to quotidian compromises and routines, an utterly disenchanted world.

So much for what is offered. But DeLillo's novels are no simple celebrations of the new Elsewhere. Indeed they seem designed, like the works of modernists such as Conrad, both to reproduce the excitements of popular romance and to reject them as unworthy: unfounded in reality and inferior to the effects produced by truer mysteries, more realistic romances. When we romanticize conspiracy, DeLillo suggests, we misrepresent it, invest it with powers and possibilities it does not possess. The great romance narratives posit a world alive with demonic and divine forces, and an inner world similarly profound and intense. They posit institutions—the faith, the court, the community—capable of satisfying individual and collective needs for transcendence: for testing, tempering, and triumph (courtly romance) or renunciation, purification, and illumination (spiritual romance). And they imply that human beings are up to these challenges. But the new intricacies are ultimately soulless, the new institutions debased. Even our capacity for trial is sadly diminished. The jungle of technical and human systems possesses only a spurious and superficial sublimity: it's the stuff of perverse fascinations and cheap thrills rather than awe and wonder. And the new orders of quest and contest, the secret agencies dedicated ostensibly to the protection of sacred cultural values, are actually no more than subsystems of a vast criminal enterprise that encompasses capitalist corporations, criminal entrepreneurs, and corrupt governments. As a character in *Running Dog* puts it, "[l]oyalties are so interwoven, the thing's a game. The Senator and PAC/ORD [a maverick intelligence unit] aren't nearly the antagonists the public believes them to be. They talk all the time. They make deals, they buy people, they sell favors. . . . That's the nature of the times." To be entangled in these systems is to be diminished—we all are. To be actively engaged is to be morally destroyed.

Within the world of conspiracy, one simply does not find the great ethical confrontations between good and evil that are at the heart of romance, nor the institutions—the secular or religious orders, legions of angels and demons, good guys and bad—that gave specific form to the struggle. Under such conditions, potential adepts drawn to conspiracy by the will to romance and by illusions fostered by popular romance find themselves "warriors without masters," their only roundtable an intelligence agency that operates by the corrupt codes of the very culture they would escape: "They didn't call it the Company for nothing. It was set up to obscure the deeper responsibilities, the calls of blood trust that have to be answered." We may mock the idea of such "calls," and see them as little more than the effects of an ideology that has long used the fictions of romance to enlist shock troops for the sordid business of conquest. But we continue to look for institutions that can satisfy such needs, and, when such institutions are absent, to settle for substitutes.

Running Dog is DeLillo's most sustained study of a single "warrior without a master." Fast-paced, scary, exciting, and grimly funny, it traces the attempts of one would-be knight, Glen Selvy, to find a channel for his aspirations. The novel invites us to be "suspicious of quests," to find "some vital deficiency on the part of the individual in pursuit, a meagerness of spirit." But it also reminds us that we are, as a culture, addicted to fantasies of quest, conspiracy, and illumination. And it appeals to us in these very terms, offering itself, at the outset anyway, as a supersophisticated version of the familiar story. Selvy, like so many recent adventure heroes—Rambo; the Robert De Niro character in *The Deer Hunter*; Hicks, the Vietnam vet of Stone's *Dog Soldiers*—wants to be a kind of knight: to practice ascetic disciplines, purify and perfect his body, join an order, serve a cause. His girlfriend casts him repeatedly as a hero of romance, "an English lancer on the eve of Balaclava," an adept trained by "some master of the wilderness." And the novel seems ready to confirm him in a contemporary version of that role: he is given a position in a secret security force, a boss named Percival, and a quest. But these possibilities are advanced only to be dashed. Both Selvy and the reader learn that in this America, in these times, there is no way to play out such dreams. The secret community Selvy joins (PAC/ORD) turns out to be every bit as corrupt and manipulative as the terror organizations it is ostensibly dedicated to destroying. Percival turns out to be a collector of pornography, and the quest that preoccupies all the major players—the Senator, the secret service, the Mafia, and Richie Armbrister, America's king of smut—is for a pornographic film shot in Hitler's bunker: "the century's ultimate piece of decadence."

Selvy, who is drawn to the ascetic life without any sense of concrete mission, at first doesn't feel "tainted by the dirt of his profession." He simply enjoys "the empty meditations, the routine, the tradecraft, the fine edge to be maintained in preparation for—he didn't know what." But ultimately, embittered and betrayed, he comes to see himself not as a modern knight, but as just another lackey of an utterly corrupt capitalist order, a servant of the god of our times, "The God of Body. The God of Lipstick and Silk. The God of Nylon, Scent and Shadow." "What's your real name?" his girlfriend asks. "Running Dog," he replies.

With this recognition, Selvy's second quest begins, and *Running Dog* turns into something of a metaromance, a quest narrative in which the aim of the quest is to find a viable romance form, a script that will enable Selvy, and perhaps the reader, to begin pursuing redemption. No longer looking for the pornographic grail of a perverse society, fleeing assassins set on him by his own employers, Selvy breaks out of the Northeastern Corridor world of the espionage thriller and out of the genre itself: "This is turning into a Western," remarks his girlfriend. But there's no longer room in the West into which Selvy flees to stage the old western romance, and besides, the players have been scrambled beyond recognition. Thus Selvy, the WASP, is pursued by two Vietnamese in cowboy hats and sunglasses through a Texas town slowly filling up with tourists, "mostly older people and eight or nine Japanese." When he retreats even further, back to the abandoned desert training camp where he once studied covert warfare, his flight takes him across yet another generic boundary, into the world of sixties shamanistic romance, the Don Juan stories. Levi Blackwater, a "gringo mystic" whose name evokes both the priestly tribe of his forebears and the Indian tribes of the land he wanders, appears at this point to warn Selvy that his final stab at living by the rules of romance, an attempt to orchestrate a spiritually meaningful death, will also fail. "There's no way out," says Blackwater.

> "No clear light for you in this direction. You can't find release from experience so simply."
> "Dying is an art in the East."
> "Yes, heroic, a spiritual victory."
> "You set me on to that, Levi."
> . . . .
> "But this is part, only part, of a longer, longer, process. We were just beginning to understand."

Selvy's attempt to write himself into Eastern rituals is hopelessly oversimplified, and he dies, ironically, thinking not about spiritual victory but about spirits—"What he needed right now was a drink." Levi's plans for Selvy—he wants to enact a burial ritual passed along to him by the "masters of the snowy range"—are similarly shipwrecked. The ceremony requires taking a few locks of the deceased's hair, but Selvy's Vietnamese assassin, who is also versed in the lore of the spirits, has decapitated his victim and carried the head away.

There are no adequate patterns for romance in the American culture to which Selvy belongs and from which he gets his bearings. The West of the western no longer exists; the new Orientalisms of the sixties celebrate disciplines Westerners cannot master; and espionage, the freshest region of romance, is a realm of all-too-familiar corruptions. Its secrets are sordid, its quests salacious, its contests little more than internecine battles between competitors who share the same mean aims. DeLillo suggests, in other words, that we have avoided rationalization without rescuing enchantment, have entered an era of aimless intensities, pornographic passions, cheap thrills, and warriors without wisdom.

DeLillo has continued to be fascinated with conspiracy, even as he warns against its fascinations. *The Names* and *Libra*, two of the three novels he has published since *Running Dog*, focus on conspiracies. They succeed, like *Running Dog*, both in conveying the excitements associated with conspiracy and in making these excitements seem spurious, disabling. They do this, in part, by working with and against the conventions of the espionage thriller, offering some of the satisfactions of the genre, denying others. They catch us up in sensational stories of conspiracy and assassination, but deny us the pleasures of compression and pacing we associate with such stories. *The Names* is a tangle of loosely integrated plot lines, unresolved conflicts, and suspended actions. And in *Libra*, DeLillo refuses to shape his subject, the first Kennedy assassination, to the forms of the conventional thriller. "If we are on the outside,"

> we assume a conspiracy is the perfect working of a scheme. Silent nameless men with unadorned hearts. A conspiracy is everything that ordinary life is not. It's the inside game, cold, sure, undistracted, forever closed off to us. We are the flawed ones, the innocents, trying to make some rough sense of the daily jostle. Conspirators have a logic and a daring beyond our reach. All conspiracies are the same taut story of men who find coherence in some criminal act.
>
> But maybe not.

Certainly not in *Libra*, which challenges the conventional "taut story" about conspiracy not only by what it depicts—a rambling, confused, and incoherent series of events, but also by its method of depiction, through a capacious and frequently meditative narrative which is anything but "taut." DeLillo structures both works in a way that challenges the romance of conspiracy, the "stories" we tell ourselves about the way things work in that mysterious domain. But he is not content, in *The Names* and *Libra*, merely to challenge the romantic representation of conspiracy. He is also searching, as Selvy does in *Running Dog*, for alternatives to conspiracy, social sites and ideologies that provide more adequate raw materials of romance. *The Names* explores "the world of corporate transients," expatriate employees of the great multinational business and government interests James Axton at first finds romantic: "I don't mind working for Rowser at all," he says, speaking of his superior in the risk analysis firm.

> This is where I want to be. History. . . . We're important suddenly. . . . We're right in the middle. We're the handlers of huge sums of delicate money. Recyclers of petrodollars. Builders of refineries. Analysts of risk. . . . The world is here. Don't you feel that? In some of these places, things have enormous power. They have impact, they're mysterious.

Axton is especially fascinated with the speech of his corporate knights-errant. He likes their habit of turning places into "one-sentence stories," a manner of speaking which suggests at once the speakers' amazing mobility (they've been everywhere), their worldliness, and their power to define and dismiss. He likes, too, their command of specialized jargons, "the technical cant" of security specialists, bankers, businessmen, and spies, which resonates with the power of the institutions that employ them. And he likes, finally, the protocols of conspiratorial exchange:

> He asked a few questions about my trips to countries in the region. He approached the subject of the Northeast Group several times but never mentioned the name itself, never asked a direct question. I let the vague references go by, volunteered nothing, paused often. . . . It was a strange conversation, full of hedged remarks and obscure undercurrents, perfect in its way.

By the end of the novel, though, Axton has had more than enough of conspiracy and, it would seem, its idioms. Before he leaves Athens, he makes a long-postponed visit to the Acropolis, and finds there examples of a strikingly different politics of discourse, resources for a different kind of romance. Axton's Acropolis is a place of congregation, free exchange, and "open expression," a language community antithetical in its purposes and principles of exchange to the conspiratorial community he is fleeing. "Everyone is talking," and the impression conveyed is one of rich heteroglossia, constructive dialogue, and catharsis. Even the stones seem to speak, and to instruct those who come to them in the purposes and powers of speech:

> I hadn't expected a human feeling to emerge from the stones but this is what I found, deeper than the art and mathematics em-

> bodied in the structure, the optical exactitudes. I found a cry for pity . . . this open cry, this voice we know as our own.

Here are the resources for a very different kind of romance, one in which people come together to share knowledge, pain, and longing on a site resonate with history and with absence. This terrain—the half-empty temple, denuded of its divinities but still filled with suppliants, still ringing, albeit silently, with a "cry for pity" addressed to absent redeemers—resembles the space that Jameson designated in *The Political Unconscious* as the terrain of authentic romance in our time. It is one of the "abandoned clearings across which higher and lower worlds once passed," and which we still visit to remember older dreams of fulfillment and to confront our impoverishment. *The Names*, like *Running Dog*, depicts a kind of transgeneric quest, but one that ends more promisingly than Selvy's. And it repudiates, as *Running Dog* does, that version of history which would offer the intricate systems and conspiracies of postmodernity as adequate sources of wonder and transcendence. If romance has a home in the present, it is not within the machinery of capitalism, but in archaic and marginal places, like the Acropolis, where memory and desire bring people together to speak openly about what they have lost and what they want.

But the episode at the Acropolis is not the end of *The Names*. It is followed by a brief fragment from a novel, being written by James Axton's son, in which the young protagonist is attending a Pentecostal revival meeting somewhere on the American plains. Here again there is a play of voices: the boy's parents and other worshipers are speaking in tongues, recreating that moment from biblical history when the spirit descended on the disciples and they began miraculously to speak in the different languages of the ancient world. But for the boy at least, this cacophony of voices is terrifying: he cannot understand, and, even worse, he cannot join them: "The gift was not his, the whole language of the spirit which was greater than Latin or French was not to be seized in his pityfull mouth." Fleeing the church, he finds himself in a bleak world without "familiar signs and safe places," but not without wonder. The last words of the fragment, and of *The Names,* describe the boy's reaction to this world: "This was worse than a retched nightmare. It was the nightmare of real things, the fallen wonder of the world."

I read this fragment as a second parabolic retort to the postmodern narrative that discovers romance in conspiracy, a counterhistory in which wonder survives the crisis of desacralization not by investing the mechanisms of multinational capitalism with all the power and mystery once ascribed to the forces of magicians and gods, but by facing the fact of our disinheritance, the emptiness of a world without God. And I imagine, even if DeLillo does not, the youngster fleeing toward the Acropolis, on his way to an encounter that will provide him with company and prepare him for the longer struggle, that of casting, in merely human speech, an image of the future as rich or richer than that which died with the gods.

Libra, DeLillo's most recent novel of conspiracy, ends on a similar note, with an extended cry for pity, and call for justice, from Marguerite, Lee Oswald's mother. Marguerite's monologue is addressed, like Job's, to an invisible judge. Of course she lacks the rich man's eloquence: she speaks in the only languages she knows, the debased languages of popular culture, the world of women's magazines and television: "Judge, I have lived in many places but never filthy dirty, never not neat, never without the personal loving touch, the decorator item. We have moved to be a family. This is the theme of my research." In her desperation she remakes and recombines the clichés she uses, fusing the fragments borrowed from so many debased utterances into an utterance which is not debasing but profoundly moving. Her voice, unlike the voices of the conspirators, is raw with emotion, resonant with memory and disappointment and confusion. "I have suffered," she proclaims, and suddenly we are back in the realm of the "open cry," the homeland of romance. "I stand here on this brokenhearted earth," she declares, and we recall that, in the genre of romance, passions are not contained in individual characters but seem to circulate through them and the world they inhabit. "You have to wonder," she says, and her words have the force of a command. Listening to her cries as she mourns her son under a wild and urgent sky, we are reminded of the young boy imagined by another young boy at the end of *The Names*, in that other country of romance where wonder is not a matter of human secrets, human institutions, machinery, but of tragic vision and open expression.

The unfashionably passionate and awkward language of the "open cry" exposes the emptiness of all the carefully closed and polished language that has preceded it, reminds us that the language of DeLillo's tough guys, so strikingly frank and transgressive in some respects, has its own decorums, effects its own suppressions. What it renders unspeakable are precisely those protests and prayers (for a Day of Judgment, a Day of Reconciliation, a salvational future) on which the great traditions of romance, sacred and secular, are founded. In giving voice to these protests and prayers, the visitors to the Acropolis, the prairie Pentecostals, the boy who flees their chapel, and Marguerite Oswald invite us to get in touch with them as well, to remember the historic vocation of romance, and to reject all romance formulas that do not reflect that vocation.

But Marguerite's monologues are not the only passages in *Libra* which point the reader toward alternatives to popular postmodern romance. Character after character in the novel comments on the role played by coincidence in the unfolding of the plot against Kennedy. "We were all linked," thinks one, "in a vast and rhythmic coincidence, a daisy chain of rumor, suspicion and secret wish." Nicholas Branch, the CIA employee assigned to write the secret history of the assassination, resists the temptation to look beyond the amazing play of coincidence for some "grand and masterful scheme," although he does come to think that "someone is trying to sway him toward superstition" by feeding him instance after instance "of cheap coincidence." But David Ferrie, the unofficial "spiritual adviser" to the conspiracy, is bolder. He insists that "there's a pattern in things. Something in us has an effect on independent events. We make things happen. The conscious mind gives one side only. We're deeper than that. We extend into time." Finally, then, "There's no such *thing* as coincidence. We don't know what to call it, so we say coincidence."

Ferrie's speculations gain credibility from their context: events in this novel (which takes its title from Ferrie's favorite science, astrology) are shaped in remarkable ways by what most characters think of as coincidence. Someone, it would seem, is trying to *sway* us toward superstition, trying to get us to see something like a grand psychic conspiracy at work in what we call coincidence. DeLillo presses us toward that familiar and academically unsavory resource of romance, the discourse of the occult. While the romance of conspiracy is rejected in *Libra*, the whole trope of conspiracy undergoes what might be called a respiritualization: we are asked to envision a world in which dark, unnameable psychic forces are in play, forces which, like those of magic and divinity, are not subject to the physical laws we think we are bound to obey.

DeLillo repudiates the romance of conspiracy and promotes certain alternatives. But while each of the novels I've discussed ends by dismissing conspiracy—the activity, the mode of speech it sponsors, the genre—in each novel DeLillo also returns to the topic. It might be argued that he has been unable to extricate himself from the spell of conspiracy, to write for long in the very different registers of romance he arrives at in the final moments of *The Names* and *Libra*. Is he trapped, then, like so many of his protagonists, outside that world of "deep wondering" and "ordinary mysteries" toward which he gestures at the end of these works? And is he driven, like many of his main characters, by a desire for the chilly disciplines, intricacies, and entanglements of the new multinational order? These are, of course, unanswerable questions. But they lead to other questions, which may be answerable. What about us—the avid readers of DeLillo's work? Does our readiness to return with him, again and again, to his chosen terrain, suggest that, like it or not, we too are enthralled by those networks of power and manipulation which we also—most of us—claim to abhor? Writing from within the enchantments of the new Elsewhere, but also against them, DeLillo helps us place ourselves, recognize our own unsavory enthrallments, acknowledge, even if we cannot embrace, some of the alternatives to this particular, historically determined enchantment.

Eugene Goodheart

Some Speculations on Don DeLillo and the Cinematic Real

Don DeLillo's characters contemplate and pronounce upon the deepest questions of life, death, selfhood, sex, violence, and history. They speak with extraordinary power and intelligence, but they seem disembodied, at times indistinguishable from one another. The very presence or absence of self is one of the themes of DeLillo's fiction. DeLillo is hardly the only contemporary writer to put the existence of the self into question. As Philip Roth's novelist-hero Nathan Zuckerman says in *The Counterlife*: "I, for one, have no self. . . . What I have instead is a variety of impersonations I can do, and not only of myself—a troupe of players that I have internalized, company of actors. . . . I am a theater and nothing more than a theater." This is not an elegy, not a lament for the death or the loss of the self. On the contrary, Zuckerman celebrates the release of new and diverse powers and energies unimpeded by the obstacle of a unitary or coherent self to which those powers and energies might have to give obeisance. The "self" as theatrical troupe is *homo ludens*.

DeLillo would endorse the view of the self as a nullity, but he would, I think, object to the theatrical metaphor. At least one of his characters, Lyle, the astronaut hero of *Players*, speaks of being bored by "three-dimensional bodies" in the theater, because they produce in him a kind of "torpor." He prefers "the manipulated depth of film." Could it be that Roth's use of the theatrical metaphor betrays an unsurmounted attachment to the substantial (three-dimensional) self? DeLillo's role players, in any case, have been completely emptied of substance. *Players* concludes with a striking image of the empty or emptying self, more radical and more convincing than what seems to me the desperate effort of Roth's alter ego to disburden himself of the guilts and sufferings that, alas, constitute his self. Here is the concluding paragraph of *Players*:

> The propped figure, for instance, is barely recognizable as male. Shedding capabilities and traits by the second, he can still be described (but quickly) as well-formed, sentient and fair. We know nothing else about him.

"But quickly" because he is already disappearing as he is described. This disembodied, disappearing self is a function of DeLillo's cinematic imagination. The cinema, as we know, is a two-dimensional space. Its quintessential subject, the cartoon character, appears and disappears at the blink of an eye. Pulverized, mashed, flattened, the cartoon character can be restored to its original dignity at a moment's notice. In a sense, even the human subjects of films have the characterless malleability of the cartoon subject, insofar as they are subject to the most incredible transformations; insofar as they possess no center of resistance to cinematic change.

Players is a novel about the absence of the quiddity of the subject, the need to make and unmake identities. A professional terrorist is characterized as "very quick," always "slip[ping] away." Part of his job is "to make up a character as he goes along." Character or identity-making is a commercial exchange, a consumer activity: "He buys a new identity, is that it?" "He knows someone who can get him whatever he has to have." And it comes with practice. Standing in "front of a mirror," he learns how to make himself look different.

The most potent mirror our culture provides is the movie screen, from which we learn to transform ourselves, to play a variety of roles at will. The consciousness of Lyle, the central male character of *Players*, is capable of turning into a split screen in which he sees himself simultaneously "as a former astronaut who walked on the surface of the moon" and "as a woman interviewing the astronaut in a TV studio." The "astronaut persona" is particularly telling, because it involves "weightlessness as a poetic form of anxiety and isolation," the screen itself being the very medium of weightlessness. This weightless, kinetic medium in turn reveals the monetary essence of our culture:

> He'd seen the encoding rooms, the microfilming of checks, money moving, shrinking as it moved, beginning to elude visualization, to pass from a paper existence to electronic sequences. . . . Lyle thought of his own money not as a medium of exchange but as something to be consigned to data storage, traceable only through magnetic flashes.

Lyle's experience of money as magnetic flashes has an uncanny resemblance to his watching television. His main pleasure is "the tactile-visual delight of switching channels, . . . transforming even random moments of content into pleasing territorial abstractions." Throughout the novel, the switching of scenes, the play of dialogue between characters or within a single consciousness (the back and forth switching of voices) takes precedence over the plot, however dramatic its potential. Like DeLillo's other books, *Players* is full of melodramatic promise, a terrorist plot to blow up the stock exchange, adulterous affairs, a particularly gruesome suicide by fire, but the promise of plot is not meant to be kept; it is subordinated to "territorial abstraction."

It is precisely the power and the desire of the cinematic medium to present *spectacular* instances of experiences, to uncover the extreme and make us feel that it represents the totality of our lives. And, indeed, to the extent that we live in the cinematic world (some households have television sets in every room) our lives become the lives of cinematic representation, as in this instance of what I would call the cinematic real from *Players*:

> She couldn't fall asleep. The long ride was still unraveling in her body, tremors and streaks. She turned on the black-and-white

> TV, the one in the bedroom. An old movie was on, inept and boring, fifties vintage. There was a man, the hero, whose middle-class life was quietly coming apart. First there was his brother, the black sheep, seriously in debt, pursued by grade-B racketeers. Phone calls, meetings, stilted dialogue. Then there was his wife, hospitalized, apparently dying of some disease nobody wanted to talk about. In a series of tediously detailed scenes, she was variously brave, angry, thoughtful and shrill. Pammy couldn't stop watching. The cheapness was magnetic. She experienced a new obliteration of self-awareness. Through blaring commercials for swimming pool manufacturers and computer trainee institutes, she remained in the chair alongside the bed. As the movie grew increasingly maudlin, she became more upset. The bus window had become a TV screen filled with serial grief. The hero's oldest boy began to pass through states of what the doctor called reduced sensibility. He would sit on the floor in a stupor, either unable to speak or refusing to, his limbs immobile. Phone calls from the hero's brother increased. He needed money fast, or else. Another hospital scene. The wife recited from a love letter the hero had written her when they were young.
>
> Pammy was awash with emotion. She tried to fight it off, knowing it was tainted by the artificiality of the movie, its plain awfulness. She felt it surge through her, this billowing woe. Her face acquired a sheen. She ran her right hand over the side of her head, fingers spread wide. Then it came, onrushing, a choppy sobbing release. She sat there, hands curled at her temples, for fifteen minutes, crying, as the wife died, the boy recovered, the brother vowed to regain his self-respect, the hero in his pleated trousers watched his youngest child ride a pony.

The real and the cinematic have become indistinguishable.

But not all lives are exclusively defined by the cinematic. Violence, emptiness, death, the terminal existential experiences are not omnipresent, though what is pervasive is the anxious sense that the end, the violent end, is always potential, about to be realized. And this sense of potentiality is exacerbated, if not created, by cinematic representation.

The deliberate insubstantiality of DeLillo's characters is compensated for by an extraordinary and eloquent plentitude of speech. Characters become meditative voices, capable of extended vatic aphorisms about the world. The meditations serve as a revelation of and a sort of defense against a killer boredom to which our consuming society vainly tries to provide an antidote. The meditation, like this one from DeLillo's first novel, *Americana*, may tell the story of a desiring empty self:

> In this country there is a universal third person, the man we all want to be. Advertising has discovered this man. It uses him to express the possibilities open to the consumer. To consume in America is not to buy; it is to dream. Advertising is the suggestion that the dream of entering the third person singular might possibly be fulfilled.

Consuming is dreaming, the deferment of actual consumption and hence the perpetuation of the feeling of emptiness.

In *White Noise* the two main sites of experience and dialogue are the supermarket and the TV screen. Jack Gladney, the protagonist, constantly runs into his friend and colleague Murray Siskind at the supermarket, where they conduct their most serious conversations about the state of contemporary culture. "This was the fourth or fifth time I'd seen him in the supermarket, which was roughly the number of times I'd seen him on campus." The soul of American society reveals itself in the supermarket: Siskind affirms "the new austerity, . . . flavorless packaging," which reflects "some kind of spiritual consensus. It's like World War III. Everything is white. They'll take our bright colors away and use them in the war effort." The talk about food is endless and indiscriminate. Pretzels, beer, peanuts, pizzas, popcorn, chocolate, featureless (generic) food, are the objects of both rampant consumerism and serious (and therefore funny) discussion.

What the supermarket gives us is not real food but its representation. The food is chemically composed, canned, packaged, advertised: we consume it all. The supermarket (a trope for all sites of consumption) is filled with an abundance of items, but the main staple of that world is not the tangible item, the real thing, but what stimulates and sustains it in an endless deferment.

The cinema, like the supermarket, is where we escape from the humdrum of "reality." It is the locus of desire. A recent book on film has the quintessential title, *The Desire to Desire*. "The twentieth century is on film. It's the filmed century," a character in *The Names* tells us. In a commercial culture dominated by the media and the values of advertising, and in an intellectual culture that textualizes the world and casts doubt about the existence of the real or of our ever being capable of knowing and experiencing it, the cinema (even more than the written text) becomes the place where we "truly live."

Whether in the movie house or on TV, film stimulates desire, arouses our imaginations, but disables our capacity for real experience. It neither satisfies desire nor makes for catharsis. Its effect is anaesthetic. In *White Noise* Siskind speaks of a "car crash in the movies as a celebration, a moment of high spirits and innocence and fun" in which "the crushed bodies, the severed limbs" are irrelevant. In the same novel a "nameless Irishman is disturbed by the prospect that the riot or terrorist act which caused his death would not be covered by the media." Not because, as one might think, the media bestow celebrity, but because they anesthetize the pain of dying.

Our age, we have been told and shown endlessly, is an apocalyptic age. The apocalypse may be the dominant media trope of our time; its endless replay has inured us to the real suffering it might entail. We repeatedly witness the assassination of Kennedy, the mushroom cloud over Hiroshima, the disintegration of the Challenger space shuttle in the sky. Repetition wears away the pain. It also perfects the image or our experience of it. By isolating the event and repeating it, its content, its horror evaporates. What we have before us is its form and rhythm. The event becomes aesthetic and the effect upon us anaesthetic. The phenomenon is sometimes called kitsch.

Kitsch is a difficult word to define. It is a term of contempt for art of little value or an art that is meretricious, a misleading, ingratiating semblance of the real thing. What makes it appealing is its pleasantness, the ease with which the consumer can assimilate it, derive pleasure from it. There are many definitions or characterizations of kitsch, but it can best be grasped through instances. Saul Friedländer conceives it as the insipidly decorative: "a branch of mistletoe under the lamps in a railway waiting room, nickled plate glass in a public place, artificial flowers gone astray in Whitechapel, a lunch box decorated with Vosges fir." Ordinary kitsch covers over reality with the appearance of art: it appeals to the desire for the pleasant and the harmonious.

There is a special case of kitsch that Friedländer calls "the Kitsch of death" that is relevant to the cinematic experiences of DeLillo's characters. Friedländer characterizes it as a "juxtaposition of the kitsch aesthetic and of the themes of death that creates the surprise, that special frisson." By death, Friedländer means violent, catastrophic death. But kitsch and death, it would seem, are incompatible. How then does one achieve "the Kitsch of death"? Maybe by aestheticizing it through an apocalyptic lyricism: "the livid sky slashed by immense purple reflections, flames surging from cities, flocks and men fleeing toward the glowing horizon," and, one might add, all confined to the safety of the screen. If genuine art and kitsch are opposed, a certain kind of aestheticizing of experience is nonetheless a condition of kitsch.

In the contemporary perspective, it may be difficult, if not impossible, to sustain the distinction and opposition between genuine art and kitsch. Such an opposition depends upon a currently disreputable elitism that assumes a cultural hierarchy of high, middle, and low, in which avant-garde art is a privileged minority activity. On this older view, art is strenuous and difficult and not available to everyone, kitsch immediate and easily consumed. DeLillo writes at a time when the oppositions are no longer secure, when the categories themselves are uncertain, when it would seem almost pretentious for something called art to separate itself from kitsch. Art has become complicit with those very things it used to despise: the commodity world and the cinematic representation of it.

DeLillo presents the pervasive experience of kitsch without being complicit with it. Contrast Friedländer's characterization of the kitsch of death with DeLillo's seeing through it in this passage from *White Noise*:

> Ever since the airborne toxic event, the sunsets had become almost unbearably beautiful. Not that there was a measurable connection. If the special character of Nyoden Derivative (added to the everyday drift of effluents, pollutants, contaminants and delirants) had caused this aesthetic leap from already brilliant sunsets to broad towering riddled visionary skyscapes, tinged with dread, no one had been able to prove it.

Beyond the illusions of desire, DeLillo portrays the omnipresence of death.

> Supermarkets this large and clean and modern are a revelation to me. I spent my life in small steamy delicatessens with slanted display cabinets full of trays that hold soft wet lumpy matter in pale colors. High enough cabinets so you had to stand on tiptoes to give your order. Shouts, accents. In cities no one notices specific dying. Dying is a quality of the air. It's everywhere and nowhere.

Jack Gladney, the hero of *White Noise*, is obsessed with the fact of death. He looks at family photos and wonders "who will die first." The question becomes a refrain in the novel. On another occasion he identifies the self with death and asks, given this identification, "how [can the self] be stronger than death?" The cinema offers a solution, by turning people into nonparticipating spectators of destruction. In film, we watch the most spectacular and apocalyptic enactments of death without being personally affected by them. DeLillo's characters (like us) comfortably watch "floods, mud slides, emptying volcanoes," while eating "take out Chinese." "Every disaster made us wish for something bigger, grander, more sweeping." Here DeLillo beautifully exemplifies Friedländer's conception of the "Kitsch of death." ("Take out Chinese" is a splendid touch, the perfect example of kitsch food.) Death and destruction in their cinematic pretenses become objects of desire. DeLillo's characters are fully invested in this cinematic play with destruction and death, but nothing can allay the persistent fear of real dying. Gladney and his wife Babette are terrified by the prospect of dying, hoping to master the fear by consuming a miracle drug Dylar, that (need we be told) turns out to be a fraud.

DeLillo has an uncanny understanding of the enormous appeal of cinematic kitsch. In *White Noise*, Gladney speaks of one of his stepchildren, who is "growing up without television. . . . [as perhaps] worth talking to . . . intelligent and literate but deprived of the deeper codes and messages that mark his species as unique." But his friend Siskind disagrees. The problem is not TV, but the quality of attention: "I tell [my students] that they have to learn to look as children again. Root out content. Find the codes and messages. . . . TV offers incredible amounts of psychic data. It opens ancient memories of world birth, it welcomes us into the grid, the network of little buzzing dots that make up the picture pattern. There is light, there is sound. I ask my students what more do you want?" (This "debate" occurs in rudimentary form in *Players*, when Lyle's wife Pammy expresses her disgust with TV. "It's so sleazy. . . . I refuse to watch. I totally do not watch." Lyle demurs: "Sometimes you see something, you know, interesting in another sense. I don't know.")

Siskind is a latter-day Walter Benjamin, who against a high cult prejudice about the cinema acknowledged its "deepening of [our] apperception." In "The Work of Art in the Age of Mechanical Reproduction," Benjamin claims that film makes "incomparably more precise statements" about a situation than does painting, and he goes on to compare the "unconscious optics" of the camera with the unconscious impulses of psychoanalysis. Benjamin, one of the true seers of the modern age, understood the enormous creative as well as pernicious power of the cinematic image.

The Siskind/Benjamin view provokes a question about what we are to make of this flood of information and "precise statement." How do we resist the anaesthetizing effect of the film? The cinema does not empower us to confront our mortality; it offers us an escape from the real contemplation of death while enjoying its melodramatic facsimiles. Siskind's response is to reject the humanist view that "a person has to be told he is going to die before he can begin to live life to the fullest. . . . [O]nce your death is established, it becomes impossible to live a satisfactory life." Survival depends on the repression of death, a truism, if not a tautology, which would not have the shock of new truth if it weren't for the vestigial power of the humanist paradox about facing death. In *Players*, one character fiercely turns an attempt to console his suicidal lover into a joke, so overwhelming is the prospect of death:

> "The consolations of time."
> "That's right. That's it. The only thing."
> "The healing hand of time."
> "Are you making fun?"
> "My time is your time."

The anaesthetizing of our experience of death (what some would call kitsch) cannot simply be dismissed as unworthy. How else can we account for the fact that the cinematic occupies so large a part of our cultural life? It satisfies an appetite which we all share. There must be something in all of us that desires kitsch. A life utterly devoid of it may be too strenuous. Cinematic kitsch may even provide us with a necessary mode of relaxation in a life governed by anxieties and fears. The real danger perhaps lies in the tumorous tendency of kitsch to overtake everything, to consume all our experiences. DeLillo suspends judgment on the value of our cinematic culture, so that we can reflect upon it.

But the reflection need not be solemn. DeLillo presents an ironic play of voices in which irony doesn't so much deflate the object as conspire with it. Contemporary life becomes sheer giddiness:

> ". . . Floods, tornados, epidemics of strange new diseases. Is it a sign? Is it the truth? Are you ready?"
> "Do people really feel it in their bones?" I said.
> "Good news travels fast."

The "good news" becomes a "ground swell," "a sudden gathering," everybody gets "right down to it." Or consider the following celebration of the Toyota Celica:

> A long moment passed before I realized this was the name of an automobile. The truth only amazed me more. The utterance was beautiful and mysterious, gold-shot with looming wonder.

> It was like the name of an ancient power in the sky, tablet-carved in cuneiform. It made me feel that something hovered. But how could this be? A simple brand name, an ordinary car. How could these near-nonsense words, murmured in a child's restless sleep, make me sense a meaning, a presence? She was only repeating some TV voice. Toyota Corolla, Toyota Celica, Toyota Cressida. Supranational names, computer-generated, more or less universally pronounceable. Part of every child's brain noise, the substatic regions too deep to probe. Whatever its source, the utterance struck me with the impact of a moment of splendid transcendence.

Is this parody or pastiche? The inflated prose seems to move beyond the absurdity of parody to lyric celebration. Is it poetry or a prize-winning TV commercial? No celebration can escape the absurd. As when Babette affirms the human brain: "I have only a bare working knowledge of the human brain but it's enough to make me proud to be an American." Or when a colleague of Jack Gladney's answers the question, "Who was the greatest influence on your life?"

> "Richard Widmark in *Kiss of Death*. When Richard Widmark pushed that old lady in the wheelchair down that flight of stairs, it was like a personal breakthrough for me. It resolved a number of conflicts. I copied Richard Widmark's sadistic laugh and used it for ten years. It got me through some tough emotional periods. Richard Widmark as Tommy Udo in Henry Hathaway's *Kiss of Death*. Remember that creepy laugh? Hyena-faced. A ghoulish titter. It clarified a number of things in my life. Helped me become a person."

Cinematic reality helps this character "get through" ordinary reality, as if the two were indistinguishable.

DeLillo's fiction is populated with the cinematic heroes of our time: not only the movie star but also the football player, the astronaut, the spy, the president, the assassin. The astronaut and the president are the exemplary heroes of our culture, the assassin and perhaps the spy in a dissonant relation to it, but all these "heroes" share a sense of extremity. Football games, spy hunts, rock performances, assassinations are presented in a prose that is at once infected by cinematic excitement and yet superior to it in its intellectuality. The rich verbal texture of DeLillo's fiction, the meditative voices that govern it, create a critical tension, an implicit negation of cinematic excitement.

To be a hero or a villain in our society is to become a presence on the screen. Early in *White Noise*, Gladney discusses with his family a murder that had taken place in Iron City. The murderer, Gladney notes, regrets having committed "an ordinary murder." If he had another chance "he would do it as an assassination." He would have liked to "kill one famous person, get noticed, make it stick." Moreover, there is "no media in Iron City." The murderer rues the fact that he will "not go down in history." The discussion anticipates DeLillo's most recent novel, *Libra*, which treats Oswald's assassination of President Kennedy.

DeLillo has characterized Oswald's ambition as the determination to get "out of the room and out of the self" and merge with history. Ironically, in order to do so, Oswald would have to be thrust back into the smallest of rooms, a jail cell. His "liberation" into history would come only with his death and his transformation into an image on the screen. The world of the small room, of the private self, is the world of anonymity, of not being recognized by others. Celebrity of whatever kind, it would seem, is the ultimate condition of being recognized.

But DeLillo understands full well that the costs of celebrity are in some ways as terrible as those of anonymity. His celebrity heroes experience the awful burdens of the images they have become, alienated from the general culture that have made them stars. The rock star in *Great Jones Street* is on the run from celebrity. The football star of *End Zone* runs away from big-time football, but cannot escape, hard as he tries, the aura of stardom even in the podunk college (portentously named Logos College) to which he has transferred.

Celebrity is what the ordinary cinematic spectator is not, what he believes he wants to be, what in actuality he would dread being, preferring hero-worship to heroism. But the spectator does not simply worship, he resents, he enjoys the vulnerabilities of the hero, the scandals and outrages that the hero performs and suffers. The private person behind the celebrity image surely experiences and suffers the spectator's passions. This, I think, is the story that *Libra* tells. It is the story of a man who feels the deep resentment of the democratic spectator toward the heroes that society brings forward. Oswald is tantalized and provoked by the images of their amazing success, their recognizability. It is Oswald's living and dying (not the President's) that incarnates the suffering of our democratic ordinariness. Oswald's extraordinariness embodies our ordinariness.

The ordinary and familiar are present in DeLillo's fiction, but with a vengeance. The narrative lingers on a quotidian event that is usually thought to be without consequence, strictly "background" and becomes filled with menace. Once again from *Players*:

> When he got home he emptied the contents of his pockets onto the dresser. Wallet, keys, ballpoint pen, memo pad. Transit tokens on the right side of the dresser. Pennies and other change on the left. He ate a sandwich and took a drink up to the roof. Four elderly people sat at one of the tables. Lyle went over to the parapet. Noise from the streets rose uncertainly tonight, muffled, an underwater density. Air conditioners, buses, taxicabs. Beyond that, something obscure: the nonconnotative tone that appeared to seep out of the streets themselves, that was present even when no traffic moved, the quietest sunups. It was some innate disturbance of low frequency in the grain of the physical city, a ghostly roar.

The ordinary, the commonplace never remain ordinary and commonplace in DeLillo's fiction. He is empowered by the medium, by the cinematic world that his imagination exposes but cannot undo. To say this is by no means to diminish his achievement or to ask him to be another kind of novelist. On the contrary, it is to assert that DeLillo is a major writer about our cultural predicament, that he has confronted it with a powerful imagination and with honesty.

DeLillo's cinematic imagination at once creates and reveals violence and death. It "says" in effect that I will express, bring to the surface the horror and terror that we repress in order to . . . ? It is not clear how this sentence should be completed. The prophets exposed horror in order to condemn it and to warn the world of its imminent destruction. But DeLillo's sense of extremity is beyond prophetic moralism; the alternative, or one alternative, it would seem, is a nihilistic complicity. In the interview for *Rolling Stone*, DeLillo proclaims an absolute neutrality toward his characters, which, given their situations, suggests a passive nihilism of the sort compellingly proffered by Murray Jay Siskind. Siskind perceives that the transformation of our culture by film is certainly one of the most important spiritual facts of the modern period. But is it an irreversible fact? The situation for art and the imagination is radically different from what it was in the past. The real disappears, or rather the real becomes the cinematic, which gives shape and texture to the imagination. The real does not escape or elude representation. This is not merely aesthetic myth: it is the "reality" constituted by our society of TV watchers who imagine the world, conceive their fantasies, shape their conduct by the coded messages and images of the medium.

Anthony DeCurtis

The Product: Bucky Wunderlick, Rock 'n Roll, and Don DeLillo's *Great Jones Street*

Perhaps the best-known passage in Don DeLillo's *Great Jones Street,* not one of his more highly regarded novels, occurs at the beginning of the book. As the novel kicks off, rock star Bucky Wunderlick is holed up in an apartment in a desolate industrial section of Manhattan—this is the early seventies; Manhattan had industrial sections then—having abandoned his band midtour in Houston. Bucky's reflections on his celebrity, which he is seeking to escape and examine, start the novel:

> Fame requires every kind of excess. I mean true fame, a devouring neon, not the somber renown of waning statesmen or chinless kings. I mean long journeys across gray space. I mean danger, the edge of every void, the circumstance of one man imparting an erotic terror to the dreams of the republic. Understand the man who must inhabit these extreme regions, monstrous and vulval, damp with memories of viola-

> tion. Even if half-mad he is absorbed into the public's total madness; even if fully rational, a bureaucrat in hell, a secret genius of survival, he is sure to be destroyed by the public's contempt for survivors. Fame, this special kind, feeds itself on outrage, on what the counselors of lesser men would consider bad publicity —hysteria in limousines, knife fights in the audience, bizarre litigation, treachery, pandemonium and drugs. Perhaps the only natural law attaching to true fame is that the famous man is compelled, eventually, to commit suicide.
>
> (Is it clear I was a hero of rock 'n' roll?)

When I read that passage to a friend of mine—a friend who is, like me, a rock fan and a reader—he said, "That's exactly what a writer would think a rock star thinks like." He wasn't being complimentary. My friend knows that rock stars' thoughts more often read like a Don DeLillo parody of an interview—of which *Great Jones Street* contains several funny examples—than like the sort of sociocultural analysis at the heart of the passage I just quoted. Even Bob Dylan, who has made albums that move me as much as any works of art I know and who is one of the figures on whom DeLillo's portrayal of Wunderlick seems to be based, typically doesn't seem to have very much to say about his own work. In fact, in interviews, he often doesn't even seem to understand his own work, or at least he affects not being able to understand it, let alone the context that helped produce it. For example, here is an exchange between Dylan and former *Rolling Stone* writer Kurt Loder that appeared in *Rolling Stone* in 1986. They are discussing Dylan's sixties albums, virtually every one of which is riveting and virtually every one of which seems to scream self-conscious intent:

> Did you feel that you had tapped into the Zeitgeist in some special sort of way?
>
> With the songs that I came up with?
>
> Yeah.
>
> As I look back on it now, I am surprised that I came up with so many of them. At the time it seemed like a natural thing to

> do. Now I can look back and see that I must have written those songs "in the spirit," you know? Like "Desolation Row"—I was just thinkin' about that the other night. There's no logical way that you can arrive at lyrics like that. I don't know how it was done.

Not even "I don't know how I did it," but "I don't know how it was done." Dylan goes on to describe how he feels his songs of that time came "through" him, which is about as characteristic a declaration from a rock songwriter as you will find. This mystical notion of creativity is one of the stances artists adopt to keep their own creative processes concealed from themselves, protected from a self-consciousness that they fear might prove paralyzing. It is also a way to maintain distance from audience expectations—one of the central, ongoing preoccupations of Dylan's career. Since artists have no control over what comes "through" them, the reasoning would seem to run, they can hardly be held accountable for deviating from the styles they previously worked in.

Wunderlick's relationship to his audience, and to the entire culture that is playing him, is central to *Great Jones Street*. In the interview included in this book, DeLillo says about Wunderlick: "The interesting thing about that particular character is that he seems to be at a crossroad between murder and suicide. For me, that defines the period between 1965 and 1975, say, and I thought it was best exemplified in a rock-music star." My friend's comment aside, Wunderlick, like so many of DeLillo's characters, is not meant to seem like a realistic, three-dimensional person; he is a notion around which DeLillo collects his ideas about how the culture was functioning at the time in which his novel is set. Wunderlick's actions, thoughts, and speech reflect those ideas, rather than anything that might conventionally be considered his own "motivations."

The interplay between murder and suicide that DeLillo mentions would seem to suggest the movement of American society from the political upheavals and turmoil of the late sixties to the dreadful cynicism, deep alienation, and desperate privatism of the seventies. Wunderlick's writing traces a similar pattern of drawing inward. His first album, a "special media kit" included in the novel informs us, is called *Amerikan War Sutra*—it's from 1968, natch, and his second, from 1970, is *Diamond Stylus*, an evident movement from political protest to a kind of aestheticism. By the time of his third album, *Pee-Pee-Maw-Maw*, in 1971—a "landmark work" in the estimation of one of the novel's characters—Wunderlick is trying to defeat language itself with a kind of minimalist gibberish.

Wunderlick's desire to strip away the rational meanings of language is related to his urge for self-attenuation—a response to the failure of the sixties' promise of ever-expanding utopian possibilities, and the suicidal pole of the dichotomy DeLillo mentioned in discussing *Great Jones Street*. He speaks of himself as potentially becoming "the epoch's barren hero, a man who knew the surest way to minimize." Near the end of the book, his desire to elude the tyranny of language and achieve a pure, perfectly unimpeded relationship with his audience reaches the point of a desire to be disembodied: "I'm tired of my body. I want to be a dream, their dream. I want to flow right through them." He speaks of wanting to become "the least of what I was." In virtually the only comprehensible lyrics on *Pee-Pee-Maw-Maw*'s title track—DeLillo provides the full lyrics—Wunderlick states, in an eerie combination of Yeats and the depressed, pragmatic wisdom of the seventies, "The beast is loose / Least is best."

What Wunderlick learns in his withdrawal is that it is finally impossible to withdraw. Great Jones Street is no different from Main Street or Wall Street; it offers no haven, no safe retreat. When he jumped off what he calls his "final tour"—though near the end of the novel he, like all good rockers with savvy managers, is contemplating going on the road again—Wunderlick had become convinced that suicide was the only meaningful performance still available to him. The basic rock-star paranoid fantasy—that the fans' wild love would somehow transform itself into murderous rage (a fantasy that proved all too real in the case of John Lennon and that is captured brilliantly on David Bowie's album, *The Rise and Fall of Ziggy Stardust*)—is turned around in Wunderlick's case.

On the "final tour," the mayhem Wunderlick's group could routinely inspire tapered off; the fans themselves withdrew, creating a vacuum that they expected Wunderlick to fill, or to internalize. "There was less sense of simple visceral abandon at our concerts during these last weeks," Wunderlick says, stricken with wonder. "Few cases of arson and vandalism. Fewer still of rape." He attributes this lessening of violence to his audience's realization that "my death, to be authentic, must be self-willed—a successful piece of instruction only if it occurred by my own hand, preferably in a foreign city"—that last detail, evidently, an allusion to the mysterious death of Jim Morrison in Paris. "It's possible the culture had reached its limit," Wunderlick speculates, "a point of severe tension."

This lessening of the fans' violence triggers a dual response in Wunderlick. The first is his suicidal, self-attenuating retreat to his room; he is one of the earliest of the "men in small rooms" that populate DeLillo's novels. The other response turns the violence toward the audience: "What I'd like to do really is I'd like to injure people with my sound," he says at a hilarious symposium at a prominent think tank, at which he is the featured guest. "Maybe actually kill some of them." Later on he says, "It's murder I've been burning to commit. I'm way beyond suicide."

But once Wunderlick retreats to the room on Great Jones Street, having reached his own limit within the context of the general cultural dissolution, it quickly becomes clear that the forces that really control events—quite independent of the whims of pop stars—have not relaxed their grip simply because he has decided to drop out. What happens is that the void he creates by his withdrawal makes the functioning of those forces more apparent—and more frightening—to him.

The first evidence of this is that Globke, Wunderlick's manager, turns up at the apartment even though Wunderlick has informed no one of his whereabouts. The very permeability of Wunderlick's room—the ultimate room of his own, an image of the sacrosanct internal world of the artist—is testimony to the failure of alternatives and escapes in this novel. On his visit, Globke informs Wunderlick that his management firm, Transparanoia, will stand by Wunderlick through this weird period—"What the hell, an artist's an artist," Globke reasons with the wisdom of a businessman who knows his product and which side his check is signed on. He also reveals that Transparanoia owns the building Wunderlick is living in. So much for escape; real estate never sleeps. Globke clearly does not share Wunderlick's desire to minimize: "It's a business thing. . . . Diversification, expansion, maximizing the growth potential. Someday you'll understand these things. You'll open your mind to these things." Transparanoia, it should be noted, is run exclusively on Wunderlick's earnings and investments. For Wunderlick's own purposes, of course, his money is "spent" or "tied up."

As in Pynchon's novels, the various undergrounds in *Great Jones Street* begin to intersect—and begin more and more to resemble flaky, sinister spin-offs on the dominant culture, rather than rebellious or subversive alternatives to it. Globke proves to be only the first of an endless series of visitors to what was supposed to be Wunderlick's secret hideaway. In the most important of those visits, Bucky, the messianic rock star turned urban hermit, is visited by a member of the Happy Valley Farm Commune—"a new earth-family on the Lower East Side that has the whole top floor of one tenement"—the book's major image of counterculture idealism gone beserk.

The Commune, whose members fled the rural life to try to find themselves in the city, holds Wunderlick in esteem for "[r]eturning the idea of privacy to American life," and asks him to stash a drug —alternately referred to as the "package" or the "product"—in his apartment. The product, as it happens, is "the ultimate drug," a drug that destroys the ability of people to speak. It was originally designed by the federal government to silence dissenters. "You'll be perfectly healthy," one character explains to Wunderlick, who eventually takes the drug. "You won't be able to make words, that's all. They just won't come into your mind the way they normally do and the way we all take for granted they will. Sounds yes. Sounds galore. But no words." In the desperate environment of a culture that has reached the breaking point, all extreme experience is desirable: "Everybody's anxious to get off on this stuff. If U.S. Guv is involved, the stuff is bound to be a real mind-crusher. . . . People are agog. It's the dawning of the age of God knows what."

More to the point: however many people want to get off on it, at least as many want to get their hands on it and sell it—or is that a false distinction? A culture under siege creates its own vital markets. The drug product becomes like the pornographic movie allegedly filmed in Hitler's bunker in *Running Dog*: an imagined commodity that, independent of its value or even its status as an object of desire, serves as a lightning rod for the greed and acquisitiveness pervading the cultural atmosphere. When the drug package becomes confused with another package containing Wunderlick's "mountain tapes"—a cache of songs Wunderlick had recorded in his remote mountain home a little over a year before his "final" tour (and based on the "basement tapes" Dylan made in Woodstock after his motorcycle accident in 1966)—the thematic center of the novel becomes clearly defined. The drug and Wunderlick's music, no matter how authentically conceived or individually created, are both products, and the buying and selling of products is what makes the world of *Great Jones Street* turn.

Eventually, every character in *Great Jones Street* is pursuing either the package containing the so-called "ultimate drug" or the one containing Wunderlick's mountain tapes. And every relationship that Wunderlick thought he had is finally seen to revolve around the possibility of business deals (legitimate or illegal, underground or mainstream, related to drugs or music: distinctions among these pairings are purely conceptual, finally) and profits. Each person is simultaneously on the make for himself and representing shadowy others. Azarian, a member of Wunderlick's band, appears one day and, after quizzing Bucky about his intentions for the group, gets around to his real point: "Happy Valley Farm Commune is holding something I'm willing to lay out money for. I represent certain interests. These interests happen to know you're in touch with Happy Valley. So they're making the offer to you through me."

When Opel Hampson, Bucky's girlfriend and the person who normally lives in the apartment on Great Jones Street, returns from her travels in "timeless lands," it is, she says, because "I've got business." That business is, of course, the product. Like Azarian, she is representing "people." "I'm bargaining agent for Happy Valley," she explains. "I have bargaining powers. I wheel and deal." Azarian and Opel eventually die for their troubles.

Fenig, the funny, failed writer who lives above Wunderlick, is likewise on the make, continually seeking to figure out the literary market—this, despite the wonderful fact that his one-act plays "get produced without exception at a very hip agricultural college in

Arkansas." In the course of the novel, Fenig's wanderings through the world of genres take him through science fiction to pornographic children's literature ("Serious stuff. Filthy, obscene and brutal sex among little kids"). The object of his obsession is fame. His meditations on the subject are somewhat less penetrating than Wunderlick's: "Fame. . . . It won't happen. But if it does happen. But it won't happen. But if it does. But it won't." But if it does: "I'll handle it gracefully. I'll be judicious. I'll adjust to it with caution. I won't let it destroy me. Fame. The perfect word for the phenomenon it describes." The final genre that captivates Fenig is, needless to say, "[f]inancial writing. Books and articles for millionaires and potential millionaires." This money literature is his "fantastic terminal fiction."

The urge to entrepreneurship also infects Hanes, a messenger for Transparanoia and an emissary for the Happy Valley Farm Commune. He takes the drug package from Wunderlick and, drugged with the power of possessing such a precious object, attempts to double-cross the Commune and make a deal for the drug on his own. As does Dr. Pepper, the scientific genius of the underground whose name is a clever conflation of the counterculture utopianism of the Beatles' *Sgt. Pepper's Lonely Hearts Club Band* and the soft-drink commodity. Pepper first signs on to analyze the drug for the Commune and then attempts to obtain and market it himself. "Everybody in the free world wants to bid," is how Pepper describes the drug's desirability. Bohack, a representative of the Commune whose name derives from a supermarket chain, threatens Wunderlick when he cannot produce the drug. Meanwhile Globke steals the mountain tapes from his own client and plots to release them. Finally, the double-dealer Hanes, in order to save his own life, informs the Commune of the whereabouts of the mountain tapes, which the Commune then destroys. The members of the Commune are angry that Wunderlick, who, after all, had restored the notion of privacy to American life, was planning to violate his own privacy and tour again.

The character who has the most to say to Wunderlick about what his life has been—and what it has become, and what determines it—is Watney. Watney is a former pop star—he pulls up to Wunderlick's building in a limousine that includes "[t]hree rooms and a dining alcove. But at the same time fairly inconspicuous"—and stands as a kind of Alice Cooper figure, an image of the decline of rock into shock spectacle, as opposed to Wunderlick's Dylan/Jagger fusion. Watney's wild, androgynous band, Schicklgruber, epitomized the notion of rock 'n roll as a mad, pointless threat to the social order: "wherever they went the village elders consulted ordinances trying to find a technicality they might use to keep the band from performing or at the very least to get the band out of town the moment the last note sounded." When he visits Wunderlick, however, it turns out Watney is done with rock 'n roll and is—in a perfect transition—"into sales, procurement and operations now. I represent a fairly large Anglo-European group." Like everyone else, he visits the former band leader to bid on the drug product.

In the course of his discussion about the product with Wunderlick, Watney explains the reasons for his move into sales:

> "I had no real power in the music structure. It was all just show. This thing about my power over kids. Watney the transatlantic villain. Schicklgruber the assassin of free will. It was just something to write, to fill up the newspapers with. I had no power, Bucky. I just dollied about on stage with my patent leather pumps and my evil leer. It was a good act all right. But it was all just an act, just a runaround, just a show."

Later on in the novel, Watney explains to Wunderlick how real power works.

> "Bucky, you have no power. You have the illusion of power. I know this firsthand. I learned this in lesson after lesson and city after city. Nothing truly moves to your sound. Nothing is shaken or bent. You're a bloody artist you are. Less than four ounces on the meat scale. You're soft, not hard. You're above ground, not under. The true underground is the place where power flows. That's the best-kept secret of our time. You're not the underground. Your people aren't underground people. The presidents and prime ministers are the ones who make the underground deals and speak the true underground idiom. The corporations. The military. The banks. This is the underground network. This is where it happens."

By the end of the novel, Wunderlick takes the ultimate drug, which provides him with "weeks of deep peace," but proves "less than lasting in its effect." Like all consumer goods, it is ultimately disappointing. The failure of the drug to transport him to a place beyond language—its failure to achieve a kind of suicide for him—is part of what Wunderlick calls his "double defeat." The other part of that defeat is the frustration, with the destruction of the mountain tapes, of his murderous desire to get back on the road. As Wunderlick himself frames the dichotomy of his failure: "first a chance not taken to reappear in the midst of people and forces made to my design and then a second enterprise denied, alternate to the first, permanent withdrawal to that unimprinted level where all sound is silken and nothing erodes in the mad weather of language." As the rumors surrounding his disappearance continue to swirl, he is back in numb isolation on Great Jones Street, sounding almost like a character out of T. S. Eliot: "When the season is right I'll return to whatever is out there. It's just a question of what sound to make or fake."

"Your life consumes itself," Watney tells Wunderlick, and the revelation of Wunderlick himself, and all artists, as objects of consumption, commodities like the ultimate drug or the mountain tapes, is part of the point of *Great Jones Street*. Like the Happy Valley Farm Commune, which moves from utopian ruralism to vicious drug dealing, each of the book's characters, with the exception of Wunderlick, who is essentially paralyzed, abandons whatever alternative seemed to be available and willfully enters the market economy. In 1990 it may not seem like much of an exercise to explore how much the sixties counterculture and its utopian hopes did or did not threaten the dominant culture. In 1973, however, such an exercise was well worth undertaking, and may still have value today. What DeLillo depicts in *Great Jones Street* is a society in which there are no meaningful alternatives, in which everyone and everything is bound in the cash nexus and the exchange of commodities, outside of which there stands nothing. Everything is consumed, or it consumes itself: murder or suicide, exploitation or self-destruction. After a decade of rampant market economics and amidst regular announcements of the worldwide triumph of capitalism—smug, dumb declarations of how the West has won—can the world DeLillo portrays in *Great Jones Street* not seem painfully familiar?

In a recent interview in *Rolling Stone*, Axl Rose, lead singer of

Guns n' Roses, the fuck-you, rebellious band of the moment—and one of the most popular bands in the world—made questionable remarks about gays, blacks, women, and immigrants, and then offered these observations about his artistic life: "I was figuring it out, and I'm like the president of a company that's worth between $125 million and a quarter billion dollars. If you add up record sales based on the low figure and a certain price for T-shirts and royalties and publishing, you come up with at least $125 million, which I get less than two percent of." A little while later Rose advises youngsters aspiring to his lifestyle of rock 'n roll revolt: "What I'd tell any kid in high school is 'Take business classes.' I don't care what else you're gonna do, if you're gonna do art or anything, take business classes."

Is it clear he is a hero of rock 'n roll?

Charles Molesworth

Don DeLillo's Perfect Starry Night

Don DeLillo's novels begin, again and again, with a solitary man being propelled headlong in a sealed chamber. In *Libra* it is the young Lee Oswald standing at the front window of a subway car as it "smashed through the dark." In *Players* the opening scene takes place aboard an airplane. And as *Ratner's Star* begins, the main character, Billy Twillig, boards a "Sony 747" en route to a gathering of scientists at work on deciphering an extraterrestrial message. In other novels, such as *Great Jones Street*, the main character is often enclosed in a room, isolated from almost everyone and very definitely cut off from society at large. Yet no other contemporary novelist could be said to outstrip DeLillo in his ability to depict that larger social environment we blandly call everyday life. Brand names, current events, fads, the society of the spectacle, and the rampant consumerism that has become our most noticeable, if not our most important, contribution to history, are all plentifully and accurately recorded throughout DeLillo's work. But his chambered isolato is more than a vestigial homage to the alienated artist figure, cut off by his own sensitivity from the blooming, buzzing confusion around him.

DeLillo has said in an interview in *Rolling Stone* that his novels "have a strong sense of place," and this is true to a large extent. What Kenneth Burke would call the agent/scene ratio, that entangled counterpoint of self and space that the realistic novel has traded on brilliantly, obtains in DeLillo's work whether the locales are ordinary to the point of squalor as in *Great Jones Street* or *Running Dog*, or clearly fantastic, as in *Ratner's Star*. Sometimes DeLillo indulges in a heightened description of landscape to convey a sharp sense of loss intermixed with fear—the Bronx scenes from Billy Twillig's childhood, for example—and sometimes to stress a thematic point, as in the final pages of the same novel, where the poverty of India and Bangladesh shatters the "placeless" virtues of the science project that has been the novel's focus for the preceding four hundred pages.

Many of his characters find their destinies shaped by or expressed not only in place—a room, a hole—but in movement. One way to read a typical DeLillo agent/scene ratio is to see the encased movement of young Oswald riding the subway in *Libra* as that of a bullet that will eventually smash through the dark of America's nightmare, or into the dark of the President's brain: unselfpropelled movement from one destination to another figures Oswald's destiny. So too with Billy Twillig, whose airplane flight in the opening sequence contains a great deal of information about the role Billy will play, for he meets (or is accosted by) Eberhard Fearing, who proceeds by turns to recognize, misappreciate, and presume to exploit Billy and his mathematical genius. The plane ride is a small version, in other words, of Billy's way of moving into the world and the history in which it is thoroughly enmeshed. The capsule is an agency of transferal that becomes an instrument of exposure, even entrapment.

In his *Rolling Stone* interview DeLillo confesses his fascination with men who live in small rooms. They function in his fiction as representative men, creatures from an atomized society that espouses a belief in individualism but as often as not produces only anomie and alienation; and they serve as the central consciousness of their books, surrogates for the author, artist figures whose drama frequently centers on their difficulties with language, their fascination with, and bafflement by, the power of naming. Seen in this double context, the rooms they inhabit are both torture chambers and contemplative retreats; they can be understood as providing an "outsider's" viewpoint for their inhabitants, allowing them to give shape and coherence to society and history, or as theaters of futility whose "inside" is always penetrated by history's distorted and overwhelming simulacra.

As for *Ratner's Star*, its structure and themes are built around the human values represented in science, especially mathematics, the field in which Billy Twillig has achieved fame and a large measure of fulfillment. The novel's plot builds to the decipherment of an extraterrestrial message, which turns out to be the encoding of an eclipse. The message, however, is not exactly extraterrestrial, since it originated from Earth, though from a now lost civilization that flourished long ago. In its larger thematics the novel suggests that science is futile, an exercise that is largely a displacement of human neurosis, and practiced by people who are otherwise gullible and thoroughly impractical. The view of science embodied in the book links it to a tradition that would include the third book of *Gulliver's Travels*, with its "projectors," and *Bouvard et Pécuchet*, with its endless round of empirical quests that only spin out onto more and more elusive phantasms.

But it is truly a more subtle and complicated novel than this brute summary would suggest. The reflections of Billy Twillig about the nature of mathematics, and the corollary philosophical issues it involves, such as the question of the unity of existence, take the reader beyond the level of science fiction satire. Billy is early on described as "more apt to be aware of pattern than brute numeration." Clearly the spirit and shadow of Pythagoras haunt the novel. But Billy also suggests at the beginning of the book that mathematics is less a case of the mysterious than the difficult. His is a temperament drawn to demystification, and his efforts are sincere and largely successful, even though they are co-opted by the project in which he is involved. DeLillo's satiric impulses are most fully displayed as the plot turns on the leaders of the project who eventually decide that the content of the message is unimportant; they have shifted their efforts to designing a language whereby they can communicate with any extraterrestrial beings, and are in fact struggling to create a metalanguage that will enable them to describe and control what they are trying to design. The third book of *Gulliver's Travels* is most distinctly echoed here, as the various scientists pursue partial projects that seem especially irrational and disconnected to any larger human purpose. This dimension of the novel enables DeLillo to speculate on serious matters even as he depicts various character types and social behaviors representative of modern capitalist societies where individualism has run amuck: the characters are all like men in isolated chambers; their attempts at interaction are frequently more than a bit surreal; their conversations frequently contain irruptions of personal or seemingly irrelevant desires or observations. Their oddball self-absorption presumably makes them easy targets for the group that wants to co-opt their scientific enterprise and control the international flow of currency.

Ratner's Star appeared in 1976, and was followed in the next two years by *Players* and *Running Dog*, novels which continue to explore some of the themes in *Ratner's Star*, especially the sense that the who and why of controlling forces are both uncontainable and signs of malevolence. Here, for instance, is a passage from *Running Dog*:

> "When technology reaches a certain level, people begin to feel like criminals," he said. "Someone is after you, the computers maybe, the machine-police. You can't escape investigation. The facts about you and your whole existence have been collected or are being collected. . . . It's the presence alone, the very fact, the superabundance of technology, that makes us feel we're committing crimes. . . . The processing machines, the scanners, the sorters. That's enough to make us feel like criminals. What enormous weight. What complex programs. And there's no one to explain it to us."

The claim that the very fact of the superabundance of technology creates guilt is a version of the Marxist notion that existence determines consciousness. What DeLillo adds to this is the idea that there is a sort of rule by no one, as Hannah Arendt put it, in which the modern bureaucracy makes explanation and responsibility impossible to locate or assign.

Beyond these fairly commonplace notions lies DeLillo's continuing sense that an explanation *ought* to be forthcoming. What drives the plot of *Ratner's Star* is just this feeling that behind it all there is pattern, and that pattern must entail purpose. Mathematics, however, can be seen as the system-making activity that hypostatizes pattern while leaving the question of purpose outside the framework. The novel never directly mentions Gödel's theorem, but its force is felt throughout, as several characters raise the possibility that a metasystem is needed in order to insure the coherence of the mathematical solutions that will be developed and to control all possible communication with extraterrestrials. What this does in effect is replace the idea of a human agent who might "explain it to us" with a higher (but impersonal) order of systematic explanation.

But a higher order of explanation might involve us in a network of paranoia and control that would effectively dehumanize us rather than provide us with a fulfilling sense of human purpose. This is one of the notions broached in *Players*, where the specter of complexity without apparent systematic resolution or control becomes another sort of evil. One of the characters in the book offers the following set of postulates and consequences:

> "When governments become too interesting, the end is in sight. Their fall is contained not in their transgressions, obviously, but in the material that flows from these breaches, one minute sinister and vicious, the next nearly laughable. Governments mustn't be that interesting. It unsettles the body politic. I almost want to say they had too much imagination. . . ."

One implication of this is that the problem is overabundance. Too much information—the flow that results from the breach is like a flood tide—results is an inability to evaluate. There are also fairly distinct echoes of the Watergate era in this passage. The sinister and the laughable commingle and eventually become indistinguishable. Information overload, in this view, has become the politically destabilizing force that is most to be avoided.

DeLillo's response to this overload, at least in some places throughout his novels, is to suggest that the patterning of art is sufficiently systematic and yet not dehumanizing, and thus offers a model for understanding the modern world. He takes this position, in its broadest form, from the modernist canon. In an interview with Tom LeClair he singles out as those novels with the greatest impact on his own aesthetic the roll call of modernist masterpieces: *Ulysses, The Sound and the Fury, Under the Volcano*. These works, as he puts it, open onto "the word beyond speech," which only the artist can lead us to, only the artist can "unsay." This privileging of the role of the artist (and some would say the mystification of the role of art in the modern world) can be read as the allegorical center of *Ratner's Star*. The following extended passage, a series of reflections from the mind of Billy Twillig, would become the hermeneutical key to the central problem and the central resolution of the novel's vision:

> The only valid standard for his work, its critical point (zero or infinity) was the beauty it possessed, the deft strength of its mathematical reasoning. The work's ultimate value was simply what it revealed about the nature of his intellect. What was at stake, in effect, was his own principle of intelligence or individual consciousness; his identity, in short. This was the infalling trap, the source of art's private involvement with obsession and despair, neither more nor less than the artist's self-containment, a mental state that led to storms of overwork and extended stretches of depression, that brought on indifference to life and at times the need to regurgitate it, to seek the level of expelled matter. Of course, the sense at the end of a serious effort, if the end is reached successfully, is one of lyrical exhilaration. There is air to breathe and a place to stand. The work gradually reveals its attachment to the charged particles of other minds, men now historical, the rediscovered dead; to the main structure of mathematical thought; perhaps even to reality itself, the so-called sum of things. It is possible to stand in time's pinewood dust and admire one's own veronicas and pavanes.

The nexus of ideas here clearly owes a great deal to Kantian formalism, as well as the notion of the transcendent subject, all filtered through Romanticism's drama of artistic despair, and even opening at the end onto something like a nihilistic, scatological vision ("to seek the level of expelled matter"). History and society are recontained in this scheme, but only in a subordinate way, just as reality ("the so-called sum of things") is present only in a subjunctive mode ("perhaps"). The importance of this passage is also attested to by the fact that the novel ends with a similar image—"the reproductive dust of existence"—as the main character is digging his way into a hole. Pinewood dust is a trope for pollen: so at the center and the closure of the novel stands the paradox of a dust that is in fact seminal.

But what is it that gives the book its dramatic tension, what resistance stands against this artist figure as a defining ground? What scene gives the agent his ratio? The answer, I think, comes in two parts: the threat of the disorder brought about by the absence of all system, and the order of nature that can only be glimpsed through the slats and lattices of human structures. The first of these defining forces is introduced in the passage when an experiment is offered Twillig whereby an electrode implanted in his head will complement his mental powers with a distinctive faculty. The result will be a new mode of sensory awareness, something very like the schizophrenia that figures in the *Anti-Oedipus* of Deleuze and Guattari.

> "The problem with the device as now constituted is that it tends to overstimulate the left side of the brain. This will result in an overpowering sense of sequence. You'll be acutely aware of the arrangement of things. The order of the succession of events. The way one thing leads to another. This is a side effect of carrying the appliance under your scalp but it's not too great a price to pay for the kind of madness ratio we're getting, not to mention scientific value. True, you'll find yourself analyzing a continuous series of acts in terms of their discrete components. Eating a sandwich will no longer be the smooth operation you've always known it to be. You'll experience . . . a strong awareness of your hands, your mouth, your throat, your stomach, whatever's between the slices of bread, the bread itself. You might even find yourself in retrograde orbit, so to speak. Bread, bakery truck, bakery, flour, wheat and so on. There is so much involved.

> . . . You'll be involved in a very detailed treatment of reality. A parody of the left brain. But is this reality any less valid than ordinary reality? Not at all."

Again, what is threatening is a superfluity of data, which can also be read as a challenge to the contemporary novelist to resist the temptation to record everything that the modern industrial world offers in all its welter of events and objects. But the immediate context, of course, is that a "mad" scientist believes that he can master the confusion of modern life by tracking it with an obsessively empirical accuracy. Empirical science thrives on contingency in time and space, for only there can the organizing principle of causality reign supreme. In place of purpose and pattern the mind is made to focus only on sequence and metonymy; causality becomes the only intelligible principle.

The other force that the artist-mathematician must face in the world of *Ratner's Star* is what we might call the plenitude of nature. Occurring only in glimpses, this plenitude often takes the form of the sublime or the ecstatic. It is what pattern feeds on, what it needs in order not to be totally empty. It is what DeLillo can call "the so-called sum of things" at one place and the "detailed treatment of reality" at another, but it is also what his style can present as a lyrical pavane of loss and ephemera:

> Through the night there had been a competition in the topiary garden, people flying box kites adorned with paper lanterns. Prizes for design, color, maneuverability, speed of ascent, time in the air. Several kites had fluttered into soft flame, every such event accompanied by sounds of pleasurable regret from below. The burning frameworks remained briefly aloft, no longer parts of flying toys but in the lazy breezes of that perfect night resembling a class of mystical invertebrates determined to burn themselves away rather than return to the porous earth, where they'd earlier shed the silk of transfiguration.

This is the world of a Renaissance pastoral masque, where the fancy toys of a court society are marshaled so as to generate the theme of memento mori. Whatever interpretive burden we would place on this passage and others like it, we can't fail to see DeLillo's undoubtable talent, the sheer skill which goes beyond control and mimicry to a lyrical excess. His starry night is perfect, or rather the human folly of bestarring the night by sending up lanterns in highly flammable kites —and thereby insuring the sighs of pleasurable regret—looks, briefly, perfect. Such lyricism breaks out in all sorts of places in his fiction, especially in scenes involving sex, but also in passages such as that in *End Zone* where a sort of scatological nightmare vision occurs to the main character.

In the view of Tom LeClair, who is one of DeLillo's most comprehensive and intelligent critics, all of the novels are explorations of systems theory. In *In the Loop*, LeClair aligns DeLillo with writers such as Thomas Pynchon and William Gaddis, creators of the novel of excess, a genre in which a surplus of information becomes the chief threat of modern life and the perfectly expressive simulacrum for it. The welter of languages, the collage of scenic juxtapositions, the affectlessness of characters, and the constant use of lists are all stylistic markers of this genre. I am generally convinced by LeClair's readings of the individual novels, and his skillful use of systems theorists such as von Bertalanffy is a useful complement to the structuralist and poststructuralist theories that are often used in discussions of contemporary fiction. LeClair's scholarly approach enables DeLillo's work to gain an academic acceptance that has been largely missing, and yet it doesn't quite address the question of DeLillo's audience. It is not only the presence of *Libra* on the best-seller list that makes this question a pressing one. Clearly DeLillo is a writer who does not directly court academic respectability, nor, it should be said, does he shun it by aping the role of an enfant terrible, or to use Phillip Rahv's term, "redskin." His work plays with popular genres even as it remakes them; like his cloistered protagonists, DeLillo wants to maintain a distance from the mundane world even as he takes it up in a bold, even haughty gesture of inspection and transcendent judgment.

LeClair's reading of DeLillo provides us with a good explanation of the fiction's intellectual concerns. But it doesn't give us that strong a purchase on the phenomenological world of the novels, nor does it always look back "out" to the social and historical particulars upon which DeLillo draws. By using systems theory as his main hermeneutical tool, LeClair is virtually forced to systematize the novels in such a way that his sense of them loses specificity, as when he describes the central theme of *Ratner's Star*:

> [The novel is] an imitative model: a looping, reciprocal whole, open in its complex diversity, differentiation of structure, and plenitude, equifinal and homeostatic in its confessed limitations. As a model that accumulates by positive feedback (abstraction leading to more abstraction) and finds its negative feedback (the recognition of abstraction's danger) late, *Ratner's Star* is a diagnostic and cautionary system, its imbalance of extremes implying some better "contact line" or steady-state relations between theory and fact.

The movement from abstraction to a recognition of the danger therein, followed by an attempt to correct the balance, is, of course, a theme that runs through many modernist works. What we also need to ask in order to particularize our sense of DeLillo's novelistic project is, first, why he feels abstraction is a danger; second, why it is attractive; and finally, how can the hoped-for balance ever have a hope of prevailing?

To his credit, LeClair is aware of some of these issues, and he tries to supply an affective center to DeLillo's work, in part to answer the criticism that the novels are empty and cold. But his reading of *Ratner's Star* focuses on fear, especially the fearful childhood experiences of Billy Twillig in the Bronx. Fear becomes pervasive in LeClair's view, serving as the chief motive of all the characters in the book. Fear drives people to pursue abstract patterns as a way of controlling abstraction's otherwise disruptive force. Fear as source of the attraction, however, is also what gives abstraction its dangerous dimension, for it can easily lead to a denial of death and the interrelatedness of our creaturely states. This explanation threatens to make the novel simply a projection of the young boy's insecurities and his increasing lack of contact with his fantasy life. (For this part of his reading LeClair draws heavily on Ernest Becker's important book, *The Denial of Death*, and the systems theory recedes far into the background.)

One way to think about systems theory is to see it in the context of the nineteenth-century argument between organic and mechanical models of totality. In this way, systems theory can be categorized as the extension and complexification of mechanistic models. The introduction of the idea of feedback loops into systems theory is a way of making the model more organic and less dependent on the reductive and linear senses of mechanical causality. But the application of systems theory can be shadowed by mechanistic determinism. This is especially true, I would argue, when the subjects being analyzed, and the mind-set of the analysts, are such that any organic conceptions aren't really allowed full play. The prime example of this would be the model of the market mechanisms under multinational capitalism. No amount of feedback loops will alter what is essentially a mechanistic conception, for the notions of supply and demand, production and consumption, remain bipolar in a machine-like way.

A sharply different alternative to applications of systems theory which remain mechanistic in their basic formulations is the Gaia hypothesis. This hypothesis argues that Earth is a self-regulating organism, complete with feedback loops, that allows for the presence and development of higher life forms by controlling such biophysical forces as the circulation of gases, the rise and fall of planetary temperatures, and so forth. While both organic and mechanistic theories treat the historical destiny of the species as a whole, only the Gaia sort finesses the question of teleology. Unlike the various forms of market analysis that depend on systems theory, which must posit some *closure* that both drives the system purposively and yet remains outside it, the Gaia hypothesis and its metaphors leave open the question of final purpose. The logic of capitalist expansion demands that the entire globe becomes a market. With Gaia the logic of a singular final goal is replaced by a sense of a steady or climax state—equilibrium which can always "fall apart" only to reassemble its systematizing energies in other ways. We can hear faint echoes of this way of thinking in passages such as the one about the lanterns in the kites, where the metaphor of the "mystical invertebrates," with their energies of transfiguration, suggests an Earth-centered fecundity that gives a distinctive shape to events. These two systems theories—multinational capitalism and Gaia—correlate, respectively, to DeLillo's focus on superfluity and on nature's plenitude.

There is, however, yet another way to think about totality. It is also a legacy of Hegelian modes, but it has a specific political and ideological content to it. This is the notion that we are now living in a period of "post-history," in which all the developmental forces have been played out. But instead of focusing on the absolute extension of capitalist markets, complete with their forces of circulation and exploitation, some post-historical schemes have a different sort of shape to bestow on history, a different formulation of modern values to celebrate. In one of its most egregious forms, post-history says that America and Western Europe have produced a conquering ideology that has taken over the world because of its essential efficacy, that we are seeing "the universalization of Western liberal democracy as the final form of human government," as Francis Fukuyama put it in the Summer 1989 issue of *The National Interest*. He set out the terms of his argument in this way:

> The triumph of the West, of the Western *idea*, is evident first of all in the total exhaustion of viable systematic alternatives to Western liberalism. In the past decade, there have been unmistakable changes in the intellectual climate of the world's two largest communist countries, and the beginning of significant reform movements in both. But this phenomenon extends beyond high politics and it can be seen also in the ineluctable spread of consumerist Western culture in such diverse contexts as the peasants' markets and color television sets now omnipresent throughout China, . . . the Beethoven piped into Japanese department stores, and the rock music enjoyed alike in Prague, Rangoon, and Teheran.

What is appalling about such a vision is not only its arrogant ethnocentrism but its complete refusal to treat difference as a separate source of value or principle of identity. But where it impinges on DeLillo is the way it has of treating multiplicity and superfluity as having their origin in a single idea. To DeLillo's credit, his way of trying to wrestle the demon of superfluity never leads him to accept the oppressive systematizing that lies behind such an idea as "post-history." Indeed, the satirical focus of *Ratner's Star* could easily be read as the totalizing impulse that must recontain all difference in a system of identity, as the directors of the scientific project eventually lose all interest in the content of the extraterrestrial message and want only to create a system that will control all possible future messages.

But what shape does DeLillo offer for history, at least in *Ratner's Star*? We can place his novel in what Fredric Jameson calls the genre of "theological science fiction," a term first applied to the Childermass trilogy of Wyndham Lewis. The category is quite limited, but at least one other work that qualifies for inclusion is James Merrill's epic poem, *The Changing Light at Sandover*. Lewis and Merrill create their own distinctive narratives, but instead of using science fiction only for satire or mere adventurism, they both use their platforms to write a version of a theodicy, in which a Supreme Being is called forth to render a final judgment on human actions and values. *Ratner's Star* is a work of the same sort: it mingles religious visionaries, such as an Eastern mystic and an interpreter of the Kabbalah, among its scientists, and it treats history in the same way Merrill treats it, as a gigantic arc or curve of repetition. One of the scandalous aspects of Merrill's poem, and one not often glossed, is its telling the story of a previous human species that had been created and then destroyed by a Supreme Being. This early human race draws somewhat on the lore of the race of fallen angels, but in Merrill it is quite clearly human, a race of our brothers and sisters, as it were, who came to perdition without any historical trace.

As it turns out, DeLillo employs this same idea, for the extraterrestrial message has in fact been sent from Earth itself, by a race of humans who have disappeared as the result of some catastrophe. Their message is an encoded date, on which an otherwise unpredicted eclipse will occur. The novel ends with an ecphrastic description of this eclipse, specifically tracing the path of its shadow across the poverty of India and Bangladesh. Thus human history is like a self-closing parabolic curve, the boomerang shape that figures in several of the scientific theories invented by DeLillo in the novel. The curve, the returning boomerang, suggests that poverty is, paradoxically, less a privation than a separate source of plenitude, a kind of superfluity. When Twillig and the director of the project react to the eclipse by digging into a hole, they are in part searching for their lost origins, engaging in a negative evolution that is less an upward line than a closing curve: a scientist proclaims at one point that this "curious juxtaposition of the primitive and the extraterrestrial is hardly a recent development." The novel seems to suggest a gnostic truth—the way down is the way up—even as it reaffirms that reality, the "so-called sum of things," has an inescapably unpleasant residue. As long as there is poverty there is history, and vice versa.

So as Billy Twillig digs himself into the hole at the end of the novel, he becomes yet another figure of the man isolated in a chamber, plunging headlong into a vortex of forces that he hardly understands. At one level it is a kind of giant visual pun: Twillig the escapist is literally burying his head in the dirt. But at another level the "reproductive dust of existence" is the redemptive ground that will keep Twillig in touch with his own mortality and the creatureliness of his fellows. There is nevertheless an image of a perfect night at the end of the book, an image of darkness: like many another DeLillo novel, *Ratner's Star* ends in a recognition that the quest for significance is futile. Whether we can see the regenerative possibilities in the very energy of the quest depends on how we read this coda, where Billy Twillig, half-illuminated and half-obscured by "the shadow bands that precede total solar eclipse," seems perfectly poised between some mystical enlightenment and some final nightmare:

> . . . laughing as he was, alternately blank and shadow-banded, producing as he was this noise resembling laughter, expressing vocally what appeared to be a compelling emotion, crying out as he was, gasping into the stillness, emitting as he was this series of involuntary shrieks, particles bouncing in the air around him, the reproductive dust of existence.

Dennis A. Foster

Alphabetic Pleasures: *The Names*

In my telephone book I find a separate listing for "CIA," as if they understand that many people who may want to contact them know only the acronym. As if they know that for aspiring informers the words "Central Intelligence Agency" say less about that fantastically uncentered, nearly autonomous disseminator of misinformation, paranoia, and terror than this trigrammaton: CIA. James Axton, first person narrator of Don DeLillo's *The Names*, calls the CIA "America's myth," suggesting its power to comfort and coerce as it sustains our culture. Particularly in its acronymic form, the CIA serves as a god, the One supposed to know the why and wherefore when all seems chaos to mortals. Like another acronymic name of god, the tetragrammaton YHWH, the letters screen, for believers, the unspeakable name. (To the Yahwist the letters mean "I am who I am": the name of God and the claim to being lie hidden and preserved in the same acronym.) The inconceivable bureaucracies, corporate conglomerates, and technological systems of our modern pantheon become both familiar and mysterious in their acronymic garbs.

The Names opens with James Axton commenting on his never having visited the Acropolis, the most visible and austere sign of Western civilization's first great flowering. It still evokes the classic gods—beauty, dignity, order, proportion—even while it is overrun with tourists. This "ambiguity . . . in exalted things" touches the complex of desire, fear, and despair that runs through the book. Politics, economics, religion, and marriage have dimensions that seem transcendent even while they remain, like language, vulgarly physical. DeLillo's metaphor for this crossing of idea and flesh is the "cult" that Axton pursues throughout the book, a group devoted to a ritual of human sacrifice. What links the cult's members to the acronymic gods is their faith in an arbitrary, alphabetic system: the initials of their victims match those of the place names where the killings occur. The violence resulting directly from the cult's faith in its acronymic method is clearly insane, but it is only a step away from the violence flowing daily from the ABC's of contemporary business and government.

Most events in *The Names* take place around a group of foreigners in Athens: bankers, diplomats, businessmen, spies. James Axton, an insurance "risk analyst" and unwitting employee of the CIA, has given up working in the United States as a freelance ghostwriter to live in Athens near his son and estranged wife, an amateur archeologist. An air of witty desperation pervades these displaced people and their acquaintances, most of them just enough beyond youth to have seen failures of marriage, career, and purpose. David Keller, for example, having just married a second, much younger wife, pursues international banking as if it were commando warfare. Ann Maitland, married to a career diplomat, structures her peripatetic life through her love affairs in each of the cities she lives in. Owen Brademas, an archeologist, has abandoned anything like an academic life, narrowing his pursuits to finding and touching strange writings in stone. Having lost touch with conventional meanings in their lives, the characters multiply their motivations in order to arrive at rationales for understanding their lives.

Such diffusion of purpose should, one would think, lead to an attenuation of action. On the contrary, the characters fulfill their roles with an intensity that seems beyond the specific drives of the individual: Axton, for instance, succeeds as a spy in spite of himself. It is as if their actions address some unspoken, or even unspeakable need that their lives of work and language—whatever it is that makes them appear as distinct individuals—know nothing of. What DeLillo explores so remarkably in this book is the complicity between the physical texture of our daily, rationally pursued lives and the needs that persist from what I am calling a "prelinguistic" life. For it is when screens of reasonableness have evidently failed, as they have for James Axton, David Keller, and others, that we see how the work of culture is sustained by this physical texture, like the alphabetic density of words that persists when words cease to make sense. More like the cultists than they would like to believe, DeLillo's characters respond to something like alphabetic coincidences that have nothing to do with the apparent failure and nonsense of their lives.

"Abecedarians," the cultists call themselves, students of the alphabet, beginners. We were all abecedarians once, chanting our ABC's in a simple rhyme that imposes order on what is thoroughly arbitrary, tying our letters to one of our earliest songs. To sing the alphabet is to feel an order in our deepest verbal memories, and an ancient pleasure. "Something in our method finds a home in your unconscious mind. A recognition," one cultist says. He continues paradoxically: "We are working at a preverbal level, although we use words." Rather than preverbal, I would say prelinguistic, by which I want to get at a use of language that functions without symbolic representation. This unconscious "home," assuming it exists, is the brick and mortar, the absolutely familiar elements of life, but which can no longer be touched except through the structure of the house. Abecedarians reach toward that primal stuff of language.

Julia Kristeva has attempted to describe such a primal level of language. She sees it as part of the preverbal experiences of the child's body, the rhythms of feeding, being carried, and particularly of the mother's voice. These first mother-words would not be heard as symbols standing in for what is absent—"mommy" for the breast's comfort, "dad" for the dark stranger—but as physical presences, the real rather than cultural construct. These verbal presences, however, soon become incorporated into language, the flow of the mother's voice articulated into distinct terms whose meaning is no longer present in the sound, but in the reference. What Kristeva shows is that even after this incorporation into language has occurred, the prelinguistic presence, which she calls the *chora*, is not extinguished but is, rather, profoundly cloaked by those symbolic meanings, by consciousness. Still, the *chora* is there, powerfully evoking, perhaps even partly reproducing earlier experiences and satisfactions that are literally unthinkable. Unlike the Freudian unconscious that shunts aside what is inadmissible to conscious thought, here we have an unconscious that inhabits the body of language, a disturbing presence carrying memories of preverbal pleasures that consciousness cannot speak of. This unconscious resembles the "home," the "recognition" that the cultist claims to find in his method: "preverbal . . . although we use words."

When James Axton, disturbed by the seeming senselessness of a series of murders, discovers the pattern linking the victim's names to place names, he first experiences an intellectual pleasure, but the effect on him is ultimately more profound. Although his intellect cannot explain it, he begins to recognize the preverbal home the cultist spoke of. He sees himself in geography—"Jebel Amman/ James Axton"—and searches newspapers for "any act that tended to isolate a person in a particular place, just so the letters matched." These recognitions return him to a lost contact with the alphabetic presence of names. When the alphabet moves from song into phonetics, writing begins to oversee voice. The early articulations of speech on paper regularize and capture the voice's indeterminacies: "Here's your name, J-O-H-N, John": a hieroglyph joined to a singsong rhyme. There is something to this early writing that exceeds the word's meaning: the mother names, and the touch of the word in the eye and ear pleases even without making sense. Later the physical word can still evoke that first "home" of alphabet and voice but banishes it to the unconscious. After we learn to speak and write, we cannot get at that home except through the words that bar our return to it. What Axton seeks in his pursuit of the cult, in looking for these alphabetic coincidences, is a method to get back to the first time of language, to circumvent reasonable thought and encounter the aural and alphabetic density of words: Axestone.

As risk analyst, James Axton works in the business of loss. He travels and collects information, "[f]acts on the infrastructure. Probabilities, statistics." His job is made necessary by the expectation that somewhere someone will be "killing Americans." No one in the novel thinks too clearly about why people kill Americans, about the specific political or economic offenses Americans may have committed. Andreas, a Greek associated with the foreign group (he sleeps with Ann Maitland, and is perhaps a terrorist), explains at one of the dinner parties that the interests of Greece have been for years subordinated to American strategic and economic interests. But as distasteful to Greeks as this is, America is only the most recent of countries to "humiliate" Greece. Owen Brademas sees the problem as a more general issue: "America is the world's living myth. There's no sense of wrong when you kill an American or blame America for some local disaster. This is our function. . . ." Both explanations of America's function may be true, but no one is really interested in reasons. Axton's job is simply to analyze the terror that results.

The object of risk analysis is not to stop the terror, however, or to lessen the risk. Rather, for insurance companies the point is to find the "cost-effectiveness of terror": without risk, there is no need for insurance. In fact, the profit of insurance companies depends on their clients' fear being greater than the actual risk, just as banks insure their loans by setting interest rates higher than the risk that the loan will not be repaid: "a complex set of dependencies and fear." Terrorism, that is, is not the enemy of international, or specifically American, business, but a component of it, and a "risk analyst" is the silent partner of terrorism, without whom the meaning of terror would be incalculable.

Our society can live with violence—or rather could not survive without it—so long as it is rationalized, represented within a myth and a technology. For instance, the cybernetic model of global interests conceives of the world as a machine stabilized by balanced responses. Insurance companies and banks are part of the world-machine's governor, sensitively adjusting the forces of instability and restraint to maintain the machine's alignment and hierarchies. The model also leads many to assume that proper world governance and American interests require the constant monitoring and intervention of the CIA both to promote and undermine revolutions. Because the interests of these groups are so deeply complicit, the fact that Axton does not know that he works for the CIA is less a matter of his boss Rowser's deceiving him than of his ignoring the nearly total coincidence of the two "companies'" practices and rationales.

Axton doesn't see and is not meant to see that insurance companies, banks, and the CIA do little to diminish the violence and chaos that blow through the nations they take under their management, and indeed contribute to violence in an international arena —thereby increasing the risk. A simple conclusion would be that whether through malevolence or the sheer inertia of bureaucratic growth, they sustain themselves by making themselves necessary. I am not suggesting that the CIA *fails* because it produces more enemies, more violence than it quells. I would rather turn the question, as Michel Foucault does, and ask "what is served by the failure" of the institution. We have difficulty comprehending nonproductive pleasures and compulsions because productivity is built into the fabric of our culture. Concepts such as freedom, progress, even humanity depend at some level on productivity and its associated terms. Except when we call it art, we usually reject explicitly nonproductive activity. So rather than accept such explicitness, we mask nonproductive institutions under the guise of "failure": in a better world, the CIA would ensure peace and universities would produce good citizens. The very concept of "failure," that is, provides a screen against recognizing drives that would otherwise have to be seen as perverse. Better not to see them at all.

Foucault's turning of the question suggests that the failures of the CIA must have some function. And that function, it is almost too evident, is that the CIA allows us to participate in a spectacle of violence both terrible and thrilling. This is one mythic function, resembling another myth Kathryn Axton discovers. She finds that the ancient Minoans who inhabited the island she is excavating sacrificed humans to the gods of fire and earthquake. The rationale, of course, is that such sacrifices appease the gods, diminishing the destructiveness of natural forces. The immediate, and perhaps only real effect, however, is to reproduce a violent spectacle within the culture. In the closed circle of institutional complicity with some more primal need, violence is both the cause and the effect, the excuse and the failure. One of the cultists says, "Let's face it, the most interesting thing we do is kill." It is an admission our culture has trouble making.

Its being interesting doesn't mean that we kill for killing's sake. The circularity of the relation just described defeats attempts to find clear causes and effects. Just as spoken language reproduces, in spite of itself, a prelinguistic world that in turn motivates speech, the CIA produces much of the violence that justifies it. In both cases, something "interesting" occurs at the same time that it is screened from view by the self-evident (and less interesting) intentions—communication, peace—of the institutions that produce it. The cult has, perhaps too simply, decided to invert the relation, bringing the interesting to the fore.

One character comes to the romantic and quite mistaken conclusion that he can get directly at this nonlinguistic world. Volterra, a filmmaker (and Kathryn's former lover), wants to make a movie of the cult. He is a one-time *enfant terrible* of film who has dropped out of commercial filmmaking to get at something he thinks more elemental.

> "Look. You have a strong bare place. Four or five interesting and mysterious faces. A strange plot or scheme. A victim. A stalking. A murder. Pure and simple. I want to get back to that. It'll be an essay on film, on what film is, what it means. It'll be like nothing you know. Forget relationships. I want faces, land, weather."

What would be left out is "relationships," the reasons, the patterns of cause and effect, the plot. What would dominate would be other kinds of patterns that belong not to representation but to what he is calling "film": "If a thing can be filmed, film is implied in the thing itself. This is where we are. The twentieth century is *on film*," which means less that it has been recorded by the paranoid's dream of "spy satellites, microscopic scanners," etc., than that film has become part of the modern idea of reality. We experience the world as film, as ourselves in film, in the infinitely repeatable, observable images that film has disclosed. Volterra wants a film that would leave out the organizing structure of plots that occupy, console, and distract the mind from the filmic image. He wants something he imagines as pure: "He wants the frenzy of the [helicopter] rotor wash, the terrible urgency, but soundless, totally. They kill him."

Volterra's conception remains unfilmed, at least in part because its fantasy of a pure killing is "sentimental," as Axton and Del, Volterra's girlfriend, realize. Volterra dreams of something like a zero degree, a pure expression—"They remain true to themselves"—in which death retains its existential value of authenticity. He never discovers what Axton did of the alphabetic pattern: the letter always occurs in the name of a real place or person. Passion is not immediacy. Rather, it lies in a movement of the body, hand, and mind tracing a form, an alphabet of arbitrary patterns that appear only within the activity of living.

Owen Brademas also realizes this embeddedness of the alphabet, and commits himself to it. He leaves the archeological site in Greece and goes to Mewar, India, to see the poem cut in the marble embankment. He is less interested in the reasons for the poem's existence—to recount the history of Mewar—than in the letters shaped by the toil of hands:

> What was it about the letter-shapes that struck his soul with the force of a tribal mystery? The looped bands, scything curves, the sense of a sacred architecture? What did he almost understand? The mystery of alphabets, the contact with death and oneself, one's other self, all made stonebound with a mallet and chisel.

On the previous page, Owen watches a woman washing clothes, beating them against the stone steps. He recalls a fisherman,

> walloping an octopus on a rock to make the flesh tender. A stroke that denoted endless toil, the upthrust arm, the regulated violence of the blow. What else did it remind him of? Not something he'd seen. Something else, something he'd kept at the predawn edge.

The imagined hammer strokes with which the cult killed? The preacher of his youth who "strokes the air as he speaks, then cuts it with emphatic gestures"? The alphabet of gestures underlies the sentences of life. Ann Maitland similarly observes that

> [t]he women kept washing floors. It seemed to be what they did in difficult times. During the worst of the fighting they kept on washing floors. They washed floors long after the floors were clean. The uniform motions, the even streaks. Unvarying things, she saw, must have deeper value than we know.

The cult and Volterra's film both appear as self-conscious perversions in the world of *The Names*, illuminating, however, in their failures to evade the religious, political, and economic systems they are enmeshed in. For DeLillo, there is no getting outside of or beyond institutions; instead he would have us recognize the underlying unreason that runs through them. Axton's son, Tap (a too bright nine-year-old), has such a recognition at one point as he watches TV weather news in Greek. He laughs, seeing that "the idea of forecasts, the idea of talking before a camera about the weather" was "gibberish." All the gestures were familiar, but until this moment they had been screened by the spoken report. Weather is gibberish. Still, something in weather reports supports a TV channel devoted exclusively to weather—the dependably irrelevant statistics, the lines of ragged blue cool fronts and rising red mounds of warm, the weatherman's merriment. More seriously, Owen Brademas says: "Masses of people scare me. Religion. People driven by the same powerful emotion. All that reverence, awe and dread." Without the blinding light of faith, the movement of the masses appears as what it is, emotion evoked by patterns devoid of reason. Gibberish. Owen talks to James about the *hadj* and its culmination in Mecca circling the Ka'bah:

> ". . . the circuit of the Ka'bah . . . has haunted me ever since I first learned of it. The three running circuits, perhaps a hundred thousand people, a swirl of white-clad people running around the massive black cube, a whirlwind of human awe and submission. To be carried along, no gaps in the ranks, to move at a pace determined by the crowd itself, breathless, in and of them. This is what draws me to such things. Surrender. To burn away one's self in the sandstone hills. To become part of the changing wave of men, the white cities, the tents that cover the plain, the vortex in the courtyard of the Grand Mosque."

"I thought it was one big bus jam, the *hadj*."
"But do you see what draws me to the running?"
"To honor God, yes, I would run."
"There is no God," he whispered.
"Then you can't run, you mustn't run. There's no point, is there? It's stupid and destructive."

Axton clings to God, to the "point" of it all, rather than admit the attraction of the pointless running, than admit that his own kind of running has a similarly pointless appeal. The point of civilized life has seemed to be the achievement of a state of peace, satisfaction, calm. But ecstasy is not calm. Etymologically, Brademas reports, it is "a displacing, a coming out of stasis." Ecstasy is being unbalanced.

In *The Names* this ecstasy occurs in an area where speech and the prelinguistic verbal meet, in glossolalia. Owen Brademas explains that it isn't necessarily a religious experience, it is "neutral," happening to "Dallas executives," Catholics, "Christian dentists." It is the brain's speech-maker producing its stuff without any allegiance to a symbolic order, without reference, and yet it is accompanied by an ecstatic sense of immediate contact with reality, of "talking freely to God," as Brademas recalls the preacher saying. In Brademas's story of his childhood encounter with this purveyor of ecstasy, the preacher moves among people for whom "[h]ardship makes the world obscure" and invites them to innocence: "He tells them they will talk as from the womb, as from the sweet soul before birth, before blood and corruption." Hardship and corruption are not the lot of just the poor: TV lets us understand that the world is also obscure to wealthy Dallas executives, and the "wonder of the world" lost to them. The world that comes into focus through ecstasy, the preacher tells them, is not "scenery," but something lost within the languages we come to speak.

Language is a kind of risk insurance, offering a sort of currency in exchange for a child's lost home. As part of the reality principle, it defers and displaces desires to safer times and situations. The losses to which life is prone, as much psychic as physical, find indemnity in the narratives that continuously restructure our lives. They give us a world more dependable than the one that nature has provided, one that grants symbolic rewards on which we count for most of our pleasures. But this symbolic, still world has a "literal" dimension that glossolalia springs from, the physicality of language that flows out of and over the ecstatic: "Get wet, the preacher says. Let me hear that babbling brook." This nonlinguistic language is a source of intense pleasure for those who learn its "inverted, indivisible, *absent*" voice.

To some extent, this other dimension of language touches even those who don't speak in tongues. The names of places carry particularly powerful presences. When Axton travels, he tells his Greek concierge a place name, a name selected not by his actual destination, but by his ability to pronounce the name properly. He worries that he is "tampering" with "the human faith in naming, the lifelong system of images" in his concierge's mind. The Greek man does not know these places in their stone and weather, but still they have a firm existence, Axton suspects, a world that resides in these names without referents. "Could reality be phonetic, a matter of gutterals and dentals?" he asks himself. Charles Maitland, a career diplomat, says something similar when he complains about the changing of names on modern geopolitical maps. An old name, Persia, evokes images and dreams from his childhood: "A vast carpet of sand, a thousand turquoise mosques. A vastness, a cruel glory extending back centuries." Changing the names is, for him, a "rescinding of memory" that removes a vital connection to the world. The political reasons for the changes don't matter beside the sense of loss he feels in the disappearance of that old story, not because the story itself was profound, but because it was his own storied Orient. The old words babble to him.

Charles's wife, Ann, literalizes this connection of pleasure to place names. Following her husband from place to place, she sees herself disconnected from the immediate reality of the situations except in the adulterous affairs she has in each city. Geography, memory, and sex are held together on a base of "sheer sense pleasure," the most complex motive Ann will admit to. The specificity of countries—Kenya, Cyprus—vanishes for her, as it does for all the peripatetic characters in this book, except insofar as a line of pleasure has been cut in her mind. Like the cultists, she has replaced logical sense with the physical sense of an action that takes her out of her social role. Reference is replaced by pattern and juxtaposition—Jebel Amman/James Axton—understanding by evocation.

Disregard of the referential dimension of language provides the power for Axton's seduction of Janet Ruffing, the dissatisfied banker's wife who took up belly dancing. The inappropriateness of her pale, angular form to the dance draws Axton's attention to her body and the simple pleasure it gives her through the excuse of the dance. When she finishes, she joins the drunken table where talk has lost "sense and purpose." They enter a circle where conversation has become a "curious intimacy, a sympathetic exchange made of misunderstood remarks." Axton tells Janet he wants to "really talk": "Say belly. I want to watch your lips." He wants the words to take on a solidity, become a part of the voice and mouth, shed the ordinary sense that screens language, just as the formal movements of belly dancing screen the body they display. Axton attempts to evoke the secret of "adolescent sex," the delight and fear in words he used when bodies were forbidden. Now, as adults for whom bodies are no longer denied, he calls on a body of words: "Say legs. Seriously, I want you to. *Stockings*. Whisper it. The word is meant to be whispered. . . . Use *names*." Pleasure, Axton thinks, must still be secreted in words once they are stripped of "sense and purpose." Absurdly, it works, both for Janet and readers, their arousal covered by amusement. And the fact that the seduction ends dismally in sex against an alley wall only emphasizes that the most intense pleasures lay in the words after all.

The consummation of his evening with Janet Ruffing is abstract after the concreteness of their conversation. It is just such concreteness that has led Axton to follow his wife to Greece. When he and Kathryn talk, they talk not about the relationship between them, but about the details of their life together: "The subject of family makes conversation almost tactile. I think of hands, food, hoisted children. There's a close-up contact warmth in the names and images. Everydayness." Conversation here is like Kathryn's excavation that lets her handle artifacts she removes from the earth, the everyday objects of specific people. The relationship between James and Kathryn is made of such objects. When they argue, the particular issues referred to are insignificant compared to the specific form of the fight itself:

> The argument had resonance. It had levels, memories. It referred to other arguments, to cities, houses, rooms, those wasted lessons, our history in words. In a way, our special way, we were discussing matters close to the center of what it meant to be a couple, to share that risk and distance. The pain of separation, the fore-memory of death.

It is not merely another, repressed emotion that is being displaced into the fight—although there is clearly a sexual tension to the argument—but the shape of the fight itself that they recognize and pursue, an old path of pleasure.

It is this path of the letter rather than some abstract spirit that guides *The Names*. Owen Brademas speaks of public storytellers who are interrupted by their audiences when the tellers begin "to examine methodically" the stories they've been telling: "Show us their faces, tell us what they said." Later he sits with a cultist squatting in the Indian desert who tells him: "The word in India has enormous power. Not what people mean but what they say. Intended meaning is beside the point. The word itself is all that matters." When interpretation is irrelevant, what becomes important is repetition, a retracing of the word's path. The word "character," as Brademas tells Tap, means a pointed stick, a scratch on the surface, not an emanation from within. This distinction between character and internal individuality is played out when Axton is attacked by a gunman while running. He thinks at first that he has been mistaken for David Keller, the banker, but when he discovers that he himself has been working all along for the CIA, he thinks that he may in fact have been the target. The shooting could be called an error only if we think of the gunman's intention as directed toward an individual identity. But on another level there could have been no mistake because Axton and Keller have the same character, take on an "exact correspondence" that voids the question. Axton's face is not his own at that moment, but one shared with all Americans: bankers, businessmen, and spies.

In a complex pun, DeLillo points to the nonabstract nature of spirit. Tap talks to a friend, Anand, about religion, about people who wanted to learn to meditate. Anand says:

> "They wanted me to teach them how to breathe."
> "Did you know how to breathe?"
> "I didn't know how to breathe. I still don't know. What a joke. They wanted to control their alpha waves."

Anand is contemptuous of this desire, a seventies fad linked to eighties biofeedback technology. But James Axton hears in this "joke" a pattern of connections. Meditation, like alpha wave production, is a matter of breath. He thinks of old men sitting in the dust, "lips moving to the endless name of God. The alphabet." And this dust leads to our "bones . . . made of material that came swimming across the galaxy from exploded stars." "Alphabreath" is the implied pun that connects in a glossolaliac enchantment the holy man in the dust to the Dallas executives to the child saying the ABC's. The concreteness of verbal repetition undermines the ostensible concreteness of the ordinary world.

Owen Brademas's own torment stems from a particular childhood memory of loss which he has spent his life trying to restore. He tells Axton, who has sought him out in India, that when he sat in a grain bin with the cult waiting for their last victim, he recalled the story of the young priest who induced glossolalia in his childhood church.

> In his memory he was a character in a story, a colored light. The bin was perfect, containing that part of his existence, enclosing it whole. There was recompense in memories too. Recall the bewilderment and ache, the longing for a thing that's out of reach, and you can begin to repair your present condition. Owen believed that memory was the faculty of absolution. Men develop memories to ease their disquiet over things they did as men. The deep past is the only innocence and therefore necessary to retain. The boy in the sorghum fields, the boy learning names of animals and plants. He would recall exactingly. He would work the details of that particular day.

The "cure" for the adult's "present condition" is a linguistic repetition of the past. Owen suggests that in seeing himself at a fictional distance, he could regain an innocence, when desire was more clearly, if already impossibly, defined. It is as if all the perversions of desire that come from the crimes and compromises of adult life might be untangled, resimplified. The preacher is also promising innocence, "talk as from the womb," through glossolalia, not in memory but in that strange babbling ecstasy, "an escape from the condition of ideal balance . . . the self and its machinery obliterated." Brademas's conversational recounting of these events misses, however, the element of reenactment, where act and recollection become the same. The careful explorations and judgments ("This speech is beautiful in its way, inverted, indivisible, *absent*") remain the enactment of the balanced self. Although Axton says that the "telling had merged with the event," he refers to an effect the story had on him, not to Owen's experience of an "obliterated" self.

Brademas's story returns with something closer to that ecstatic quality in the form of Tap's novel based on Brademas's life. What is immediately striking in Tap's version is the alphabetic energy of his misspellings: "gang green." While those around Tap's hero, Orville Benton, reach a state of "glossylalya," "breathing words instead of air," he is unable to "yeeld" and is overwhelmed with despair and fear. Tap's language is on the border between the comforting beat of childhood voices and the world of adult rationality. The logic of plot and the running stream of story both ride upon a disconcerting murmur of obsession and repetition, distress and pleasure. At a moment when Orville Benton is struggling out of childhood, trying to find an order to replace the child's vanishing certainties, the preacher invites him to return to the babble of "childs play." In a panic, he runs from the church:

> Why couldn't he understand and speak? There was no answer that the living could give. Tongue tied! His fait was signed. He ran into the rainy distance, smaller and smaller. This was worse than a retched nightmare. It was the nightmare of real things, the fallen wonder of the world.

At that moment of exclusion from the Eden of Adamic speech (Brademas recalled "the boy in the sorghum fields, the boy learning the names of plants and animals"), language has ceased to tie Tap's hero to the world of "real things," and it stands for the first time bewilderingly distant. But Tap has already begun to compensate for that loss by preserving the archaic voice ("The worldwind") within a larger tale.

This structure of loss and preservation that runs throughout the book is at the heart of the most intense joys and the most profound and insidious confusions the characters experience. A cure, finally, is not the point, whether we speak of psychoanalysis, marriage, business, the CIA. As activities, however, they preserve simultaneously both the culture that has developed around them and the encrypted words that are our only access to a lost pleasure. The best work of culture can be seen as an exfoliation of this deep obsession—the making of the Acropolis; the love that "comes down to things that happen and what we say about them." But also, and indiscriminately, it produces the worst behavior. Brademas says of the cult:

> These killings mock us. They mock our need to structure and classify, to build a system against the terror in our souls. They make the system equal to the terror. The means to contend with death has become death.

He sees the cult as a demystifying parody of civilized systems. It replicates our institutions' motivations, revealing civilization's "systems against terror" to be systems, like the cult, for producing terror, and ecstasy, and death. The CIA, America's constant defense in a world condemned by Mutually Assured Destruction to peace between the superpowers, has no role except to produce the paranoia that makes life worth living: making secrets, not discovering them; unearthing enemies, terrorists, wars where they might otherwise go unnoticed and unfought. And because our institutions respond so obviously to our anxieties about the future—war, poverty, madness: real threats—we need never notice the more primary needs they answer.

Axton moves in his world as a mild-mannered skeptic, conditioned by his Canadian wife to doubt American values. But his doubt does no more than set him up, a dupe for the CIA, an institution he would prefer to condemn. He is conned in part because he resists knowing the extent to which he has already been shaped by the world he inhabits. He is, for example, a literal character, the Arabic letter *jim*, as if already written into words that are not his meaning; he is a tool, "Axestone"; a set of initials, Jebel Amman. His father, he notes, lives within him: a genetic sentence, a set of memories, a character "occupying" his mind. He is the words that speak of family, a list of "27 Depravities" (all conventional) that he provides for his wife to call him by. These, his ABC's, precede his claims to a rational, individuated self and are always ready to emerge in the obsessive persistence of a prelinguistic past. They are some of the "real things" that have become nightmares in the fallen world. Unlike, Tap, Axton and the others remain complicit with the languages of our institutions. But for Tap (and DeLillo) who engraves his alphabet in his own text, those nightmares are occasionally still "wonders."

John Frow

The Last Things Before the Last: Notes on *White Noise*

> The edges of the earth trembled in a darkish haze. Upon it lay the sun, going down like a ship in a burning sea. Another postmodern sunset, rich in romantic imagery. Why try to describe it? It's enough to say that everything in our field of vision seemed to exist in order to gather the light of this event.
> —Don DeLillo, *White Noise*

G*ötterdämmerung*. Why try to describe it? It's been written already, by Conrad, among others. Postmodern writing always comes after, the postmodern sunset is another sunset, an event within a series, never an originating moment but mass-produced as much by the cosmological system as by the system of writing. But the word postmodern here means more than this: this passage from *White Noise* refers back to an earlier one about the effects of an industrial (or postindustrial) disaster:

> Ever since the airborne toxic event, the sunsets had become almost unbearably beautiful. Not that there was a measurable connection. If the special character of Nyodene Derivative (added to the everyday drift of effluents, pollutants, contaminants and deliriants) had caused this aesthetic leap from already brilliant sunsets to broad towering ruddled visionary skyscapes, tinged with dread, no one had been able to prove it.

The conditional clause structure and the repeated negation convey a pessimistic sense of undecidability, but it seems clear that industrial poison is a crucial component of the postmodern aesthetic, "rich in romantic imagery"—and vice versa. We could as well say "another *poisonous* sunset," or speak of an "airborne *aesthetic* event." It is not that the postmodern marks the return of aestheticism, a non-ironic deployment of the full romantic cliché, but rather that it is the site of conjunction of the beautiful and the toxic, of Turner's *Fire at Sea* (1835), his "broad towering ruddled visionary skyscapes" and our postindustrial waste. This is thus, in Lyotard's sense, an aesthetic of the sublime: "With the sublime, the question of death enters the aesthetic question." It involves *terror* (the skyscapes are "tinged with dread") and ineffability, "the unpresentable in presentation itself." Why try to describe it? The twist here is that the sense of the inadequacy of representation comes not because of the transcendental or uncanny nature of the object but because of the multiplicity of prior representations. Priority of writing, priority of television, priority of the chain of metaphors in which the object is constructed. "We stood there watching a surge of florid light, like a heart pumping in a documentary on color TV."

Nor is there a lack of irony so much as a kind of self-effacement before the power of the stories which have gone before. The DeLillo passage I quoted at the beginning continues: "Not that this was one of the stronger sunsets. There had been more dynamic colors, a deeper sense of narrative sweep." Far from declining, the great nineteenth-century narratives continue to infuse the world with meaning, with a meaningfulness so total that the only possible response is ambivalence. The skies of this belated world are "under a spell, powerful and storied." They take on

> content, feeling, an exalted narrative life. The bands of color reach so high, seem at times to separate into their constituent parts. There are turreted skies, light storms, softly falling streamers. It is hard to know how we should feel about this. Some people are scared by the sunsets, some determined to be elated, but most of us don't know how to feel, are ready to go either way.

Malign and beautiful, interpretable not so much to infinity as within an endless loop between two contradictory poles, this labile postmodern object causes "awe, it is all awe, it transcends previous categories of awe, but we don't know whether we are watching in wonder or dread." Singular but recurrent, an event (a change, a deviation, a production of newness) within the serial reproduction of sameness, it announces (but how typically *modernist* a gesture) nothing but its own gesture of annunciation: "There was nothing to do but wait for the next sunset, when the sky would ring like bronze."

> In a town there are houses, plants in bay windows. People notice dying better. The dead have faces, automobiles. If you don't know a name, you know a street name, a dog's name. "He drove an orange Mazda." You know a couple of useless things about a person that become major facts of identification and cosmic placement when he dies suddenly, after a short illness, in his own bed, with a comforter and matching pillows, on a rainy Wednesday afternoon, feverish, a little congested in the sinuses and chest, thinking about his dry cleaning.

White Noise is obsessed with one of the classical aims of the realist novel: the construction of typicality. What this used to mean was a continuous process of extrapolation from the particular to the general, a process rooted in the existence of broad social taxonomies, general structures of human and historical destiny. Social typicality precedes the literary type—which is to say that the type is laid down in the social world; it is prior to and has a different kind of reality from secondary representations of it. First there is life, and then there is art. In *White Noise*, however, it's the other way round: social taxonomies are a function not of historical necessity but of style. Consider this description of the parents of Jack Gladney's students:

> The conscientious suntans. The well-made faces and wry looks. They feel a sense of renewal, of communal recognition. The women crisp and alert, in diet trim, knowing people's names. Their husbands content to measure out the time, distant but ungrudging, accomplished in parenthood, something about them suggesting massive insurance coverage.

This type is not a naive given, an embodied universality, but a self-conscious enactment; the middle-class parents *know* the ideality they are supposed to represent, and are deliberately living up to it. But this means that the type loses its purity, since it can always be imitated, feigned; or rather that there is no longer a difference in kind between the social category and the life-style which brings it into everyday being: the type ceaselessly imitates itself—through the ritual assembly of station wagons, for example, which "tells the parents they are a collection of the like-minded and the spiritually akin, a people, a nation."

It is thus no longer possible to distinguish meaningfully between a generality embedded in life and a generality embedded in representations of life. The communal recognition that constitutes the social class is part of a more diffuse system of recognitions conveyed through an infinitely detailed network of mediations. When Jack tries to characterize the convicted murderer his son Heinrich plays chess with, he draws on a range of mass-cultural information, like those psychological "profiles" that construct, above all for television, a taxonomy of criminal types: "Did he care for his weapons obsessively? Did he have an arsenal stacked in his shabby little room off a six-story concrete car park?" A computer operator "had a skinny neck and jug-handle ears to go with his starved skull—the innocent prewar look of a rural murderer." Those who would be affected by the airborne toxic event would be "people who live in mobile homes out in the scrubby parts of the county, where the fish hatcheries are." The type of the bigot, embodied in Murray Siskind's landlord, is "very good with all those little tools and fixtures that people in cities never know the names of," and tends to drive a panel truck "with an extension ladder on the roof and some kind of plastic charm dangling from the rearview mirror." The whole of this world is covered by a fine grid of typifications, so detailed and precise that it preempts and contains contingency.

If the type is susceptible to minute description, then the traditional novelistic tension between detail and generality falls away, and Lukács's account of typicality becomes unworkable. For Lukács, typicality is best embodied in the category of particularity (*Besonderheit*), which stands midway between philosophical generality (*Allgemeinheit*) and descriptive detail, or singularity (*Einzelheit*); in a postmodern economy of mediations, however, where representations of generality suffuse every pore of the world, the opposition between the general and the singular collapses as they merge into a single, undialectical unity. The *petit fait vrai* of the realist novel, the meaningless detail whose sole function is to establish a realism effect, is no longer meaningless. Reconstructing the scene of his wife's adultery, Jack mentions objects like "the fire-retardant carpet" and "the rental car keys on the dresser"; the definite article here marks these—as it does in much of Auden's poetry—not as concrete particulars but as generic indicators; they are not pieces of detail broken off from the contingent real but fragments of a mundane typicality.

The complexity and intricacy of the type—whether it is a character, a scene, or a landscape—is made possible by the constant repetition of its features: it is reproduced as a sort of amalgam of television and experience, the two now theoretically inseparable. At its simplest, this inseparability gives us something like the image of the grandparents who "share the Trimline phone, beamish old folks in hand-knit sweaters on fixed incomes." This is of course a joke about typicality, or rather about its construction in Hollywood movies and television advertising. A somewhat more complex play with typification is this:

> A woman in a yellow slicker held up traffic to let some children cross. I pictured her in a soup commercial taking off her oilskin hat as she entered the cheerful kitchen where her husband stood over a pot of smoky lobster bisque, a smallish man with six weeks to live.

This description depends on the reader's recognition of the particular soup commercial, or at least the genre of commercials, that is being parodied by role reversal, and by the substitution of the traffic warden's yellow raincoat for the traditional and stereotyped fisherman's yellow raincoat—a substitution of the urban and feminine for the premodern world of masculine work. But part of the effect of this passage, as of that quoted at the beginning of this section, lies in its stylistic trick of pinning down the type (welcoming spouse at hearth) to an absurdly particular detail. What most of these typifications have in common, however, is their source in a chain of prior representations. Jack's dying, for example, is projected through a characterology taken from the movies, as in Murray's line to him that people "will depend on you to be brave. What people look for in a dying friend is a stubborn kind of gravel-voiced nobility, a refusal to give in, with moments of indomitable humor." The cliché is a simulacrum, an ideal form that shapes and constrains both life and death.

Let us say that this new mode of typicality has two features: it is constructed in representations which are then lived as real; and it is so detailed that it is not opposed to the particular. The name usually given to it in the genre of postmodernity is the simulacrum. Here are some notes:

(1) Early in *White Noise* Jack and Murray visit the most photographed barn in America. They pass five signs advertising it before reaching the site, and when they arrive there find forty cars and a tour bus in the car park, and a number of people taking pictures. Murray delivers a commentary: "No one sees the barn," he says. "Once you've seen the signs about the barn, it becomes impossible to see the barn. . . . We're not here to capture an image, we're here to maintain one. Every photograph reinforces the aura. . . . We've agreed to be part of a collective perception. This literally colors our vision. A religious experience in a way, like all tourism. . . . They are taking pictures of taking pictures. . . . What was the barn like before it was photographed? . . . What did it look like, how was it different from other barns, how was it similar to other barns? We can't answer these questions because we've read the signs, seen the people

snapping the pictures. We can't get outside the aura. We're part of the aura. We're here, we're now." To this should be added another comment: "Murray says it's possible to be homesick for a place even when you are there."

(2) At the center of Walter Benjamin's argument about the mechanical reproduction of representations was the thesis that it would have the effect—the liberatory effect—of destroying the quasi-religious aura surrounding the work of art. It is clear that the opposite has happened: that the commodification of culture has worked to preserve the myth of origins and of authenticity.

(3) In the main street of DeLillo's Iron City is "a tall old Moorish movie theater, now remarkably a mosque"; it is flanked by "blank structures called the Terminal Building, the Packer Building, the Commerce Building. How close this was to a classic photography of regret."

(4) The evacuation of Jack and his family is conducted by an organization called SIMUVAC, which is "short for simulated evacuation. A new state program they're still battling for funds for." When Jack points out to one of its employees that this is not a simulated but a real evacuation, he replies: "We thought we could use it as a model"; it gives them "a chance to use the real event in order to rehearse the simulation."

(5) For Plato, the simulacrum is the copy of a copy. Violating an ethics of imitation, its untruth is defined by its distance from the original and by its exposure of the scandal that an imitation can in its turn function as a reality to be copied (and so on endlessly).

The most influential contemporary account of the simulacrum and the chain of simulations is that of Baudrillard. His is a melancholy vision of the emptying out of meaning (that is, of originals, of stable referents) from a world which is henceforth made up of closed and self-referring systems of semiotic exchange. In a state of what he calls hyperreality the real becomes indefinitely reproducible, an effect, merely, of the codes which continue to generate it. From the very beginning Baudrillard has been hostile to the scandalous opacity of systems of mediation. His is a historical vision: there was a referent; it has been lost; and this loss, as in Plato, is the equivalent of a moral fall.

By contrast, the account that Deleuze gives of the simulacrum in

Différence et répétition, while retaining the formal structure of the Platonic model, cuts it off from its ties to a lost original, and cuts it off, too, from all its Baudrillardian melancholy. The world we inhabit is one in which identity is simulated in the play of difference and repetition, but this simulation carries no sense of loss. Instead, freeing ourselves of the Platonic ontology means denying the priority of an original over the copy, of a model over the image. It means glorifying the reign of simulacra, and affirming that any original is itself already a copy, divided in its very origin. According to Deleuze, the simulacrum "is that system in which the different is related to the different through difference itself."

(6) The most horrifying fact about the evacuation is that it isn't even reported on network television. "Does this thing happen so often that nobody cares anymore?" asks one man. "Do they think this is just television?"

(7) The smoke from the chemical spill is initially called a "feathery plume," then a "black billowing cloud," and finally an "airborne toxic event." Steffie and Denise, Jack's daughters, keep experiencing the symptoms described in the bulletin preceding the current one. One of these symptoms is *déjà vu*, and Jack wonders, "Is it possible to have a false perception of an illusion? Is there a true *déjà vu* and a false *déjà vu*?" Later his wife Babette has a *déjà vu* experience of *déjà vu*.

(8) "The phone rang and I picked it up. A woman's voice delivered a high-performance hello. It said it was computer-generated, part of a marketing survey aimed at determining current levels of consumer desire. It said it would ask a series of questions, pausing after each to give me a chance to reply." Steffie, answering its questions, reads the label on her sweater: "virgin acrylic."

(9) Peter Wollen writes that in "an age marked by an ever-increasing and ever-accelerating proliferation of signs, of all types, the immediate environment becomes itself increasingly dominated by signs, rather than natural objects or events. The realm of signs becomes not simply a 'second nature' but a primary 'reality.' (The quotes around 'reality' mark the effacement of the traditional distinction between reality and representation in a world dominated by representations.)"

(10) Lighted by helicopters, the airborne toxic event moves like an operatic death ship across the landscape: "In its tremendous size, its

dark and bulky menace, its escorting aircraft, the cloud resembled a national promotion for death, a multimillion-dollar campaign backed by radio spots, heavy print and billboard, TV saturation."

The world of *White Noise* is a world of primary representations which neither precede nor follow the real but are themselves real—although it is true that they always have the *appearance* both of preceding another reality (as a model to be followed) and of following it (as copy). But this appearance must itself be taken seriously.

Consider these two passages about an adult looking at sleeping children: "I looked for a blanket to adjust, a toy to remove from a child's warm grasp, feeling I'd wandered into a TV moment." And "[t]hese sleeping children were like figures in an ad for the Rosicrucians, drawing a powerful beam of light from somewhere off the page." Both moments are mediated by another moment, a memory or a metaphor which shapes them, endows them with a certain structure; this structure is a part of their reality. It is quite possible to distinguish one reality (the sleeping children) from another (the TV moment, the ad for the Rosicrucians), just as we can in principle distinguish literal from metaphorical language; it is possible for the novel to be ironical about the gap between these two realities. But this distinguishing and this irony are insecure. Real moments and TV moments interpenetrate each other—and it is, in any case, another (novelistic) representation which offers us this reality and this distinction. The world is so saturated with representations that it becomes increasingly difficult to separate primary actions from imitations of actions.

Indeed, it seems that it is only within the realm of representation that it is possible to postulate a realm of primary actions which would be quite distinct from representation. During the evacuation Jack notices groups of refugees:

> Out in the open, keeping their children near, carrying what they could, they seemed to be part of some ancient destiny, connected in doom and pain to a whole history of people trekking across wasted landscapes. There was an epic quality about them that

> made me wonder for the first time at the scope of our predicament.

What he is seeing is of course a movie; and it is precisely because it is cinematic, because of its "epic quality," that the scene is real and serious to him. "Epic" here perhaps means something like "naive," lacking self-consciousness, and above all lacking any awareness of the cinematic nature of the experience. This paradox is even clearer in the case of Jack's fantasy about the death of Attila the Hun: "I want to believe he lay in his tent, wrapped in animal skins, as in some internationally financed movie epic, and said brave cruel things to his aides and retainers." The image is again of a heroic lack of self-consciousness, a naive immediacy to life and death:

> No weakening of the spirit. No sense of the irony of human existence. . . . He accepted death as an experience that flows naturally from life, a wild ride through the forest, as would befit someone known as the Scourge of God. This is how it ended for him, with his attendants cutting off their hair and disfiguring their own faces in barbarian tribute, as the camera pulls back out of the tent and pans across the night sky of the fifth century A.D., clear and uncontaminated, bright-banded with shimmering worlds.

It is only in the movies, only through cultural mediation, that a vision of nonmediation is possible—and therefore absurd.

The central mediating agency in this world is television; indeed, for "most people there are only two places in the world. Where they live and their TV set. If a thing happens on television, we have every right to find it fascinating, whatever it is." The major statement is a speech made by Murray. He tells his students that

> they're already too old to figure importantly in the making of society. Minute by minute they're beginning to diverge from each other. "Even as we sit here," I tell them, "you are spinning out from the core, becoming less recognizable as a group, less targetable by advertisers and mass-producers of culture. Kids are a true universal. But you're well beyond that, already beginning to drift, to feel estranged from the products you consume. Who are

> they designed for? What is your place in the marketing scheme? Once you're out of school, it is only a matter of time before you experience the vast loneliness and dissatisfaction of consumers who have lost their group identity."

The assumptions are astounding: we know that human worth can't be measured in terms of our relation to consumption—to money and commodities—and that the order of things transcends "the marketing scheme." But all that Murray is doing is stating the central, the deadly serious principles of a capitalist society. This is really how it is, the marketing scheme really does work, for most purposes, in a capitalist society, as the scheme of things; the whole social organization is geared to this equation. The propositions are monstrous, but only because we find it so hard to believe in the true and central awfulness of capitalism.

Television comes into this because of its crucial role in marketing—and this is to say that its importance lies not in the sheer quantity of representations that it generates, nor even in their content as messages, but in the fact that they are always directly linked to commodity production and the generation of profits, and that in order to serve these ends they work as an integral part of a system for the shaping and reshaping of human identity. Murray's students are thus "beginning to feel they ought to turn against the medium, exactly as an earlier generation turned against their parents and their country." When he tells them that "they have to learn to look as children again. Root out content. Find codes and messages," they reply that television "is just another name for junk mail."

But cultural criticism—the moralistic critique of the mass media that has been the stock in trade of liberal journalism—is of course not an option, certainly not for this novel, which is much more interested, in its own ironic but unconditional way, in, for example, Murray's quasi-mystical experience of television. It is, he says, "a primal force in the American home. Sealed-off, self-contained, self-referring." Television

> offers incredible amounts of psychic data. It opens ancient memories of world birth, it welcomes us into the grid, the network of little buzzing dots that make up the picture pattern. There

> is light, there is sound. I ask my students, "What more do you want?" Look at the wealth of data concealed in the grid, in the bright packaging, the jingles, the slice-of-life commercials, the products hurtling out of darkness, the coded messages and endless repetitions, like chants, like mantras. "*Coke is it, Coke is it, Coke is it*." The medium practically overflows with sacred formulas if we can remember how to respond innocently and get past our irritation, weariness and disgust.

A whole aesthetic is elaborated here, although unfortunately it's made up of the dregs of other aesthetic systems. Murray has the quixotic ability to disregard the banal surface of television and, with all the innocence of a formalist semiotician, to discover a cornucopia of aesthetic information in its organization. The key term here is "data," a meaningless word which suggests that the relevant level at which to decode the television message is that of the physical structure of light on the screen—but in fact the word has the effect of conflating this level with other levels of information. Gestalt and perceptual psychology mingle with genre theory and a mysticism of the proper name in Murray's postcritical celebration of the medium. For his students, however, television is "worse than junk mail. Television is the death throes of human consciousness, according to them. They're ashamed of their television past. They want to talk about movies." Murray is a postmodernist. His students, wishing to return to the high modernism of cinema, are postpostmodernist.

> The smoke alarm went off in the hallway upstairs, either to let us know the battery had just died or because the house was on fire. We finished our lunch in silence.

When the jug-eared computer operator taps into Jack's data profile (his history—but what history? "Where was it located exactly? Some state or federal agency, some insurance company or credit firm or medical clearinghouse?") he finds that "[w]e have a situation": "It's what we call a massive data-base tally." This tally doesn't actually *mean* anything except that Jack is "the sum total of [his] data." Like so many signifying structures in *White Noise* it offers a profound interpretability but withdraws any precise meaning, or is at best deeply ambivalent. It's nothing but data, raw and unreadable. And what constitutes data is of course not something given, as the word suggests, but a set of constructs, figures whose significance lies not in their inherent structure but in the decision that has been taken to frame them in a certain way. The word embodies all the pathos of an impoverished and institutionalized empiricism. Its faultiness is caught in a joke about the search for contamination in the girls' school; the search is carried out by men in Mylex suits, but "because Mylex is itself a suspect material, the results tended to be ambiguous."

Whereas the sign causes unease, a sense that there is more to be known, the proper name is the site of a magical plenitude. Proper names tend to come in cadenced triads: "The Airport Marriott, the Downtown Travelodge, the Sheraton Inn and Conference Center." "Dacron, Orlon, Lycra Spandex." "Krylon, Rust-Oleum, Red Devil." They appear mysteriously in the midst of the mundane world of novelistic narrative, detached, functionless, unmotivated. At the end of a paragraph on Babette's fear of death, "the emptiness, the sense of cosmic darkness," occurs the single line: "MasterCard, Visa, American Express." The sonorous, Miltonic names lack all epic content, and they are intruded into the text without any marker of a speaking source. In a later episode the sleeping Steffie, speaking in "a language not quite of this world," utters two words

> that seemed to have a ritual meaning, part of a verbal spell or ecstatic chant.
>
> *Toyota Celica.*
>
> A long moment passed before I realized this was the name of an automobile. The truth only amazed me more. The utterance was beautiful and mysterious, gold-shot with looming wonder. It was like the name of an ancient power in the sky, tablet-carved in cuneiform.

Here there is a definite source for the utterance, but in another sense Steffie is not this source: the words are spoken through her, by her unconscious but also, as Jack recognizes, by the unconscious of her culture. Yet for all their commercial banality (the same that echoes gloriously through a phrase caught on the radio: "It's the rainbow hologram that gives this credit card a marketing intrigue"), the names remain charged with an opaque significance, so that Jack remarks: "Whatever its source, the utterance struck me with the impact of a moment of splendid transcendence."

The question of the source of enunciation of these proper names remains an interesting one, as there seems to be a definite progression in the novel from an apparently impersonal enunciation to more localized points of origin. In a description of the supermarket, "full of elderly people who look lost among the hedgerows," the words "Dristan Ultra, Dristan Ultra" occur on a separate line but are enclosed within inverted commas, which indicates a diegetic source—probably a public address system in the supermarket. The words have the same sort of status as the voices emanating from the television and the radio that punctuate the life of the house. At other times a psychological source seems to be indicated—when the words "leaded, unleaded, super unleaded" intrude into Jack and Babette's desperate lovemaking; or when the spelled out acronyms "Random Access Memory, Acquired Immune Deficiency Syndrome, Mutual Assured Destruction" cross the text as Jack is crossing the slum districts of Iron City. At other times there seem to be verbal associations flowing between the proper names and their textual context: "I watched light climb into the rounded summits of high-altitude clouds. Clorets, Velamints, Freedent." The movement is not just the phonetic one from clouds (perhaps "cloud turrets") to Clorets but is also a circuit between the novel's imagery of sunsets and the poetry of advertising. Another example: Jack experiences "aural torment" as he imagines Babette making love to the mysterious Mr. Gray:

> . . . Then gloom moved in around the gray-sheeted bed, a circle slowly closing.
>
> Panasonic.

Like the syllables of the Proustian name, the last word is multiply motivated. "Pana-" is the circle slowly closing, "sonic" is Jack's aural torment, and there are overdetermined traces of "panoramic" and, of course, television. But as with the name in Proust, the point is the excess of the poetic signifier over its component parts, its transcendental character, its plenitude. The poetic word comes from elsewhere, and if it seems to be spoken by a character (like the woman passing on the street who says "a decongestant, an antihistamine, a cough suppressant, a pain reliever"), this is nevertheless only a proximate source, a relay. The proper name is its own absolute origin.

At lunchtime Wilder sits surrounded by "open cartons, crumpled tinfoil, shiny bags of potato chips, bowls of pasty substances covered with plastic wrap, flip-top rings and twist ties, individually wrapped slices of orange cheese." Meals in this house lack the monumental solidity of the meals in *Buddenbrooks* or even in the James Bond novels; they are depthless, physically insubstantial. At times the staple junk food is opposed to the "real" (but never achieved) lunch of yogurt and wheat germ, but the truth of the matter is that eating has entirely to do with surfaces. Even chewing gum is described in terms of its wrappings.

The supermarket is the privileged place for a phenomenology of surfaces. Murray is a devotee of generic brands, and he takes their "flavorless packaging" to be the sign of a new austerity, a new "spiritual consensus." The packaging on supermarket goods, he says, "is the last avant-garde. Bold new forms. The power to shock." But even unprocessed and unpackaged foods take on the *form* of packaging: "There were six kinds of apples, there were exotic melons in several pastels. Everything seemed to be in season, sprayed, burnished, bright." And later: "The fruit was gleaming and wet, hard-edged. There was a self-conscious quality about it. It looked carefully observed, like four-color fruit in a guide to photography. We veered right at the plastic jugs of spring water." The kitchen, too, is a place of containers and packagings—the freezer, for example, where "a strange crackling sound came off the plastic food wrap, the snug covering for half eaten things, the Ziploc sacks of liver and ribs, all gleaming with sleety crystals."

But the force of this is not a sentimental regret for a lost world of depths, a nostalgic opposition of surface to substance. There *is* a depth to be found in this world (this house, this novel), but it is not a fullness of being; rather, it's the other end of the packaging process, a sort of final interiority of the wrapping. Jack comes across it when he searches through the trash bag of the compactor:

> An oozing cube of semi-mangled cans, clothes hangers, animal bones and other refuse. The bottles were broken, the cartons flat. Product colors were undiminished in brightness and intensity. Fats, juices and heavy sludges seeped through layers of pressed vegetable matter. I felt like an archaeologist about to sift through a finding of tool fragments and assorted cave trash.

This is the heart of domesticity:

> I found a banana skin with a tampon inside. Was this the dark underside of consumer consciousness? I came across a horrible clotted mass of hair, soap, ear swabs, crushed roaches, flip-top rings, sterile pads smeared with pus and bacon fat, strands of frayed dental floss, fragments of ballpoint refills, toothpicks still displaying bits of impaled food. There was a pair of shredded undershorts with lipstick markings, perhaps a memento of the Grayview Motel.

The list is of an accretion of wastes that have come full circle from the supermarket but which still retain the formal structure (and even the "undiminished colors") of the presentation of surfaces. At the heart of this inside is nothing more than a compacted mass of outsides.

White Noise is a domestic novel, continuously concerned with the secret life of the house—with the closet doors that open by themselves, with the chirping of the radiator, with the sounds of the sink and the washing machine and the compactor, with the jeans tumbling in the dryer. The narrator writes of the "numerous and deep" levels of data in the kitchen, and speaks of the kitchen and the bedroom as "the major chambers around here, the power haunts, the sources." But the center of the life of the house is the voice of the television. This is what it says:

> Let's sit half-lotus and think about our spines.
>
> . . . .

If it breaks easily into pieces, it is called shale. When wet, it smells like clay.

. . . .

Until Florida surgeons attached an artificial flipper.

. . . .

(In a British voice): There are forms of vertigo that do not include spinning.

. . . .

And other trends that could dramatically impact your portfolio.

. . . .

This creature has developed a complicated stomach in keeping with its leafy diet.

. . . .

Now we will put the little feelers on the butterfly.

. . . .

Meanwhile here is a quick and attractive lemon garnish suitable for any sea food.

. . . .

Now watch this. Joanie is trying to snap Ralph's patella with a *bushido* stun kick. She makes contact, he crumples, she runs.

. . . .

They're not booing—they're saying, "Bruce, Bruce."

Television is about everything. It is about the ordinary, the banal, information for living our lives. It is rarely the voice of apocalypse.

Frank Lentricchia

Libra as Postmodern Critique

Two scenes in Don DeLillo's fiction are primal for his imagination of America. The first occurs in his first book, *Americana*, in a brief dialogue the ostensible subject of which is television but whose real subject is the invention of America as the invention of television, which "came over on the Mayflower," as one of his characters says. And that is the first mark of his fiction—the presence of witty characters who talk obsessively about cultural issues in a funny and colloquial English and who do on a regular basis what Melville's characters couldn't keep themselves from doing: they think. And what they think about tends to be concerned not with what goes on domestically in the private kitchens of their private lives—small, good things, or even small, horrible things—but with what large and nearly invisible things press upon the private life, the various coercive contemporary environments within which the so-called private life is led. In the dialogue from *Americana* the genius of television emerges as nothing other than the desire for the universal third-person—it is *that* which "came over on the Mayflower," the person we dream about from our armchairs in front of the television, originally dreamt by the first immigrants, the pilgrims on their way over, the object of the dream being the person those pilgrims would become, could the dream be fulfilled: a new self because a new world.

Sitting in front of the TV in our armchairs is like a perpetual Atlantic crossing. For if, as DeLillo writes, "[t]o consume in America is not to buy; it is to dream," then the pilgrims were the ur-American consumers in the market for selfhood. Which is to say that it is not the consummation of desire (for the pilgrims, the actual grinding experience of being here) but the foreplay of desire that is TV advertising's object. To buy is merely an effect, but to dream is a cause—the motor principle, in fact, of consumer capitalism. TV advertising taps into and manipulates the American dream; it is the mechanism which triggers our move "from first person consciousness to third," from the self we are, and would leave behind, to the self we would become. Unlike the movies, which blow up the image of the third-person ideal to larger-than-life proportions, the TV ad is realistic because it never tries to encourage you to think of yourself as a movie star who can go to bed with another movie star in Acapulco; instead, it tells you "that the dream of entering the third person singular might possibly be fulfilled," that it is entirely possible for you to have "two solid weeks of sex and adventure with a vacationing typist from Iowa City." Advertising "discovered" and exploited the economic value of the person we all want to be, but the pilgrim-consumer dreaming on the original Mayflower, or on the new Mayflower in front of the television, "invented" that person.

If, in F. Scott Fitzgerald's words at the end of *The Great Gatsby*, the "fresh, green breast of the new world" had "pandered in whispers to the last and greatest of all human dreams," if Gatsby's life is the meretricious but typical incarnation of that dream—the self he made out of the self he repressed: James Gatz become Jay Gatsby, the "first person" (in two senses) become "third"—then those pilgrims were his ancestors and we in TV land are his real-life progeny. The pilgrims, Gatsby, almost any character in Stephen Crane or Theodore Dreiser, ourselves in front of the television, JFK and Lee Harvey Oswald: the distinction between the real and fictional cannot be sustained; its undesirability is the key meaning, even, of being an American. To be real in America is to be in the position of the "I" who would be "he" or "she," the I who must negate I, leave I behind in a real or metaphoric Europe, some suffocating ghetto of selfhood figured forth repeatedly in DeLillo's books as some shabby and lonely room in America, a site of dream and obsession, a contemporary American origin just as generative as the Mayflower. The Mayflower may or may not have been the origin of origins—surely it was not—but, in any case, for America to be America the original moment of yearning for the third-person must be ceaselessly renewed.

The second primal scene for DeLillo's imagination of America comes in *White Noise* in a passage which extends a major implication of the surprising history of television he had explored in *Americana*. "The most photographed barn in America" is the ostensible subject of this scene; the real subject is a new kind of representation as a new kind of excitement: not any given representation as some inert object upon which we might apply our powers of analysis (say, the particular barn in question), but the electronic medium of representation as the active context of contemporary existence in America. TV, a productive medium of the image, is only one (albeit dominant) technological expression of an entire environment of the image. But unlike TV, which is an element in the contemporary landscape, the environment of the image *is* the landscape—it is what (for us) "landscape" has become, and it can't be turned off with the flick of a wrist. For this environment-as-electronic-medium radically constitutes contemporary consciousness and therefore (such as it is) contemporary community—it guarantees that we are a people of, by, and for the image. Measured against TV advertising's manipulation of the image of the third person, the economic goals of which are pretty clear, and clearly susceptible to class analysis from the left—it is obvious who the big beneficiaries of such manipulations are—the environment of the image in question in *White Noise* appears far less concretely in focus (less apprehensible, less empirically encounterable) and therefore more insidious in its effects.

The first-person narrator of *White Noise*, Jack Gladney, professor of Hitler Studies, drives to the tourist attraction known as the most photographed barn in America, and he takes with him his new colleague, Murray Jay Siskind, professor of popular culture, a smart émigré from New York City to Middle America who identifies himself as the incarnation of the problem of stereotypical representation, as "The Jew. Who else would I be?" The tourist attraction is pastorally set, some twenty miles from the small city where the two reside and teach, and all along the way there are natural things to be taken in, presumably, though all the nature that is experienced (hardly the word, but it will have to do) is noted in a flat, undetailed, and apparently unemotional declarative: "There were meadows and apple orchards." And the traditional picturesque of rural life is similarly registered: "White fences trailed through the rolling fields." The strategically unenergized prose of these traditional moments is an index to the passing of both a literary convention and an older America. The narrator continues in his recessed way while his companion comments (lectures, really) upon the tourist site which is previewed for them (literally) by several signs, spaced every few miles along the way, announcing the attraction in big block letters. When they arrive the attraction is crowded with people with cameras. There is a booth where a man sells postcards and slides of the barn; there is an elevated spot from which the tourists snap their photos.

Gladney's phlegmatic narrative style is thrown into high relief by the ebullience of his friend's commentary. Murray does all the talking, like some guru of the postmodern drawing his neophyte into a new world which the neophyte experiences in a shocked state of half-consciousness situated somewhere between the older world where there were objects of perception like barns and apple orchards and the strange new world where the object of perception is perception itself: a packaged perception, a "sight" (in the genius of the vernacular), not a "thing." What they view is the view of a thing. What Murray reveals is that "no one sees the barn" because once "you've seen the signs about the barn, it becomes impossible to see the barn." This news about the loss of the referent, the dissolving of the object into its representations (the road signs, the photos) is delivered not with nostalgia for a lost world of the real but with joy: "We're not here to capture an image, we're here to maintain one. Every photograph reinforces the aura."

In between Murray's remarks, Jack Gladney reports on the long silences and the background noise—a new kind of choral commentary, "the incessant clicking of shutter release buttons, the rustling crank of levers that advanced the film"—and on the tourists ritually gathered in order to partake, as Murray says, of "a kind of spiritual surrender." So not only can't we get outside the aura, we really don't want to. We prefer not to know what the barn was like before it was photographed because its aura, its technological transcendence, its soul, is our production, it is us. "We're part of the aura," says Murray, and knowing we're a part is tantamount to the achievement of a new identity—a collective selfhood brought to birth in the moment of contact with an "accumulation of nameless energies," in the medium of representation synonymous with the conferring of fame and charisma. "We're here, we're now," says Murray, as if he were affirming the psychic wholeness of the community. "The thousands who were here in the past, those who will come in the future. We've agreed to be part of a collective perception." We've come home to the world, beyond alienation.

Oswald also thought he would come satisfyingly into the world and do so according to the terms of the classic Marxist directive: "Happiness," Oswald wrote in a letter to his brother which DeLillo uses as the epigraph for the first part of *Libra*, "is not based on oneself, it does not consist of a small home, of taking and getting. Happiness is taking part in the struggle, where there is no borderline between one's own personal world, and the world in general." Marxist Oswald will become, in his last moment of lucid consciousness, just before Ruby shoots him, postmodern Oswald—a man who wants to, and does enter "the world in general," not through striking a blow in class warfare, however, on the side of the working oppressed, but by entering the aura. For on that weekend of 22 November 1963, Lee Oswald—the name he was known by to that point—thanks to the fathering power of the media becomes rebaptized, forever now "Lee Harvey Oswald," a triple-named echo of another media child, "John Fitzgerald Kennedy."

Libra is a fiction of social destiny, but one which largely sets aside the usual arguments of determinism based on class, social setting, ethnicity, and race. Bobby Dupard, a friend Oswald makes in the brig while serving in the Marines, is poor and he's black, but when Oswald asks him if he did the crime he was accused of, Bobby's answer—despite the unmistakable style of his idiom—marks him less as black, poor, and big city ghetto than as another victim of the American epidemic metaphorically named by *Libra*'s title. In answer to Oswald's question—did you do it?—Bobby replies with the book's wildest representation of itself: "In my mind I could like verbalize it either way." The social forces which obsess writers like Dreiser and Dos Passos—whom DeLillo most resembles in this book—are treated in *Libra* as forces whose capacity to shape as they differentiate the individual is decidedly on the ebb. The social environment of the typical naturalist character is displaced in DeLillo by the charismatic environment of the image, a new phase in American literature and culture—a new arena of action and a power of determination whose major effect is to realign radically all social agents (from top to bottom) as first-person agents of desire seeking self-annihilation and fulfillment in the magical third.

DeLillo's American tragedy is much more Oswald's than it is Kennedy's; much more America's than it is the tragedy of an isolated psychopath. Unlike Dreiser's, DeLillo's American tragedy is classless, not because he refuses to recognize the differences that class can make, but because the object of desire, what is insistently imagined in *Libra* as the conferrer of happiness, is never located in the privileged social space of those Fitzgerald called "the very rich" who he thought "different from you and me." Oswald is different from Kennedy, all right, and in exactly the way that Fitzgerald would have chosen to report their difference, but in his fantasy life he never longs for Kennedy's place as, say, Clyde Griffiths in *An American Tragedy* longs for the place of his wealthy relatives. In his fantasy life Oswald is focused on his similarities with JFK: their wives were pregnant at about the same time in the late summer of 1963; they were bad spellers; they had bad handwriting; they both did military service in the Pacific. And "Lee was always reading two or three books, like Kennedy." Oswald's desire is implicitly utopian, its object a place where he and Kennedy—who both had brothers named Robert—could themselves become brothers.

One of the voices that speaks inside Oswald is a voice out of the movies, out of Howard Hawks's *Red River*, none other than the voice of John Wayne, and it says (as Oswald practice-fires his rifle) "*Take 'em to Missouri, Matt.*" The voice inside Kennedy (whose Secret Service code name, Lancer, DeLillo insists upon, as in "*Lancer is hit*") is a voice out of a book, a Shakespearean voice from *King John*, scribbled on a scrap of paper that Kennedy carried in his wallet, and it says: "*They whirl asunder and dismember me.*" The real Oswald and the real Kennedy were of course in some part the inescapable inheritors of family, but in *Libra* the genealogy that counts is literary—with Kennedy's Arthurian and Shakespearean fantasies marking him as a seeker of traditional cultural sanction and empowerment, and Oswald's fix on John Wayne marking his desire as the product (DeLillo's postmodern turn on naturalist convention), the plaything even, of Hollywood's image factories. Unlike JFK, Oswald is the genuine American article.

Sometime during the enormous vogue of *Peck's Bad Boy* in the 1880s and 1890s, a Philadelphia newspaper reported that upon apprehension a juvenile delinquent, when asked who he was, said, "I am Peck's bad boy." The paper's editorialist, like other editorialists who responded to similar evidence of infectious writing, like librarians all over the country, was not amused. He already knew what DeLillo's right-wing critics Jonathan Yardley and George Will would learn a century later about *Libra*: that *Peck's Bad Boy* and *Huckleberry Finn* were bad influences—acts, even, of bad citizenship. He knew that literature sometimes makes something happen. DeLillo's Oswald is the latest avatar of a very bad boy, the Tom Sawyer of our time, though John Hinckley who saw *Taxi Driver* and then shot Ronald Reagan as a lover's offering to Jody Foster might wish to claim the honor for himself.

Why did Oswald shoot at, if not kill John Kennedy? What movies had *he* been seeing? *Libra* repeatedly forces those questions upon us. For despite his transformation of naturalism's traditional social scene of determination, DeLillo has not written in *Libra* a book that will please the classic liberal (now "conservative") mind. *Libra* is the story of the context and the setting of an action, not the story of an autonomous lone gunman operating in a social vacuum. To take up the question of Oswald's motivation is to take up what motivates the question: not the conspiracy theory that DeLillo invents (one version or another of it has been bruited about for twenty-five years) but *Libra*'s double narrative structure—the story of two narratives becoming fatally one: the story of Oswald beginning in his early teens in the Bronx, in the early 1950s, and ending on 24 November 1963 in Dallas; and the story of the conspiracy hatched on 17 April 1963, the second anniversary of the Bay of Pigs, by a disaffected CIA official who believes an "electrifying event" is needed to reverse the administration's increasingly accommodationist posture toward Castro. The word DeLillo likes is not "story" or "narrative" but "plot" in its several senses. The conspiracy plot (intention, design, narrative), ideologically pure Cold War politics at its inception, becomes something else when it is extended from theory to practice—when it engages its agents: Cuban exiles furious with blood lust because they are convinced JFK betrayed them; the New Orleans Mafia boss (DeLillo calls him Carmine Latta) who wants Cuba returned to a Battista-like status—"back in the firm." ("A whole city to pluck like a fruit," says his bodyguard; a "whole country," says the boss.) And another CIA agent whose essential interests in Cuba are not rooted in Cold War ideology, who had used the agency's intelligence-gathering power to bring down hostile Central American regimes in return for substantial kickbacks from the multinationals—his lucrative stake in Cuban oil being so derived but now put out of reach by the hostility to American interests of Castro's revolution: this agent, in other words, is Carmine Latta's socially acceptable double in that government agency called "the Company" by those who work for it. The conspirators: not a collection of nut cases, but the interlocked representatives, as in Iran-Contra, of American power.

One of *Libra*'s more uncanny effects is anachronistic: DeLillo's wager is that we will read his book out of the political history that Watergate and Iran-Contra has made, as if Watergate and Iran-Contra preceded 22 November 1963, as if the novel's narration of the events of twenty-five years past made that day in November contemporaneous with its retelling. *Libra*'s politically caustic and unsettling point is therefore inextricable from DeLillo's effort to focus our culture's interpretation of its political history through the lens of post-Watergate America, so that even the reader inclined to believe that Oswald acted alone, but now grown accustomed to rogue government conspiracies of anti-Soviet demonologists, American intelligence, and multinational business and criminal interests, will be likely to grant DeLillo that the CIA, the Mafia, and the Cuban exile community in Miami, either individually or in concert, possessed sufficient motive and resources to plan and execute the murder whether or not they in fact did so. As hatched, the plot is not to kill the president but to lay down fire on the street, to stage a spectacular miss. But as the operation moves from theory to execution it passes into the hands of one T. J. Mackey, a CIA agent who is also a Bay of Pigs veteran, and his Cuban recruits, the shooters who are supposed to be actors but whose politically triggered passion for revenge, like Mackey's, turns assassination theater, the representation of violence, into the real thing—the violent lurch backward, exploded brain tissue, and the dead who persist through history's ambiguities.

DeLillo builds his conspiracy plot with relentless inevitability, making good on the original plotter's theory that all plots tend deathward. The Oswald plot, on the other hand, is so utterly episodic in character that it couldn't be approved by Aristotle, much less by the conspirators; it certainly doesn't deserve to be called a "plot" in DeLillo's senses of the word. What he has done in *Libra* is given us one perfectly shaped, intention-driven narrative while folding within it, every other chapter, a second narrative, his imagined biography of Oswald, a plotless tale of an aimless life propelled by the agonies of inconsistent and contradictory motivation, a life without coherent form except for the form implied by the book's title: Oswald is a "negative libran, somewhat unsteady and impulsive. Easily, easily, easily influenced. Poised to make the dangerous leap." DeLillo writes that Oswald "wanted to carry himself with a clear sense of role." But who is this "he" who wanted a "role," just who is it that stands in the wings waiting for a part in the theater of self? It doesn't much help to say that he is someone named "Oswald" who can get up from a chair where he's been reading a book, calmly walk over to his wife, pummel her with both fists, then return to the chair and resume his reading, quietly. The identity of the negative libran is the nonidentity of sheer possibility—of the American who might play any part. The negative libran is an undecidable intention waiting to be decided.

And astrology is the metaphor in *Libra* for being trapped in a system whose determinative power is grippingly registered by DeLillo's double narrative of an amorphous existence haphazardly stumbling into the future where a plot awaits to confer upon it the identity of a role fraught with form and purpose.

The double narrative virtually forces us to read in order to catch up with the future; in order to find out how the drifting episodes of Oswald's life in the 1950s and early 1960s will be gathered on 22 November 1963 into the rigors of causality; in order to give Oswald's life everything that it lacks and that the conspirators' plot has: the literary wholeness of a beginning, middle, and end. We find ourselves seduced into reading with the hope of seeing Oswald made into a product of an environment in which paranoia is a reasonable response to the structure of the world. The original plotter (one Win Everett) sees himself as something of a novelist/playwright who has scripted a fiction, one of whose characters was an illusory lone gunman, a man of paper who a trail of carefully planted clues would lead authorities to conclude was real, that he was Castro's hit man, and that after the attempt on Kennedy's life had escaped to Cuba. The point was to get Castro blamed; Mackey's people would set up the play. The actual Oswald was irrelevant. But Oswald materializes as the real-life counterpart of a fictional lone gunman whose appearance almost turns history into designed narrative, almost makes believers of us all in astrology.

With his double narrative DeLillo toys with conventional political and novelistic expectations. He has written a book about the triggering event of our political paranoia in the context of a recent political scene which can only reenforce that paranoia. DeLillo did not invent Watergate, Oliver North, Albert Hakim, Richard Secord, or William Casey, who my father (a reasonable sort of guy) told me offhandedly at the Christmas dinner table had most certainly been murdered by Reagan's operatives, with the consent of Casey himself. DeLillo has written this book, moreover, in the context of a contemporary fiction scene decisively shaped by the paranoid styles of Orwell, Burroughs, Mailer, Pynchon, and Didion. So *Libra*'s double narrative primes our desire for a paranoid finish to what the great naturalists always feared: that we lead lives arranged by and for the interests of others, that they are making history behind our backs. But unlike some of his predecessors in the paranoid novel (particularly Pynchon), DeLillo refuses to force a clinical reading of everyday life.

The true paranoid does not believe in chance or accident. DeLillo, however, does not tell us that his conspirators arranged for Oswald's job at the Texas School Book Depository. Nor does he tell us that the conspirators had the power and contacts to arrange for the motorcade to pass under Oswald's elevated view (in other words, that they could rig the president's closest personal aides and the Secret Service). Nor does he permit us to conclude, absurdly, that the conspirators could arrange for good weather so that the bubble top from the president's limousine could be removed. In DeLillo's version Oswald's presence at Dealey Plaza is an awesome coincidence; he is used as a last-minute, redundant, back-up shooter who fires at the motorcade, wounds, but does not kill Kennedy: the fatal bullet comes from the fabled grassy knoll, fired by one of the embittered Cubans. So though he lays out a paranoid plot for our delectation, one calculated to titillate the left—the decisive plotters are multinational capitalists of both legitimate and Mafia stripe—DeLillo, by his insistence on the chancy appearance of Oswald, presses us to rethink the question of Oswald outside the framework of conspiracy. After the assassination, the major plotters virtually disappear, the book rounds to its conclusion wholly focused on Oswald, and the reader is forced to confront the familiar mystery of his identity. Left with a book more about Oswald than about conspiracy, we learn that the question is not what happened in Dallas on 22 November 1963—DeLillo gives us a theory about that. The question is not even, who is this Oswald? It is, who is *Lee Harvey Oswald*?

In the radical sense of the word, Lee Harvey Oswald is a contemporary *production*, a figure who is doubled everywhere in *Libra*, even, most harrowingly, in strategic places, in the narrative voice that DeLillo invented for this book. The question, who or what is responsible for the production of *Lee Harvey Oswald* (or *John Fitzgerald Kennedy*), is inseparable from the question of where DeLillo imagines power to lie in contemporary America. His answer, brutal as it may seem, makes the matter of the assassination and who may have done it very nearly beside the point. One of the Cubans says, "Someone has to die"; another says, "This Kennedy has things to answer for"; and Carmine Latta says, "You cut off the head, the tail doesn't wag." Latta, like another fictional godfather much given to proverbial discourse, is a sentimentalist of power, a survival from an era when decapitation was the favored method of execution, a man likened by conspirator David Ferrie to a "fairy-tale pope, able to look at you and change your life, say a word and change your life." Latta imagines the world as a place run by epically forceful men—Sam Giancana, JFK, Fidel, himself—a world whose fortunes are inseparable from the fortunes of such powerful individuals. Hence the political usefulness, every so often, of cutting off a head. In an odd way, it is a comfortable view of the world because it provides a pretty workable program for social change. But *Libra* doesn't locate power in isolate male heads, whether of the state or of the Mafia, a distinction DeLillo undercuts, even more savagely than does Mario Puzo, in a passage in which the sublimely comic and innocent force he invents as Jack Ruby, when informed by Latta's bodyguard that JFK has been "ramming this woman that's Sam's [Giancana's] mistress. . . . Two years, Jack. They did it in the White House," is stunned into this reflection: "Jack could not conceive of a situation whereby the President of the United States would be fucking the girlfriend of Momo Giancana." That President Kennedy should emerge from this novel not "like" a Mafia don but *as* a Mafia don—had he not put himself in "the arena of blood and pain" by making it known that he wanted Fidel "on a slab"?—this, too, is treated with an irony that moves the issue beyond traditional takes on power (get the right head and you won't have to cut it off). Not only is the distinction between Sam Giancana and JFK irrelevant but so is their metaphorical sameness, because the action is finally somewhere else—at a level of power, beyond the conspiracies of agents, where there is no head to cut off.

The disturbing strength of *Libra*—DeLillo gives no quarter on this—is its refusal to offer its readers a comfortable place outside of Oswald. DeLillo does not do what the media right convicts him of doing—imply that all Americans are would-be murderous sociopaths.

He has presented a politically far more unsettling vision of normalcy, of an everyday life so utterly enthralled by the fantasy selves projected in the media as our possible third-person, and, more insidiously, an everyday life so enthralled by the charisma of the media, that it makes little useful sense to speak of sociopathology or of a lone gunman. Oswald is ourselves painted large, in scary tones, but ourselves. It may be that Mailer and Pynchon are shamans of the paranoid novel, but it is not the case, as a critic for the *New York Review of Books* has written, that with *Libra* DeLillo has become chief of the shamans. Though used often as a description of a major vein of contemporary writing, and even of something called the contemporary sensibility, "paranoia" distorts DeLillo's efforts in *Libra* because it has the effect of trivializing what he has done by deflecting attention away from the public, institutional targets of the book and by focusing attention instead on some strange bit of terrain situated somewhere in the author's putative inner self. The literary shamans of paranoia are dismissable as fascinating oddballs. As for DeLillo, he has played with the conventions of paranoia in several of his books, has inserted a few certifiable types into *Libra*—Oswald is not one among them—but has himself, as writer, never assented. *Libra* does not finger a conspiracy as much as it incarnates a cultural scene of action in the electronic society within which assassination is one of the extreme but logical expressions of the course of daily life.

DeLillo succeeds in large part in *Libra* because he has created on almost every page, in all the minor moments, a novelistic texture which evokes a cultural context totally saturated by the very thing that preoccupies him in the novel's major invention, Oswald himself. What that thing is which makes contemporary culture what it is, is not easy for me to define, but it is encountered repeatedly in *Libra*, beginning with Oswald in his early teens, in the Bronx, listening to a would-be street-tough look forward to his sixteenth birthday and to the self he would become, talking about himself in the third-person: "The kid quits school the minute he's sixteen. I mean look out. . . . The kid gets a job in construction. First thing, he buys ten shirts with Mr. B. collars. He saves his money, before you know it he owns a car. He simonizes the car once a month. The car gets him laid. Who's better than the kid?" Then there is Wayne Elko, one of the shooters, supposed to kill Oswald in the Texas theater—that day showing a movie Elko happened to know—but the police get to Oswald first, not because Elko didn't have time to do the job but because he wanted to do it at the movie's climactic moment: Wayne Elko, whom the narrator introduces at one point as a man whose "experience in life and in the movies told him that. . . ." And there is Guy Bannister, FBI agent, who was at the scene when John Dillinger was gunned down coming out of Chicago's Biograph, who replays that scene for a bartender, cautioning the bartender all the while that "whenever there's a famous finish in the vicinity of a movie house, it behooves you to know what's playing," because "this is history with a fucking flourish." And there is the moment of the President arriving at Love Field on 22 November, striding confidently off the tarmac away from his security, toward the fence against which the crowd surged, "smiling famously into the wall of open mouths," and DeLillo assuming the voice of the crowd, DeLillo becoming the crowd gaping at Kennedy, and creating the kind of comedy that is organic to *Libra*'s vision: "He looked like himself, like photographs, a helms-man squinting in the seaglare. . . ."

Most of all, though, there is the moment of Marina Oswald's initiation to America, her assumption of true citizenship occurring on a stroll in downtown Fort Worth with Lee and the baby. Looking in a department store window she sees "something so strange she had to stop and stare, grab hard at Lee. It was the world gone inside out. There they were gaping back at themselves from the TV screen. She was on television. . . . She kept walking out of the picture and coming back. She was amazed every time she saw herself return." Each of these small moments in *Libra* condenses the whole, none with more concentration than the single sentence which registers the crowd's stunned response to what it learns at Love Field—that Kennedy looked like himself, that he must therefore be himself because he looked like the photographs of himself. *Libra* dramatizes the experience of everyday life in a "world gone inside out," of life lived totally inside the representations generated in the print and visual media. The book's cultural logic encourages us to reread JFK as a postmodern figure and Ronald Reagan, the actor who was known to gloss affairs of state with lines from his old movies, as the president we had to have, the chief executive of postmodernism. The value of the episode in which Marina Oswald discovers herself as an image is that it condenses the entire American story that began on the Mayflower with the spiritual invention of television and that concludes in the actual electronic society of real television, where the romantic third-person of the pilgrims and Fitzgerald is literally imaged as ourselves on TV. What is shocking to Marina is also seductive: she can't keep herself from walking back into the picture in order to give audience to her own charismatic self.

Libra is a novel of at least three endings: the shooting of JFK, the shooting of Oswald, and the burial of Oswald, the actual ending graced by his mother's elegiac lyricism ("I stand here on this brokenhearted earth and I look at the stones of the dead"), who speaks the name of her son as "Lee Harvey Oswald," and in so doing implicitly acknowledges the authenticity of an alternative genealogy and her loss of motherhood—his strange new media birth. But this literal ending is prefigured in a moment that can claim more of *Libra*'s logic as the true ending than any of the others. It begins just before Oswald is shot, when, as DeLillo imagines it, Oswald looks above the place where Ruby stands and sees the TV cameras and imagines himself on the news; then the moment of the shooting itself, when he imagines himself on TV being shot: "He could see himself shot as the camera caught it. Through the pain he watched TV. . . . Lee watched himself react to the auguring heat of the bullet." He remembers another triple-named celebrity of the time, baptized by the press "Francis Gary Powers." And more: he imagines, in a jump to the future, the fame that would be conferred upon him after death by the memories of those who would see it happen on TV. In this jump to the future, just before loss of consciousness, Oswald makes his final move into a world without exit from representation, the world gone inside out: he propels himself into someone else's "darkish room, someone's TV den"; he becomes his audience, he witnesses his own birth as media star. A few pages later, Oswald's media fantasy is confirmed: we cut to the living room of one of the CIA plotters, where his wife sits alone, watching the shooting and then its endless replays. And she thinks that there was something in Oswald's face, "a glance at the camera before he was shot, that put him in the audience, among the rest of us, sleepless in our homes. . . ." She thinks that "he is outside the moment, watching with the rest of us." She felt she couldn't leave the TV room; she felt swept into the image, and that she, that all of us, had been made a "part of his dying."

There is a character in DeLillo's seventh book, *The Names* (1982), both a filmmaker and a theorist of film, who says that "film is another part of the twentieth-century mind. . . . If a thing can be filmed, film is implied in the thing itself. This is where we are. The twentieth century is *on film*. You have to ask yourself if there's anything about us more important than the fact that we are constantly on film, constantly watching ourselves." The thing itself in which film is implied is the consciousness formed in the century in which film has become culturally dominant. Film, in other words, is the culturally inevitable form of our self-consciousness, the medium of our "constantly watching ourselves" in future filmic time perform the role of a self-to-be. It is the form of self-consciousness that marks all the major players of *Libra*, including Win Everett, the original plotter, and Jack Ruby, who just before he shoots Oswald—in the excitement of reporters, cameras, and flashbulbs—"saw everything happen in advance." Filmic self-consciousness constitutes, then, the contemporary form of self-making and a new kind of storytelling about the magical third-person pitched by and to the audience of the first-person, who is none other than the ordinary moviegoer or TV viewer. To enter the mind of Oswald is to enter an especially intense—literary—version of such self-consciousness, a mind so preoccupied with the possibilities of its theatrical futurity that the actual Oswald, the physical being in the kitchen, seems to his wife lifelessly mechanical, somehow not there, seen from a distance.

Film may be the dominant, but is not the only mediator of self. Oswald's environment seamlessly blends into an alluring setting for self-reflection John Wayne movies, Karl Marx, and unnameable thriller novels of shadowy men in raincoats who "cross rooftops in the rain" and walk "rain slick streets," a detail so freighted that, once established, DeLillo can simply cite it, without context, in order to draw back all of Oswald's melodramatic reveries: "He had a little vision of himself. He saw himself narrating the story. . . . The future inside the present." Reading Marx as a teenager altered his room, charged it with meaning, propelled him into a history shaped by his imagination: he suddenly saw capitalists, oppressed workers, class struggle. When they learn of Oswald, the conspirators believe they can script him ("We could put him together . . . help him select a fantasy"), but Oswald has already been written, his fantasies already selected. With the "future inside the present," then, and only then, with a firm sense of narrative closure, does life begin to make sense to him. If *Libra*'s author would make sense of his lead character's aimlessness by containing it inside the portentous logic of classically driven narrative, then Oswald, in his desire for a perfectly distilled, scripted self— propelled by itself as its own novelist/prime mover—is a figure of the assassin as writer, a man isolated by his passion, room-bound, a plot schemer.

After he defects to Moscow, Oswald begins to keep a self-described "historic diary" whose misspelled discourse is an unintended pastiche drawn without self-irony from commercial fiction—"*My fondes dreams are shattered*"—and B-movies: "*Somewhere a violin plays.*" He stops shaving, chooses to take but one meal a day, develops the role of "revolutionary in exile," a role that he soon learns will not play. So he leaves Russia in disillusionment, with a new jargon of self in tow: "My Russian period was over," he thinks. He becomes now an "ex-Marine who has penetrated the heart of the Soviet Union," returns to Texas, and begins to develop a new role as the assassin who will do Fidel a favor by killing the fanatic racist/anticommunist General Edwin Walker. Oswald buys a rifle through the mail. He practices its bolt-action over and over in front of his baby in her high chair (she's not there because he's not), poses for a photo, rifle in one hand, radical newspaper in the other, that will appear (he imagines) in *Time* or *Newsweek* after he is apprehended as Walker's killer. (The photo in fact becomes famous.) Self-constructed, constantly revised, Oswald's narrative is a search for the very thing—a well-motivated, shapely existence—whose absence is a mark of the negative libran. In the world of *Libra*, Oswald's patched voice produces the presiding tone of the postmodern absence of substantial and autonomous selfhood; Oswald is the representative man among a company of negative librans. Whether born under the sign or not, DeLillo implies, you are a libran because you are an American. Was JFK moving toward a settlement with Castro or was he planning his assassination? Not even Ruby's balding head can escape the metaphor: "He took scalp treatments that he felt were doing some good although he doubted it."

If the libra-like status of the American complements, maybe because it is motivated by, the primal American condition—the dynamic of third-person desire—and if that dynamic is excruciatingly intensified by contemporary media America, then is there any place beyond such desire where we can stand freely in order to take its critical measure? The usual answer to that question in American fiction is that the place of freedom is within the author's evaluative perspective which judges the dynamic of desire for what it is: within the values of the "omniscient" author who displays the workings of the dynamic but is not himself subject to them. The author, then, is a transcendent figure, someone the reader is implicitly asked to identify with on the promise that, if he does, he will, like the author, be freed to be himself, autonomously disengaged from the need (everywhere narrated in *Libra*) that constantly throws us forward into some other, some imagined existence. This exit is sealed off from us in *Libra*. For the narrator of *Libra* is not DeLillo but DeLillo in quotation marks: "DeLillo" as a voice crafted to perform virtuoso changes of point of view that function as disconcerting repetitions of his characters' obsessive shifts from first-person to third. The omniscient third-person narrator "DeLillo" becomes first-person consciousness trapped in the system, without the warning of "he thought" or "he felt," or the safety of quotation marks, in the midst of a paragraph, often in the midst of a sentence: "DeLillo's" voice fades into his major characters, he becomes Ruby or Oswald, or the crowd gaping at Kennedy, or Mrs. John Connolly in the limousine speeding to Parkland Hospital ("those dying men in our arms"). This narrative strategy is the book's most politically generous gesture, DeLillo's undercutting of himself as the traditional authority who is supposed to guide the reader safely through the maze. And the shock is beyond calculation when DeLillo-the-narrator slides into Oswald as if he were a third-person ideal in the same way that JFK was Oswald's. The effect is not unlike T. S. Eliot's in *The Waste Land*, where at one famous point the reader is addressed first as a hypocrite, then as the narrator's likeness, his brother even. The reader's conventional, necessarily unthinking identification with DeLillo the omniscient author becomes an identification with DeLillo in quotation marks, becomes, in turn, identification with Oswald, *mon semblable, mon frère:* that same reader who, like Oswald, desires, at a minimum, his own fifteen minutes of fame.

At the end of the lyric preface to his *USA* trilogy Dos Passos wrote: "But mostly USA is the speech of the people." By "USA" he meant both his novel and his country, and by "speech of the people" he meant his ensemble of variegated voices whose distinctions could be traced to specific regional and ethnic locales; speech as natural expression; speech out of blood and earth. One of the good old-fashioned pleasures of *Libra* derives precisely from DeLillo's ability to invent his own ensemble of variegated American voices, but so does *Libra*'s terror because DeLillo also succeeds—again in the smaller and often hilarious aesthetic textures as well as in the life of Oswald—in showing how the expressive forces of blood and earth are in the process of being overtaken and largely replaced by the forces of contemporary textuality. Lives lived so wholly inside the media are lives expressed (in the passive mood) through voices dominated by the jargons of the media.

When Bannister the FBI agent's secretary and mistress speaks of Oswald as a "thought-provoking individual," when she labels his pro-Cuba leaflets "inflammatory reading matter," when she says that blacks have it tough enough without having to add a "communistic tinge," and when she declares that the place she works at "tended to draw people from a colorful range of backgrounds," then the question becomes how much does it really count anymore that this good old girl is from New Orleans? Likewise, who really is the father of Oswald, that one-man ensemble who renders his botched suicide in Moscow in the present tense as if he were writing his "historic diary" while submerging his slashed wrists in a warm tub of water—and he doesn't forget to add the crucial stage direction: "*I decide to end it all. . . . Days of utter loneliness. . . . A sweet death (to violins). . . .*

I watch my life whirl away" (this last a weird, pulpy echo of JFK's Shakespearean sense of self); who imagines a desperate last-minute phone call to his mother in Texas: "It's me, Mother, lying in a pool of blood"; who imagines a press conference in which he says, "I won't answer questions about my family but I will say this for publication."

In his inner voice Oswald speaks of the "fears and aspirations of a man who only wanted to see for myself what socialism was like," imagines writing an exposé on the Soviet Union—the story, as he tells himself, of "the purposeful curtailment of diet in the consumer slighted population of Russia." This is the same Oswald (but what can it mean to say *same* in this context?) who when interviewed on a radio talk show in New Orleans, shortly after his arrest for contributing to a disturbance following his attempt to distribute leaflets on behalf of the Fairplay for Cuba Committee, says, "Certainly it is obvious to me having been educated in New Orleans and having been instilled with the ideals of democracy," and who says, "You know, when our forefathers drew up the Constitution. . . ." When his mother asks, "Who arranged the life of Lee Harvey Oswald?" the answer is that, like Francis Gary Powers and John Fitzgerald Kennedy, Lee Harvey Oswald is a political and cultural "chapter in the imagination of the state," a chapter done in the preferred modernist mode of montage, and, as he wishes, a personage of world-historical significance.

In the voice of Jack Ruby, DeLillo appears to have opened an escape hatch back to the earth of the robust ethnic life. The illusion of the essential health and purity of the ethnic voice—its self-possession—is strengthened by the narrative strategy in the Ruby sections of the book, DeLillo's virtual disappearance as a narrator: not into "DeLillo" but into the objective dramatist who writes pure dialogue, almost without intervention, and for long stretches. The illusion is of the ethnic voice's accessibility, its sincere public *thereness*. It feels good to be released through Ruby from the "world within the world," all those inner voices of men who harbor secrets their wives can only guess at, and who never are where they appear to be (say, at the breakfast table, very carefully buttering their toast). The ethnic familiarity and charm of Ruby's voice is a sort of code that tells us we are at last outside the subterranean world of power, a claustrophobic presence in *Libra* so dominant that when the book's historic public moment finally comes (Win Everett's assassination theater, JFK's answering heroics of the open car motorcade), it comes as creepily unreal, a manipulated world of show whose only exit is blood.

Here is Ruby in dialogue that sounds transparent, aboveground, with another Jack, a financial counselor for the Mafia and also a Jew. The two Jacks are hard to tell apart, which is the point:

> "What is the first thing people say about this tragedy? What does my mother say, eighty-eight years old, in a nursing home? She calls me on the phone. Do I have to tell you what she says? 'Thank God this Oswald isn't a Jew.'"
>
> "Thank God."
>
> "Am I right? How many people are saying the exact same thing these last two days? 'Thank God this Oswald isn't a Jew.'"
>
> "Whatever he is, at least we know he's not a Jew."
>
> "Am I right? These are the things people say."
>
> "When I think of my father," Jack Ruby said.
>
> "Of course. This is what I say."
>
> "Always drinking, drinking. Out of work for years. My mother talked Yiddish to the day she died. She couldn't write her name in English."
>
> "This is exactly the situation we find ourselves today. I'm saying there are things that need protection."
>
> "I'm a great believer in you have to stand up for your natural values."
>
> "Don't hide who you are."

But the escape hatch is quickly closed. Jack of the Mafia is a plotter whose Jewishness is theater, here to talk to Jack Ruby in order to rescript his ethnicity, take him into the world below, sign him on to do the hit on Oswald. Ethnicity is a manipulable jargon of self, and Jack of the Mafia knows how to manipulate it. In his hands, ethnicity becomes rhetoric, a tool for execution, the device that will bring closure to the plot:

> "As things now stand, Jack, what are you worth to the city of Dallas? You're a Chicago guy to them. You're an operator from the North. Worse, a Jew. You're a Jew in the heart of the gentile

machine. Who are we kidding here? You're a strip-joint owner. Asses and tits. That's what you mean to Dallas."

"Who are we kidding?"

"Who are we kidding here?"

"When I think of my mother."

"Exactly what I'm saying."

Ruby, too, is a negative libran, poised to go either way, comically figured in his doubts about his sexual identity:

> "Do I look swishy to you, Janet? What about my voice? People tell me there's a lisp. Is this the way a queer sounds to a neutral person? Do you think I'm latent or what? Could I go either way? Don't pee on my legs, Janet. I want the total truth."

This is the "same" Ruby who after JFK's death will talk out of some Cagney film about Oswald as "the weasel" and "the little rat," who on the morning of the day he will kill Oswald shaves with a Wilkinson sword blade, "for the name appeal." Jack Ruby, the ethnic self unselved. John Dos Passos's America, good night.

From the literal landscape of desire in Emerson (where standing in the woods a man may imaginatively recover the youth he never had—early America's favorite third-person, the yearned-for Adamic self in the yearned-for Eden of the new world), to Dreiser's cityscapes in *Sister Carrie* or *An American Tragedy* (where his unprivileged chief characters, Gatsby's literary parents, typically glimpse in passing the interiors of expensive restaurants and sumptuous mansions, where high-class food, clothing, and homes stand not so much for the material advantages of the wealthy as for the imagined romance of their lives—vehicles of selfhood, access to the fabulous third-person), to DeLillo's mediascapes where characters compose equally fabulous selves from the flood of ego ideals represented in movies, TV, popular fiction, and cheaply reproduced classic literature—the literary representation of the American dreamer has persisted. David Ferrie, *Libra*'s Emerson, was right when he told Oswald that he, Oswald, didn't want to merge with history, he wanted to get out. Oswald does not have the woods as the ideal space of solitude that brings self-renewal; the world of *Libra* is a world where nature has been almost perfectly displaced. What he has, finally, is his cell in the Dallas Police and Courts building, "the same room he'd known all his life" but now, in idealized form, the place where he felt himself "growing into the role as it developed." Oswald becomes the strange semblance of the obsessed author-figure who is ensconced in a room piled high with documents (he is called Nicholas Branch), who appears intermittently in *Libra* as DeLillo's double: Oswald, the double of a double, another man in his lonely writer's room who would tell the true tale of Dallas. Lee Harvey Oswald was his name, his fame "charged him with strength": he "would fill his cell with books about the case"; they "will give him writing paper." And at long last he will have actualized his desired vocation: not by becoming a realist "short story writer on contemporary American life," as he had once hoped, or the author of a "historic diary," but by becoming a writer in the romantic, Emersonian vein who will sing his self because he will have been its original author. "This," DeLillo writes, "was the true beginning."

Don DeLillo's Novels

Americana (1971)

End Zone (1972)

Great Jones Street (1973)

Ratner's Star (1976)

Players (1977)

Running Dog (1978)

The Names (1982)

White Noise (1985)

Libra (1988)

Notes on Contributors

DANIEL AARON is Emeritus Professor of English at Harvard University.

HAL CROWTHER writes his syndicated column for the *Independent Weekly* of Durham, N.C. He was previously a staff writer at *Time*, media editor and television critic for *Newsweek*, and a columnist for the *Buffalo News, Spectator, The Humanist*, and *Free Inquiry*. On the other side of the fence, he worked as a scriptwriter for films and television, and an editorialist for radio and public television.

ANTHONY DECURTIS is a Senior Writer at *Rolling Stone*, where he also edits the record review section. He holds a Ph.D. in American literature from Indiana University and has taught at Emory University. His essay accompanying the Eric Clapton retrospective *Crossroads* won the 1988 Grammy Award in the "Best Album Notes" category.

DENNIS A. FOSTER is Associate Professor of English at Southern Methodist University. He has written *Confession and Complicity in Narrative* (1987) and essays on modernist writers and pedagogy. Currently, he is working on a book on structures of the perverse in contemporary American writing.

JOHN FROW is the author of *Marxism and Literary History* (1986) and is Professor of English at the University of Queensland, Australia.

EUGENE GOODHEART is the Edytha Macy Gross Professor of Humanities at Brandeis University. He is the author of a number of books, among them *Culture and the Radical Conscience* (1973), *The Failure of Criticism* (1978), *The Skeptic Disposition in Contemporary Criticism* (1984), and, most recently, *Pieces of Resistance* (1987).

FRANK LENTRICCHIA is the editor of *SAQ* and Professor of English at Duke University. His books include *The Gaiety of Language* (1968), *Robert Frost: Modern Poetics and the Landscapes of Self* (1975), *After the New Criticism* (1980), *Criticism and Social Change* (1983), and *Ariel and the Police* (1988).

JOHN A. MCCLURE is Associate Professor of English at Rutgers University, New Brunswick. He is author of *Kipling and Conrad: The Colonial Fiction* (1981) and is completing a study of contemporary political fiction entitled *Imperial Projections*.

CHARLES MOLESWORTH is the author of the forthcoming *Marianne Moore: A Literary Life* (1990), the first full-length critical biography of this poet. He is also Chairperson of the Department of English at Queens College, City University of New York. He has published books on Gary Snyder, Donald Barthelme, and contemporary American poetry.

Index

Derrida - The Gift of Death

coat = 71
Dolores = 180
fees = 300
$551